Wildfire

Criminal Utopia II
Wildfire

J. ARTHUR SQUIERS

DEDICATION

This book is dedicated to everyone who has supported my Criminal Utopia series.

ACKNOWLEDGMENTS

I have a great group of people who have put significant time and effort into helping me create this novel. My goal is to put out the most polished work of art I possibly can, and I could not do it without them.

CHAPTER 1

L acy's lips parted and she tried to cry out, but no sound came from her mouth. Her eyes flew open and she looked all around her, trying to figure out where she was. There was a smash of breaking glass as she kicked her leg outward. She braced herself for an attack, her body seizing up. Then she recognized her surroundings.

Lacy had fallen asleep on the couch again. Running her hand through her sweat soaked hair, she squinted at the glowing television set across the room. A rerun of *Law and Order* blared back at her with the volume turned up way too high. She lay there on her back, her right leg resting on a coffee table nearby. A beer bottle had been knocked over onto the hardwood floor and green chunks of broken glass were scattered in a circle, looking shiny and wet. Lacy closed her eyes and willed the image of Nian's face to leave her mind.

With a grunt, Lacy rolled off the couch and onto her knees. She sucked in deep breaths and remained slumped on the floor, waiting for her head to stop pounding. Finally, she stood up and shuffled to the kitchen. She peered at the clock on her microwave and a blurry 5:05 a.m. stared back at her. A sound like fingernails tapping on glass caused her to flinch out of her stupor. Icy snowflakes were blowing against her window with wild gusts of wind. It was April in Night Harbor, and this was not uncommon. Lacy sighed and rubbed her aching forehead with the palm of her hand. She needed coffee and she had five blocks of brisk, snowy cold between her and that first warm cup. Grabbing her gray hoodie off the chair by her kitchen table, she made for the door. As she passed her backpack on the floor, she picked it up and swung it onto her shoulder before ducking out into the bitter air.

Once outside, Lacy decided she would jog through town. Her Volkswagen Beetle was parked in the lot behind her house, but finding a parking spot at the coffee shop was often difficult. Besides, the fresh air and exercise would help snap her out of the fog that was clouding her mind. She would still get there earlier than usual this morning, probably even earlier than Emily. That would be a first.

Emily walked through the front door of the coffee shop and saw Lacy sitting at a table in the corner. Lacy waved to her and Emily waved back with a frown and a crinkled forehead. It was then that Lacy realized she looked like a slob, with her ratty blue hair hanging wildly over her shoulders—not to mention that she was wearing the same jeans and t-shirt she had worn yesterday. Emily closed her eyes and shook her head, then stepped up to the counter and ordered a cup of coffee. After a few minutes, Emily came back to Lacy's table.

"You're having the dreams again?" Emily said. She sat down and looked at Lacy with raised eyebrows.

"How'd you guess?" Lacy said.

"Well, honey, it's Monday morning and you look like you're going to a Pink concert." Emily sniffed and wrinkled her nose. "And you smell like stale beer."

"I'm sorry," Lacy said. "The dreams usually go away after a week."

"I know, hon." Emily dug in her purse, pulled out a

perfume bottle, and held it out toward Lacy.

Lacy eyed the bottle for a second before taking it. She sprayed a couple of squirts on her neck and handed it back to Emily. The fragrance had a strong, fruity smell and Lacy thought she was going to sneeze.

Emily stuffed the perfume back into her purse. "Does your boss care if you show up looking like that?"

Lacy shrugged.

Emily lifted her coffee cup to her lips, her long lashes looking immaculate as her eyelids fluttered in reaction to the piping hot beverage. "What about your martial arts? Are you still training?"

Lacy shook her head. "Charlie's been on a case in New York for three weeks. I've been running on the trails, but that's about it lately."

Emily sighed and reached out her hand, placing it on Lacy's arm. "I've got an idea," Emily said with a smile. "Let's go shopping."

Lacy looked up from the table and smirked at the excitement in Emily's eyes.

"I'm not working today," Emily said. "I suppose it's too late for you to ask for the day off?"

"I don't think anyone would care," Lacy said.

"Really?"

Lacy shook her head. "I try to keep a low profile there because I don't want anyone to know what I'm really capable of. Since I can write more code in one day than the other programmers write in two weeks, I spend most of the time not working."

Emily snorted in the middle of another sip of coffee. She grabbed a tissue out of her purse and wiped her nose. "What do you do during all that time then?"

"I listen to audiobooks and hack people for fun," Lacy said.

"Oh goodness."

"It's okay," Lacy said. "It's a nice paycheck and I get to live in peace."

Emily eyed Lacy's clothes, her unruly hair, and her bloodshot eyes. "Peace?"

Lacy scratched her forehead and forced a smile. "Let's go to the mall, Emily."

Emily nodded. "I just worry about you, Lacy. Sometimes you go down a dark hole and it feels like you might not ever come back. You know what I mean?"

"Yeah," Lacy said. "I do."

Emily clicked her tongue. "Oh, sweetie." She stood up and leaned over to kiss Lacy on the cheek.

When Emily's lips touched her skin, Lacy put her hand on Emily's head, holding it there for a moment. Lacy took a deep breath through her nose.

"Thank you, Em," Lacy said.

"Of course," Emily said, resting her warm hand on Lacy's back. Then Emily straightened up and grabbed her purse from the table. "Come on, let's go have some fun."

CHAPTER 2

L acy carried her shopping bags as she walked along the sidewalk next to Emily, trying not to think about going back to her empty house. Emily had helped in taking her mind off of things for a while, and she was grateful for that. Yet she also hated having to rely on Emily, or anyone else for that matter. Lacy stopped in the middle of the sidewalk and gave Emily a hug before turning to walk away.

"Shoot," Emily said. "My phone just died. Can you text Jim and let him know I'm on my way home?"

"Yeah, sure." Lacy pulled her mobile out and typed on the screen with her thumbs. She slid the device back into her pocket. "Done."

"Thanks, hon," Emily said.

Lacy looked at Emily, then down at the ground, stuffing her hands into her pockets and shivering. An icy feeling of envy crept into Lacy's heart, though she despised herself for it and tried to cast it away. She wondered how Emily could do her makeup so perfectly every single day. Sure, Lacy could hack into any computer system in the world, but she could never make herself look as beautiful as Emily. Lacy shuddered again, this time intentionally as she tried to shake off the dark feelings that sickened her. She loved Emily and would be lost without her. How dare she resent her like that?

Emily stepped forward and put her hands on Lacy's shoulders. "Why don't you come and stay at our place tonight?" She rubbed Lacy's arms, trying to warm her. "I don't want you going back to that cold house by yourself right now."

There was nothing Lacy wanted more at that moment, but she shook her head. "No, I can't depend on you like that. I have to push through this on my own."

Emily's eyes started to brim with tears.

"Don't do that," Lacy said, a half smile forming at the corner of her mouth. "You'll ruin your mascara."

They both laughed.

"Lacy, you know I love you."

"I know, Em." Lacy stepped back from Emily's warm glow, which felt like stepping away from a warm campfire on a freezing cold night. "I'll see you tomorrow, at the cafe."

"Yes," Emily said. "I'll see you then."

Lacy gave a quick nod, turned, and strode down the sidewalk. Her pace grew quicker as she fought to keep her lower lip from quivering. Once she had gotten more than a block away, she started to run. The howling wind caught her breath and she let out a silent shout of despair that rattled around inside her mind. Behind her, a street lamp caused Lacy's shadow to extend far out in front of her. She watched the caricatured silhouette of herself gliding over the ground, before another shadow appeared next to her own.

Jumping into the air, Lacy twisted her head around to look behind her. She caught a blur of someone tall and agile jumping sideways into the alley, ten paces away. Burning heat spread through Lacy's body as her finely tuned adrenaline system revved up. Her feet landed back on the cement and she froze, staring at the opening of the alley. She listened as the wind whipped around her and whirred between the buildings, causing some of the street signs to rattle. The sidewalks were now empty and abandoned looking, with most people having ducked into buildings for cover from the frigid gusts.

Resisting the urge to go after the mysterious figure, Lacy waited. She could go toe-to-toe with just about anyone in a fair fight, but charging into a dark alley, having no idea what you are dealing with, would be stupid—and Lacy was the opposite of stupid.

Circling wide, Lacy moved around the opening of the alley, going slow and staying quiet. She dropped her bags and held her hands out in front of her, relaxed yet ready. When she was almost to the point where she could get a clear view between the two buildings, she heard the sound of metal clanging on the pavement, like someone had kicked a wrench. She leapt out in front of the alley, ready to attack, but nothing was there except a dumpster and scattered newspapers.

Lacy stood there trembling, the chattering of her teeth echoing in her head. She yanked out her phone, intending to call Emily at first. But Emily's phone was dead, so she dialed Jim's number. His voicemail announcement blared back at her.

"Jim," Lacy said into her phone. "I need help. Please meet me at The Foyer Bar in thirty minutes."

Lacy hung up and hurried down the street, leaving her purchases from the mall behind.

J. ARTHUR SQUIERS

CHAPTER 3

L acy opened the door to the bar and a gust of wind nearly tore it out of her hand. She fought to pull it closed as she entered. The place was packed, wall to wall with people. She tried to spot an open seat, but it was no use. After pushing her way through the crowd, she saw a small unoccupied table in the back corner. Sighing, she made her way back to the open spot, sidestepping clusters of people who were roaring with laughter and shouted conversations. Finally, she plopped down in the open seat and waited.

A hipster looking guy, a little older than Lacy, was sitting at the table next to her. He wore stylish Gucci glasses and had curly blonde hair. Since everyone in the bar was scrunched in tight, this guy was practically on top of her. Lacy smirked, thinking he looked both cute and flustered. He had an impressive array of tattoos on his forearms, which Lacy spent a few moments studying with interest. A guitar case sat on the floor, next to his feet, covered in band stickers that were worn and peeling. Groaning, the guy kept hammering the keys on a laptop in front of him. After a while, he started hitting the keyboard harder. Then he was mashing them with the palm of his hand. Finally, he threw his hands in the air and swore.

Looking around him, he locked eyes with Lacy. She let her blue hair fall in front of her eyes, trying to hide the fact that she had been staring.

"I'm sorry to bother you," he said.

Lacy tried to act like she didn't hear him.

"Do you know anything about computers?"

Lacy swallowed hard, rolling her eyes, which were still hidden behind her hair. She could feel him looking at her. With a sigh, she flicked her head to the side, swinging her hair out of her face.

"Please," he said.

Lacy shrugged. The guy's eyes were pleading and his desperation was kind of adorable. Plus, she had some time to kill while she waited for Jim.

"I have to go on stage in ten minutes." His eyes darted over to a small platform, with a microphone, at the front of the bar.

"You're singing?" Lacy said.

"Yeah, but I'm trying to get my sound mix running. The software keeps freezing up."

Lacy glanced at his laptop, a MacBook Pro. She looked at him with a wry smile. "What's your name?"

"It's Ethan."

"I'm Lacy." She held out her hand. "Give me your MacBook, Ethan."

Ethan handed the silver laptop to Lacy. She set it on the table in front of her, cracking her knuckles and tilting her head to one side, then the other, producing a loud pop from her neck in each direction. Her fingers began to type. "You know, Mac OS is built on top of Unix."

"Um, no, I didn't—"

"The only way it should freeze up like this is if you are running way too much crap, overloading the CPU." Her fingers danced across the keys.

"Well," he said, "I do use it for—"

"I'm killing all this stuff you're running. It's like you started every app you could."

"I couldn't shut them down. They were all frozen."

"That's why I'm using the command line terminal."

"The what?"

"The command line," Lacy said. "It lets you enter commands directly into the Unix system."

Lacy clicked the enter key and a drum beat started playing.

The owner of the bar, whom Lacy knew as Big Jerry, walked up to them, wiping his hands off on a towel. "Ethan, you're on."

Ethan jerked his head up to look at him. "Oh, okay." Grabbing his laptop, Ethan fumbled with the handle on his guitar case and stood up. His forehead was shiny with sweat. He looked at Lacy, raising an uneasy eyebrow. "Wish me luck."

Lacy winked. "Good luck." She felt queasy in her stomach and realized she was nervous for him.

Ethan shuffled through the crowded tables, sidestepping a waitress with a tray of drinks, causing her to tilt back and almost spill a glass of wine on a grizzled looking biker with a leather vest.

As Ethan climbed up onto the stage, Lacy's palms became slick with sweat. Ethan plugged a speaker cable into his laptop, pulled his guitar out, and scooted up to the microphone.

"Hi, I'm Ethan," he said. "I'm going to play a few songs. Uh . . . . I hope you enjoy them."

The crowd continued its loud roar. Nobody seemed to notice Ethan on stage.

Strumming his guitar once, Ethan tightened the D-string a few turns. He tapped a key on his laptop next to him, said "check" into the microphone, and strummed his guitar again.

Ethan started playing a melody on his guitar and Lacy recognized the tune on the second note. Several of the other people did as well, and they groaned in disapproval.

"You've got to be kidding me," she said, her mouth dropping open.

Big Jerry, still standing next to Lacy, looked at her and laughed.

"This crowd is going to eat him alive," Lacy said.

"Just wait," Big Jerry said. "Wait for it."

Lacy listened, closing her eyes to shut out the horrible scene.

Ethan started to sing the first verse of "Let It Go."

The noise of the crowed faded.

Ethan's voice was pure and rich. He had a deep tone that made Lacy raise her eyebrows and sit up straight. Ethan was putting a hard rock slant on a song that only a fool would dare to attempt in a place like this. He started strumming the chords harder, faster.

When he hit the chorus, Ethan belted out with such power and control, that it made Lacy's entire body tingle. He was unbelievable. Everyone was staring at him; they were all still and silent.

When Ethan finished the song, the entire bar erupted with applause. One man jumped up, standing on his chair, clapping above his head. Several others stood up as well.

Ethan looked around the room, nodding his head to the crowd and mouthing "thank you." His gaze swept to the back of the room, locking eyes with Lacy. She felt her chest get warm as she gave him a thumbs-up. Ethan gave her a wide, sparkling smile and waved.

Ethan made his way back through the crowd, having finished his set. He received pats on the back and big smiles from people as he passed by them. Finally, he collapsed into the chair next to Lacy.

"Whew!" Ethan said.

"You were unbelievable," Lacy said. "And you were such a frantic mess beforehand. I never would've guessed you could sing like that."

"I always get that nervous before I perform," Ethan said. "I just can't seem to shake it."

"Well, you killed it up there."

"Thanks," Ethan said. "Can I buy you a drink?"

Lacy glanced out the window. "I don't know. I'm waiting for someone."

"Oh?"

"Yeah, a friend."

"Your friend has been keeping you waiting quite a while. You could have one drink with me and then I'll be on my way."

Lacy thought for a moment. "Let me try calling them one more time first."

Ethan tucked his guitar back into the case. "Fair enough."

Getting up, Lacy made her way back to the restroom. She pulled out her mobile and decided to try calling Emily this time. Emily would be home by now and would have started charging her phone. Lacy got Emily's voicemail.

"Guys," Lacy said, leaving a message, "I'm sorry about this, but I need you. Please call me back." She tried Jim's number and got the same result.

Lacy came back to the table and Ethan already had a drink in front of him, whiskey by the looks of it.

"Well," Ethan said. "Can I order something for you?"

Lacy peered through the window one more time and exhaled through her nose. "Okay, just one."

"Do you live around here?" Lacy said.

"Only for a few months," Ethan said. "Moved here from Omaha. I knew a guy who was into the music scene in this area and he got me started with some gigs."

Ethan's phone buzzed in his pocket. He pulled it out and looked at it before typing a response.

"Looks like I'm singing again tonight, someone cancelled at Jimmy Bean's." Ethan pulled his guitar onto his lap and tucked his laptop under his armpit. "You want to come watch?"

Lacy smiled and shook her head. "Thanks, but I think I'm going to head home. It's been a weird night."

Ethan's face fell. "Okay." He paused. "Can I get your number then?"

"I don't give out my number," Lacy said. "But you can give me yours."

Ethan pursed his lips and then smiled, rattling off ten digits. "Aren't you going to write it down?" he asked.

"I have a good memory," Lacy said. "I won't forget."

Ethan nodded. "Okay, talk to you later." He set two ten dollar bills down on the table and headed for the door.

Lacy breathed a deep sigh and watched him through the window as he hustled down the sidewalk. She glanced at her phone one more time before getting up and making her way outside. The crisp chill of the air pierced through her clothes like icepicks. Lacy ran down the road, never looking back until she reached her house.

Bursting through her front door, Lacy bolted the lock and tapped the keypad on the wall to set her alarm. She hated feeling scared, more than anything. Lacy clenched her fist into a ball and slammed it into her oak door. She let out a cry and slumped down to the floor, sitting with her head between her knees. Her house was quiet, dead quiet, and empty. A chilling sensation tickled the back of her neck; was it really empty? Lacy lifted her head from her knees and stared into the dark kitchen, her eyes adjusting enough to make out the shapes of her table and chairs. The silence was so thick that it made her ears hurt. She jumped when a deep grating noise blared right next to her. Even though she knew right away it was her refrigerator starting up, her heart took much longer to catch on. With a grunt, Lacy pushed herself to her feet and flicked on the light switch, waiting for that brief moment to pass where she imagined seeing armed men standing in her kitchen under the bright incandescent glow.

Lacy was starving, not having eaten anything since the stale salad she had at the mall. She went to the fridge and opened it, then slumped her shoulders. It was empty except for sour cream, margarine, ranch salad dressing, and taco sauce. Standing there, letting the refrigerator air cool her face, she closed her eyes. The grocery store was still open. She could make it in time. The person by the alley must have been a fluke, some creep just looking for money. She was not going to let that incident paralyze her.

Looking out her window, she saw her car, sitting in the dark under a birch tree. A flutter erupted in her chest when something moved in the back seat. She froze and watched, not daring to breathe. The wind picked up and the trees swayed, causing the shadows in her car to shift again. Lacy exhaled in relief. She decided to take her motorcycle instead, which was parked out front. Though it was frigid and windy outside, she felt safer on her bike, preferring to be agile and free to make quick maneuvers. Just in case.

J. ARTHUR SQUIERS

CHAPTER 4

The front wheel of the shopping cart squeaked and pulled to the left as Lacy pushed it along the snack aisle. She gritted her teeth as the shrill sound reverberated across the polished floor and seemed to fill the entire grocery store. Squeezing the handle of the cart with both hands, she went faster, hoping the wheel would spin smoother and the noise would calm down. It got worse. Just as she was about to send the cart flying into a stack of Pringles cans and run off to get a new one, she spotted the item she had been looking for. Lacy grabbed a box of Cheez-It crackers from the shelf, tore the top off, and pulled the bag open with a popping sound. She looked around, realizing how quiet and empty the store was. It was almost closing time and she needed to hurry.

Making her way to the dairy section, Lacy stuffed handfuls of orange crackers into her mouth. She grabbed a few cartons of Greek yogurt and headed for the register. By the time she got to the checkout, the Cheez-It box was empty and her hunger pains had subsided.

The elderly lady at the register made a scowling face of reproach while she swiped the empty box across the barcode scanner to ring up the price. Lacy shrugged and smiled. She was used to people reacting to her with disapproval, and it no longer bothered her. What did get to her was fear, and she was trying hard to push that feeling away. It always started in her stomach, a tightness which spreads out and finally overtakes her. She had avoided it for quite a while, and now she was furious that it had appeared again, all because of some stupid creep in a dark alley. Lacy had spent every spare moment training herself to be a skilled fighter who could handle any situation. Yet, just like that, her dreaded enemy was taking root again. With a swipe of her arm, Lacy snatched up her bags of food in clenched fists and headed for the door. She banished the fear from her mind. After all, she had sworn she would never give in to it again.

Lacy walked out of the grocery store holding a plastic bag in each hand. It was now eleven o'clock and the night had gone pitch black with clouds blocking out the moon and the stars. The street lamps glowing overhead were dim and did little to illuminate the parking lot. A howling gust of wind slammed into Lacy from the side, causing her hair to blow in her face, blinding her even further. She blew air from her mouth, trying to move some of her hair out of the way so she could see. When she was finally able to spot her motorcycle up ahead, she froze. Something was wrong. Her bike looked different. She wasn't sure what it was, but she knew it had been tampered with. Lacy stood still, listening and waiting. The wind whistled in her ears, preventing her from hearing anything, but she saw a shadow move behind the van parked to her right. There was a blur of motion behind her and she spun around, her groceries flying in all directions.

The barrel of a pistol stared back at her.

"Don't move," said a hoarse voice.

Screw that, Lacy was going to move. It takes one-fourth of a second for someone to pull the trigger when reacting to a visual cue. Plenty of time.

Lacy's right hand made a sudden clockwise circle and her

forearm slammed into the back of the hand that was holding the gun. At the same time, she spun around so her back was facing the man and reached up with her other hand, grabbing his wrist. She yanked down with both hands, snapping the ulna bone of his forearm over her shoulder.

As the gun fell from his hand, Lacy grabbed it and turned back around, pointing it at him. He was wearing a dark overcoat and a black stocking cap. He had a bony face with sharp features. It was hard to tell in the dark, but she thought he looked Russian. He was gritting his teeth in pain and holding his arm. His gaze moved from Lacy to something far off in the distance behind her. It only took Lacy a moment to realize what he was looking for. More people were coming.

Keeping the gun pointed at her attacker, Lacy backed up toward her motorcycle. The man didn't move. He just waited, watching down the highway. Lacy put her key in the bike and kicked down the starter. The engine came alive with a deep rumble. Lacy swung her leg over the bike and gunned the throttle. Leaving a thick rubber track, she sped out of the parking lot and onto the street.

Lacy raced down the highway, heading for the road that led down into the harbor. She saw the street lights changing to red up ahead and prepared to accelerate through them anyhow. When she cranked the throttle, the engine started to sputter. Her legs felt cold and she looked down to see that her pants were soaked.

"Dammit," she said. Her gas line had been cut.

A loud roar startled her from behind. As she twisted her head around, a huge truck was bearing down on her. Her bike finally died and she was coasting on the wheels. The truck was now ten feet from Lacy's back tire; it was a tan Humvee with a cable winch on the front bumper.

Lacy steered her motorcycle off into a deep ditch on the side of the road. As she flew down the steep incline, the front tire of her bike slammed into the mud and the back end of her bike catapulted her through the air. She rolled as she hit the ground, then sprang up to her feet and ran. Her gas soaked jeans were slowing her down, so she gritted her teeth and pumped her arms hard.

Looking over her shoulder, Lacy saw the Hummer skid to a stop, sliding into the gravel on the side of the road. The doors opened and slammed shut. She turned back around and ducked her head down, leaning into her sprinting stride. A grove of pine trees loomed ahead. In an instant, she had burst into a sea of spruce branches, with prickly needles clawing her face and hands. Ignoring the pain, Lacy pressed on at full speed. After ten strides, she broke out of the tangles and found herself in someone's backyard.

Breathing heavy and ragged, Lacy took a quick scan of the area. There was a small pond in the corner of the lot. She ran to the edge of it and stepped in with her left foot, gasping as ice cold water soaked into her shoe. Shouts came from the trees behind her and she flinched. They were getting close. Lacy stepped into the pond with her other foot and stood there, waist deep among the reeds. She heard branches snapping in the pine trees and loud footsteps thudding on the ground.

Lacy lowered herself into the water and tipped her head back, so that only her lips were above the surface. The freezing water felt like hundreds of daggers against her skin and she willed herself not to shriek out loud. The muffled sound of shouting voices penetrated the water and seeped into her numb ears. A flashlight beam moved back and forth overhead before stopping in the middle of the pond. For a brief moment, the beam was right in her eyes. Then it was gone. Lacy waited another ten minutes, her head pounding from the drop in body temperature. Everything around her had become still and quiet. She clenched her fists as hard as she could, fighting to stay conscious as hypothermia threatened to engulf her.

Finally, deciding it would be deadly to stay in the water any longer, Lacy crawled out of the pond with spastic movements. She crept across the yard, into a forest of maple and oak trees. Her body jerked with violent shivering and her numb feet caused her to wobble as she walked. She stopped and listened, her teeth chattering in her skull, trying to think. Looking up at the moon, its bluish light barely visible through the clouds, she decided to head west and get to the highway that led into the harbor through the backside of town.

When Lacy reached the road, she started to run. She picked up her pace until her body started to warm up and stop shaking. Lacy's frame was small, but she had put on some muscle by lifting weights with Charlie for the past two years, and muscle mass generates heat when it's working. During that time, Charlie himself had gotten massive. Maybe he sensed the inevitable danger that Lacy had been preparing for, and wanted to be able to protect her, because Charlie became an animal in the gym. Even though he was in his mid-forties, the man was now a monster. Lacy did not know what supplements Charlie was taking, nor if it was all considered legal, but whatever he was doing, the results were astounding.

Lacy squinted as headlights approached from the distance, and her heart hammered against her ribs. She watched to see if they were going to slow down. When the lights sped past her, she breathed out a sigh. After a minute, another set of headlights approached. Lacy held her breath, blinking into the beams. These lights started to slow down. Lacy prepared herself to jump into the ditch. Red lights flashed on above the beams and Lacy relaxed, coming to a stop. A police car, thank goodness. She waved her arms above her head as the blinding lights came closer. The squad car pulled over and stopped in front of her. After a brief pause, an officer got out of the driver's side.

"Ma'am, are you okay?" he said.

Lacy rested her hands on her knees, gasping for air. "No," she said. "Some guys tried to kidnap me." She heaved and coughed. "I don't know who they are, but you've got to get me out of here. There's a lot of them and they keep chasing me."

The passenger door of the squad car opened and a second police officer stepped out. He was tall, lanky, and spoke in a soft, friendly tone. "Miss, you look pretty banged up. We should call an ambulance."

"No," Lacy said. "We've got to go, right now. I just need you to take me to a friend's house."

"But your forehead is bleeding," said the first officer.

Lacy wiped her brow with her right hand and looked at it. There was some blood, but not much. "It's just a scratch, I'm fine." Lacy's face grew hot and her voice was tense. "We're all in danger right now, please, listen to me."

"Sweetie, we've got to do this by the book." The first officer pressed the button on the CB radio clipped onto his shoulder. "We need an ambulance on sixteen." Then he looked at the other officer and nodded.

Lacy saw something in the first officer's eyes that made her heart sink. She looked over at the second officer and her legs went numb; he was aiming his gun at her.

Lacy shifted her weight, preparing to dive into the ditch at an angle that might get her out of the second officer's line of sight.

The first officer shouted, "Freeze, or I'll kill you."

Lacy looked over and saw that he had also pulled out a gun and was circling wide, cutting off any chance of escape.

"Put your hands up," said the second officer.

Lacy obeyed. "Why are you doing this?"

"Shut your mouth," said the second officer.

A black van came roaring up behind Lacy, screeching to a halt.

Lacy turned her head, looking at the van out of the corner of her eye. A huge man with a ski mask got out of the driver's seat. He was holding a big taser gun, a unique type that Lacy had seen only once before.

"It can't be," Lacy whispered, just before fifty thousand volts of electricity coursed through her body.

J. ARTHUR SQUIERS

CHAPTER 5

Lacy's hands were bound behind her back with zip ties. She lay on her stomach, with two men kneeling on either side of her, holding her down against the floor of the van. There were no seats in the back, and her face was pressed against the cold steel, which smelled like it had been bleached. A third man, whom Lacy assumed was the leader, was crouched next to her head.

"Stay still and you won't get hurt," the leader said.

Lacy was silent. She knew that was not true.

The leader leaned toward the driver. "Take a right up here," he said.

"Yes, sir," the driver said.

Lacy fought to stay calm. She focused on the positions of the three men, analyzing hundreds of scenarios in her mind. Realizing that all of her choices for a course of action would require some form of luck, she chose her escape plan.

Craning her neck, Lacy looked up at the leader's throat, which was bare and exposed at the bottom of his knitted mask. She waited. Having a good idea of where they were on the road, she knew her opportunity would come in less than a minute. She just hoped the driver would not slow down too much. If he kept this speed, the physics would make everything much easier.

There was a boom as the van flew over the railroad tracks at full speed, sending everyone into the air for a split second and causing their grips on Lacy to loosen. She twisted her body around hard so that she landed on her back, while bringing her knees up above her head. As their momentum came crashing back down, Lacy slammed the heel of her boot into the throat of the leader, collapsing his trachea. Her primary threat was neutralized. Lacy's next move was her biggest gamble. She had to flip up to her feet, and she had never done that with her hands tied behind her back. If the move failed, she was toast. Lacy kicked her feet up, arching her back before crunching forward into the air. She had assumed that the steep uphill climb, immediately after the railroad tracks, would help her get all the way to her feet—it did. In fact, she over rotated and landed in a position where she was falling forward into the man that was on her right; this would add a lot more force into what she was about to do. But that was his problem, not hers. Lacy was terrified for her life and she was not going to hold back. She brought her knee up into the man's nose with all the power of her momentum behind it. It felt like her knee smashed into a pumpkin as cartilage and bone gave way, and he went down without making a sound.

Lacy turned just in time as her back slammed into the corner of the van, knocking the wind out of her. The remaining guy had been allowed a moment to react, so he would be the most difficult to predict. He lunged at Lacy, trying to drive his shoulder into her stomach. Lacy dropped to the ground, rolling to the side as the man collided with the unforgiving steel of the van. The uphill angle of the van had also given him too much momentum, which he failed to foresee. As the man fell to one knee, Lacy leapt at him from behind, feet first, and wrapped her legs around his neck. She squeezed and grunted while he struggled to get free. There was a gurgle and the man went limp.

Meanwhile, the driver had been trying to recover from the shock of sailing over the railroad tracks at full tilt, not having known they were there. Realizing there had been a fight, which had lasted only four seconds, the driver turned around to look. Lacy was crouched down, sliding her tied hands under her legs to get her arms in front of her. The driver reached down and came up with a gun, pointing it back at Lacy. She rolled to the side and a deafening sound stung her ears as a bullet hole appeared in the floor of the van, right where she had been. The driver aimed again, and Lacy rolled the other direction, slamming into one of the men's bodies as another bullet ricocheted off the floor. When Lacy looked up, she caught sight of a U-Haul truck pulling in front of the van, right before they smashed into it. The driver flew out of his seat, breaking through the windshield. Lacy was thrown forward into the back of the driver's seat, her ribs cracking as her abdomen slammed against the headrest. She screamed in pain.

Lying on her back, Lacy opened her eyes and saw the ceiling of the van. She stirred, trying to remember what had happened. Her head rolled to the side and she saw the night sky through the busted out windshield. The van was on its side, and the bodies of the three men Lacy had fought were in a heap next to her. Lacy started to crawl toward the front of the van, sucking in air through her teeth at the pain in her side, when one of the men stirred. It was the one she had choked out with her legs. Hurrying between the front seats, Lacy pulled herself through the hole in the windshield. She got to her feet and stood on the blacktop, turning in a circle and looking all around her. The U-Haul truck that the van had crashed into was about thirty feet down the street, its driver's side completely smashed in. A man was slouched over the steering wheel, not moving.

Lacy looked around for the van driver that had been shooting at her, but she didn't see him. She hurried back to the van and rubbed the zip tie, binding her hands, against a sharp piece of the windshield until it came off. A twig snapped in the thick brush on the other side of the ditch, causing Lacy to stumble backwards away from the sound. She had to get out of there. Pitching herself into a run, she held her hand against her aching side and raced down the road toward town, which was two miles away.

Gasping for air as she stumbled along the highway, Lacy made two decisions. Her first decision was that she needed to steal a car. She was done hoofing it all over the place in the middle of the night with crazy people chasing her. The second decision was that she had to go into hiding, at least until she figured out what was going on.

Lacy knew now that Jim was not getting her texts, and going to his and Emily's house was not an option. Whoever was after her seemed to be very good at finding her. Leading her pursuers to Jim and Emily's place would only put them in terrible danger. If Charlie were home, he could certainly help. But he was out of state and undercover. There was only one other person left that she trusted, and that was where she decided to go.

First, Lacy had to get a car, and hopefully some food. There was a gas station on the outskirts of town, where it was secluded with almost no traffic. Nodding her head, she decided to go there and get herself some wheels.

Lacy crept up to the parking lot of the gas station and crouched behind a row of shrubs on the edge. The paved area in front of the store was crumbled and uneven, with weeds growing up anywhere the tar had cracked. There were two vehicles parked outside the store, a bright red pickup truck and a small car. One of them must have belonged to the store clerk, and a customer must have driven the other. Lacy would wait for the customer to leave and take the vehicle that remained. After five minutes, a giant man in a sleeveless shirt ambled out the door. He heaved himself into the pickup, started it up, and drove off. Staying low, Lacy crept up to the car. When she got close, she pulled her smartphone out of her pocket. The device was still wet and the screen was dark. She pressed the power button, hoping her decision to get a waterproof model would pay off. The phone powered up and she felt a tinge of relief. Grabbing a key ring out of her other pocket, Lacy pushed a few keys aside and clasped a square, plastic object that was hooked to the ring. Lacy plugged the square into the bottom of her phone.

Glancing up at the gas station window, Lacy made sure the cashier was not looking. He was bent over the counter, writing something on a piece of paper. Lacy stood up and held her phone camera over the VIN number of the car, letting it scan the digits. The phone buzzed and started cycling through number combinations. Lacy counted the seconds while stealing quick glances into the store. One .... two .... three .... four .... five .... six. The car unlocked with a click.

Lacy lifted the handle of the car door, when another vehicle came rumbling into the parking lot, pulling up next to her. Lacy cursed. She opened the door of the car she had unlocked and climbed in. When she turned and looked at the vehicle that had pulled up, she flinched and slouched low in the seat. It was Ethan, and he was waving at her with a bright smile. Lacy tried to act like she had not noticed him. She pressed a button on her phone, starting the car engine.

Jumping out of his silver Honda Civic, Ethan ran over and knocked on Lacy's window. She looked at him, jerking her head backward in mock surprise. He made circles in the air with his hand, trying to get her to roll down the window. Lacy glanced up at the store. The employee was coming toward the window, squinting to see what was going on outside. Groaning, Lacy pushed the car door open, causing Ethan to jump backward to get out of the way. She popped out of the car and slammed the door shut in one swift movement.

"Ethan, what are you doing here?" Lacy's voice trembled as she spoke.

"I'm on my way back from playing a gig in Bear County." He gestured with his hand toward the highway. "I stopped here to get a Coke." Ethan rubbed his eyes with the palm of his hand. "I was starting to fall asleep at the wheel." Ethan moved closer, looking at Lacy's face. "Whoa, what happened? Are you okay?"

Lacy looked around, fidgeting and shifting her weight from one foot to the other. "You have to get out of here right now."

"What?" Ethan squinted at Lacy "Why?"

"Just trust me, it's not safe to be around me. Please, get in your car and go."

"Are you in danger?"

"Ethan, just leave. They'll kill you if they find out you even talked to me. They'll kill you after they torture you for information." Lacy looked at the roof of the gas station, searching for a security camera.

Ethan followed Lacy's gaze. Then he turned back to her and looked at the car behind her.

"Is that yours?" Ethan said.

"You have no idea how determined these people are. I have to get out of here any way I can, and so do you."

An engine roared on the highway, coming toward them. Lacy started to step backward as Ethan moved in front of her, blocking her from the sight of anyone driving by. A brown, rusty diesel truck appeared out of the darkness and rumbled past the gas station, continuing on down the road.

Ethan turned around and looked Lacy in the eyes. "You do realize how ridiculous this all sounds, right? You're not high, are you?"

Lacy puffed out her cheeks and squeezed her hands into fists. "No," she said through a clenched jaw. "I am not high.

They had me in a van. It crashed and I escaped."

Ethan's eyebrows almost disappeared under his mop of hair and his mouth opened to speak, but he thought better of it and said nothing.

"I know it's a lot to swallow," Lacy said. "But it's all true."

"I want to believe you." Ethan put a hand on her shoulder. "I want to help you."

"Then get out of here and forget you saw me."

"I can't leave you here. Look, I'll give you a ride."

"You'll drop me off where I tell you to?"

"First, I need you to show me where the crash happened."

"Why?"

"Because I'm scared," Ethan said.

"Well, you should be," Lacy said.

"I'm scared this is all in your head. I need to know if it's real."

Lacy's mouth twisted into a scowl. "It doesn't get more real than this."

"Then show me."

"Fine, but keep your distance when we get close, and be ready to get the hell out of there." Lacy stepped up to Ethan's car and yanked his passenger door open.

"Okay," Ethan said, hurrying around the front of his car. "Just show me the way."

Ethan's car idled along the highway as the intersection came into view far up ahead. Lacy gripped the dashboard and leaned forward, peering into the darkness beyond Ethan's headlights. She sucked in a gasp. There was nothing there, the intersection was empty.

"That's not possible." Lacy's muscles started to twitch.

Ethan looked at her. "It's okay, I can get you help." He put his hand on her arm.

Lacy yanked herself away from his touch. She thought

about all of the details from that night. Her ribs were screaming in pain. She put her fingers to her forehead, feeling the
sting of the deep scratches. It was all real.

"Pull up closer," she said.

"Lacy, please—"

"Do it." She glared at him.

"Okay," Ethan said. "Just remember, I'm here for you. I'm
trying to help."

Ethan drove up to the intersection and stopped. Nothing
out of the ordinary could be seen in any direction. Lacy
stumbled out of the car and staggered into the middle of the
road. She snapped her head side to side, looking all around her.

"It can't be." She put her hand on her broken ribs, pressing
a little to intensify the pain enough so that it jolted her mind,
reminding her that it was real.

Ethan got out of the car and sighed. His eyes were soft,
caring, and worried. "Lacy, I'm sorry. I don't know what to
say."

"No." Lacy was walking across the pavement, examining
every inch. "No, no, no . . . . it was right here!"

"Please, let me bring you to a hospital. Maybe you fell and
hit your head."

"There has to be something," Lacy said. She bent over,
brushing her fingers across the tar. Then she got down on her
hands and knees, examining every crack. There was no trace
of an accident anywhere. She straightened up, looking into the
darkness behind her. "I need more light." She turned and
looked at Ethan. "Turn your high beams on."

"Lacy, I—"

"Dammit, Ethan. Humor me, please." She stood up and put
her hands on her hips, her breathing deep and heavy. "Give
me ten minutes, and if I can't prove that it all really happened,
you can take me to the psych ward."

Ethan ran his fingers through his hair and shook his head.

"Okay, Lacy." He opened the door to his car and reached inside. "We have a deal."

The headlights flashed and blinded Lacy as the area filled with light. She looked around and something caught her eye in the ditch, something reflecting the light. Lacy walked with quick strides into the grass, reaching down and pushing the green blades apart. She picked up a piece of glass, holding it up to the light.

"A broken windshield," she said.

Ethan started walking toward her, rubbing the back of his neck. "That could have been there for months, years even. This is crazy."

Lacy slammed her fist against her ribs and cried out. "I'm not crazy."

Ethan stopped at the edge of the road, leaning forward as though he were standing on the edge of a cliff and peering down into a canyon.

Lacy looked to her left and saw that an area of grass appeared to have been disturbed. There were matted down spots, as though people had been walking around in a circle. She got closer and knelt down. There was a circular matted down spot, the size of basketball, where the grass was a dark blackish color. Lacy touched the spot, feeling a sticky substance. She lifted her finger to the light and held it toward Ethan.

Squinting at Lacy, Ethan shrugged. "What is it?"

"Blood," Lacy said. "Lots of it."

Ethan jogged down into the ditch and stopped in front of Lacy. He leaned over and examined her finger for a moment, saying nothing. Finally, he started moving around, pushing the tall grass to the side with his foot.

"Do you believe me now?" Lacy said.

"I don't know." Ethan moved faster, covering more ground, searching in a wide circle. "I don't see any dead animals. No roadkill."

"You've got to get me out of here."

"Wait one second. We don't know what type of blood it is."

Lacy put her face closer to the blood spot. Something else caught her eye, two white spots. She pinched one and her hand started to tremble. With her free hand, Lacy plucked up the other one. Holding both objects up to the light, she turned toward Ethan with big, wide eyes. She looked at him in silence.

"What are those?" Ethan asked.

"Teeth," Lacy said.

Ethan's cheeks lost all color, turning as white as the molars in Lacy's hands. His arms fell limp to his sides and he turned away from Lacy, vomit spraying out of his mouth. He choked and coughed. "You're sure they're human?" he said, trying to breathe.

"Yes," Lacy said.

Ethan inhaled, deep and long. He straightened up and wiped his mouth with his sleeve. "Okay, let's get out of here."

Lacy stood up and started climbing out of the ditch. Ethan followed close behind her.

Far off in the distance, a car appeared, heading their way. Lacy stiffened and took off running for Ethan's car. They both jumped into their seats and Ethan floored the gas. Lacy took one last look back at the ditch, as Ethan's speedometer climbed higher and higher.

"You promised you'd drop me off where I told you to," Lacy said.

"I know, I know." Ethan kept scratching the back of his neck and drumming his fingers on top of the steering wheel as he drove. "It's just so crazy."

"Bring me to the airport. Just drop me off at the front doors and drive away."

"Just like that," Ethan said. "I feel so sick about this. How will I know you're okay?"

"You won't," Lacy said. "But it's the only way. Look, I'm really sorry that you got involved. The less you know, the safer you are. Please, just go back to your life and act like nothing ever happened."

"That's not going to be easy," Ethan said.

Lacy looked at Ethan and forced a smile. His soft features and brown eyes twitched as he drove. She knew he wasn't used to these situations, though she unfortunately was. And she was scared, so he must be terrified.

Lacy put her hand on Ethan's leg. "You can do this."

Ethan gave her a quick nod. "Okay." He chewed on his lower lip, his jaw muscles twitching as he focused his eyes on the road ahead.

They pulled up to the glass doors at the front entrance of the airport. Lacy looked around, examining every car and person in sight. Deciding nothing seemed suspicious, she reached over and placed her fingers under Ethan's chin, gently pulling his face toward hers. Leaning over, she kissed him on the lips. He kissed her back, his hand going to the back of her head, his fingers sinking into her hair. Lacy felt her neck and chest fill with heat as her pulse quickened. She pressed against him harder for a moment, then pulled away. He looked at her, blinking, his cheeks flushed.

"Thank you for helping me," Lacy said. "Someday, when things are safe again, I'll find you."

"I sure hope so," Ethan said.

Lacy turned away and opened the car door. She dashed inside the airport terminal and disappeared amongst the crowd.

Lacy was going to do one last thing before she went into hiding; she'd leave a message for Charlie. Jim was obviously not getting her calls, so his phone was probably hacked, as well as Emily's. Maybe Charlie could still be reached.

Lacy walked along the stores inside the airport until she

came to a cell phone kiosk. She purchased a prepaid phone and walked to the restroom. Checking each toilet stall, she made sure she was alone. Then she dialed Charlie's secure line. There was no announcement on his voicemail, just a beep.

"Charlie," Lacy said into the phone. "They're after me, and they're everywhere—professionals. I'm going away—"

Lacy heard the door to the restroom slam open. With a flick of her wrist, she sent the phone flying into the garbage can. When she looked up, four men wearing security guard uniforms came around the corner, their boots scraping on the tile floor. Lacy stumbled backward, her foot slipping on a puddle of water.

CHAPTER 6

J im was wearing only boxer shorts as he stood in the middle of his living room, looking around in the dark. He had been restless and unable to sleep. Now he was shivering from the chilly air on his legs and torso, and wondering why he felt so edgy. Something was wrong.

He made his way to the front door and checked to make sure it was locked. Satisfied that it was, Jim crept back through the house, shuffling around the couch and coffee table as he headed toward the bedroom. The shadows on the walls seemed to loom over him, and he resisted the urge to turn on a light switch. There was a feeling in his gut; a feeling that he could not place at first, but then it hit him. He had a sensation that someone was watching him from outside the house.

Scratching his head and yawning, Jim decided he was being ridiculous—his tired brain was just playing tricks on him. Just to be sure though, to give himself peace of mind so he could go back to sleep, Jim went up to each window and peered outside. Each time he looked out, he saw nothing but the other houses in his neighborhood and empty streets. It did seem quite windy out there; perhaps that was causing noises that were tricking his subconscious into thinking people were creeping around outside. Finally, fed up with his paranoia, Jim went back to bed.

He had just rested his head on his pillow and closed his eyes when a clinking sound penetrated the silence. Jim sat up and looked toward the window, his heart hammering in his chest. The sound stopped for a few seconds, then started again— metal tapping on glass. He tried to move, but fear paralyzed him. He tried to listen, but his pulse was thumping in his ears. Then the old instincts, which had been buried deep down for two years, came rushing back to him.

Jumping out of bed, Jim crept to the closet and reached into the corner. His hands felt along the wall, behind a row of pants on hangers, until his fingers touched cold steel. Gripping a long barrel, Jim pulled his twelve gauge shotgun out and slid the pump action down, causing Emily to murmur. He waited, listening in the silence as the chill of the room started seeping into his bare skin. The tapping resumed, louder than before. Jim slid the pump of his shotgun upward, loading a shell.

Emily had always protested against keeping a gun in their room, but Jim had never been able to shake the feeling of being hunted by Kraig. He needed it there in order to sleep.

Jim held his breath as he moved across the room, staying close to the wall. When he got near the window, another set of loud taps sounded out.

"Jim?" Emily's voice echoed through the room.

"Emily, stay still," Jim whispered.

She went silent.

Jim took a deep breath and moved the curtains to the side with the barrel of his gun.

A face stared back at him.

The face ducked when it saw the shotgun. Jim sucked in a deep, loud breath, causing Emily to scream.

Jim realized right away that it was Charlie outside the window, but it took some time for his body to shake off the initial shock of seeing a pale white face staring back at him.

Lowering the barrel of his shotgun, Jim unlatched his window and slid it upward.

"Charlie, what the hell are you doing?" Jim said. "I almost blew your head off."

Emily rustled on the bed, throwing the covers off of herself and scrambling up next to Jim.

Charlie popped his head back up, his chiseled, muscular jaw rippling with tension. "Dammit, Jim. Why is your phone off?"

"What?" Jim said. "It's not off."

"I've been trying to text you and call you," Charlie said. "Did Lacy leave you a message?"

Jim paused, then looked at Emily. "Can you grab my phone?"

"Yeah," Emily said. She ran over to the nightstand and came rushing back, handing Jim his phone. He took it and looked at the screen.

"I haven't gotten any texts or calls since yesterday afternoon," Jim said.

"Shit," Charlie said. "How about you, Emily?"

Emily was tapping her screen. "No, nothing."

"I bet you guys have been hacked," Charlie said.

"Why would we be hacked?" Jim said.

Charlie got closer to the house, leaning his head inside the window. "I got a message from Lacy while I was out of state. She was in trouble. She said they were after her, and they were everywhere."

"Who is they?" Emily said.

"I don't know," Charlie said. "But she was always worried about something like this. It took her a long time to tell me, but she has been training for this exact thing. That's why she's been busting her ass all this time, earning every type of black belt in existence, training like fricking Rocky."

"She knew someone would come after her?" Jim said.

Charlie rubbed one eye with his thumb and the other with his forefinger. "I think so. She said if the wrong people found out about that program she wrote, they would hunt her down."

"Her program? The one that saved us?" Emily said. "She mentioned it to me once—said I could never speak of it. What did she call it?"

"Wildfire," Jim said.

"Yeah, wildfire," Emily said. "But how did someone find out about it? The three of us were the only ones who knew."

Charlie grunted. "There's one other person alive that knew."

Jim put his hand on the window sill and rested his forehead against the wall. "Kraig," he said.

CHAPTER 7

J im stuffed his trembling hands into his pockets and forced himself to keep walking down the narrow corridor deep under the prison. It was like a winding dungeon hallway, and the walls were not smooth, but made of rough-hewn stone, like the blocks had been cut with a giant chainsaw. The air had an earthy, damp smell to it that made Jim's nose tingle. Whoever had made these passageways had done so on a minimal budget, probably because not many people were privy to the fact that they existed.

"Are you sure you're okay with going in alone?" Charlie said.

"Yeah, I think it's best," Jim said. "I think I can convince him. He won't respond to intimidation."

"What, me intimidate?" Charlie gave an exaggerated smile.

Jim's gaze went to Charlie's broad shoulders and thick chest, then to his military style haircut. There was no denying it, Charlie looked like a bonafide ass-kicker.

"Yeah," Jim said. "I think keeping Arnold Schwarzenegger and his waterboarding interrogations out of the room is the best approach."

"Really? Did you just say that?" Charlie said. "That's pretty offensive, you know. I look nothing like Arnold."

Jim tried to smile and took a deep breath as they neared the iron door. "Oh man, am I nervous," he said, his voice shaking.

Charlie turned to him. "You can do this, man. He's just a guy with a messed up brain. Don't make him into something bigger than that."

Jim nodded. "He's a cold-blooded killer and he hates me more than anyone on the planet."

Charlie put his hands on Jim's shoulders, giving him a squeeze. "Let's not forget that he has an IQ of 220."

Jim's forehead was cold with sweat. He shuddered.

"Take a slow, deep breath and hold it as long as you can," Charlie said.

Jim breathed in deep and held it. He started to feel light headed and exhaled.

"Feel a little better?" Charlie said.

Jim nodded.

"Okay, let's do this." Charlie lifted a rusty iron latch and pushed the door open; it grated loudly on the hinges.

Jim stepped into the room, and Charlie closed the door behind him with an echoing clank.

Kraig knelt on the cement floor, looking up at Jim with a sneer. His long black hair was greasy and wet, hanging over his face. It looked like he had taken a beating earlier that day. His eyes were puffy and he had scratches on his cheek.

"What the hell do you want?" Kraig said.

Jim hesitated, breathing deep through his nose. He closed his eyes. "We need your help."

Kraig laughed and then choked on his spit, causing him to go into a coughing fit. When the coughing stopped, Kraig shook his head. "What could possibly be that important, that you would come to me? You realize if my hands weren't shackled behind my back, you'd be dead by now. Well, dying slowly and painfully, at least."

"Lacy is missing," Jim said.

42

Kraig shrugged.

"Nian is dead," Jim said.

Kraig froze, then looked up at Jim, raising an eyebrow.

"That right, he's gone. He's not the one who has Lacy."

Kraig's lips spread into a sly smile. Jim assumed he was thinking about where Nian's death put him on the list of the world's best hackers. Probably at the top.

"Do you know who else would have taken her?" Jim said.

Kraig was silent for a moment, staring at the floor. His eyes were darting back and forth. Then his eyes widened and his head jerked up, his piercing gaze fixating on Jim.

"You don't want to get involved in this," Kraig said. "As much I would relish in seeing you suffer, I'm telling you; you do not want to get involved in this."

"What?" Jim leaned forward. "What are you talking about?"

"Just walk away, Jimbo. Walk away and forget about it."

"What about Lacy?"

"She's already gone," Kraig said. "Trust me, that little twat is not worth going where this rabbit hole will take you."

Jim took three steps forward and slammed his fist into Kraig's face, knocking him backward. Kraig lay on his back, his hands bound underneath him, laughing. Blood streamed out of his nose. Jim leaped onto Kraig's chest, wrapping his hands around his neck.

"Go ahead, kill me," Kraig said. "If you do, this face is what you'll see every night when you close your eyes and go to sleep." Kraig's mouth spread into a crimson smile and he winked. "Unless that's already the case."

Jim's hands relaxed.

"There's nothing you could do to make me help you." Kraig laughed as blood ran into his mouth.

Jim gritted his teeth. "I could get you into a different cell block."

Kraig stopped laughing and his eyes narrowed at Jim.

"That's right, I can get you away from those guys who are

visiting you every night."

"How?" Kraig said.

"I know people who have connections," Jim said. "How do you think I got a meeting with you down here?"

Kraig studied Jim's eyes, thinking for a moment. "Charlie," Kraig said.

Jim said nothing.

"I'll need a smartphone," Kraig said. "If I get online, I can search the subnets and figure out what's going on."

Jim stood up, pulled a shrink wrapped silver mobile device out of his pocket, and set it on Kraig's stomach. "You know where you'll have to hide that to get it past the guards?"

Kraig turned his head and spit a stream of blood onto the floor. "I've had much worse things there, trust me."

Jim stepped out of the room, closing the heavy door behind him.

"So much for not using intimidation," Charlie said.

"You heard all that?" Jim said.

"Oh yeah."

CHAPTER 8

Kraig lay on his bunk bed, with his blanket over his head, tapping on the screen of the smartphone. He had the display of the device turned down to the dimmest setting possible, just to make sure he didn't wake up the stinky, nasty pile of crap snoring on the bunk beneath him.

A tingling sensation filled Kraig's body as he felt the thrill of finally being back online; a simple thing which gave him unimaginable power. Although hacking from a touchscreen was not ideal, it was still a window into a world in which Kraig was the king.

He had modified an old FM radio so that he could hide the phone inside it, connecting it to power wires that would keep it charged during the day. At night, Kraig could traverse the entire world of cyberspace. He felt a rush every time he broke into a network or took over a server. Two years had been way too long to go without his beloved technology, and it had only pushed him deeper into madness.

While Kraig hated Jim more than anything, and the thought of helping him was infuriating, Jim was right about one thing. Charlie Prentice could get Kraig into a better spot; the man did have connections within the prison. Given that Kraig was a cold, calculating man—he could set aside his feelings and do whatever it took to make his situation better.

Besides, figuring out where Lacy had been taken would be an exhilarating challenge. A hacking mission that difficult was a thrill he had not enjoyed in a long time. He would accomplish the task, even though he knew that Lacy would still die in the end. In fact, none of them would survive. Jim and Charlie were also as good as dead. If Kraig was right about who took Lacy, there was nothing on earth that could stop them from killing off all of the loose ends.

Kraig's thumbs drummed on the touchscreen all night. First, he hacked the local cell towers to make sure his phone would always have connectivity, even if they tried to shut off his service. Then he installed packet sniffers on primary servers, trying to find any messages that were related to Lacy Chase. Finally, his fingers began to shake as he prepared to penetrate a server that he had only heard about through a strict warning from Nian.

"Never touch it," Nian had warned him. "Don't even ping that server. If you do, I won't be able to save you. You will soon disappear from the face of the earth."

To Kraig, something like that would have normally seemed like a dramatic exaggeration, but Nian was never one to exaggerate. So, Kraig had left it alone. Not out of fear, but because going against a warning from Nian was stupid, and counterproductive to Kraig's own ambitions.

But now he didn't care. He simply craved the ecstasy of hacking into something that Nian had dared not mess with.

CHAPTER 9

J im stood in the middle of the dank, cold room, his arms folded in front of him. Kraig sat in a steel chair, staring up at Jim, his wrists and ankles both secured this time. Charlie had told the guards they were too careless with Kraig on the last visit and explained to them just how dangerous Kraig was.

"Are we going to get violent again?" Kraig said.

"That depends," Jim said. "Did you find anything?"

"I did." One corner of Kraig's mouth curved into a smirk. "It's a shame you wouldn't understand the genius that was required to get the information."

Jim ran his fingers through his hair and sighed. "Just tell me."

"Fine," Kraig said. "There is a set of warehouses fifty miles north of Night Harbor. Operations have been running out of there for three months with the primary mission of capturing Lacy Chase."

"How many people are there?"

Kraig shrugged. "I don't know. It could be three hired goons, or it could be a whole army."

"You don't know?"

"Nope. I don't even know if they're still there," Kraig said. "If they already got her, they may have just packed up and gone home by now. The information I found was a week old."

"Great," Jim said.

"It doesn't matter, Jim." Kraig leaned his head back and looked at the ceiling, giving his cuffed hands a tug and rattling his chains against the chair.

Jim flinched.

"You're all dead anyhow," Kraig said. "These people. You don't realize their power—their reach." Kraig moved his head forward so that it was under the pale light. The shadows on his face were ghastly; his eyes looked like cavernous sockets. "They will kill you, Jim."

Jim's throat tightened up, choking his voice. "Well you already tried to kill me," Jim said.

Kraig tossed his head back and started laughing. His loud cackle echoed against the stone walls. Jim felt a chill race across his skin, causing him to shiver.

"I'm nothing compared to them." Kraig coughed and then spit a wad of phlegm onto the floor. "Absolutely nothing."

Jim clenched his jaw together, his breath seething between his teeth. "Who are they?"

"The Supremalus," Kraig said. His eyes flitted all around the room as though the walls could hear him.

"Supremalus?" Jim said.

"Yesss," Kraig said. "And they secretly rule the world."

Jim looked at Charlie as they wound through the corridors of the prison. "Have you ever heard of The Supremalus?"

"No," Charlie said, squinting up ahead at the glass doors that led outside. "What is it?"

"Apparently, it's a group that rules the world without anyone knowing it."

Charlie grunted. "I've taken orders directly signed by the president. I think I'd know if we were up against something like that."

Jim rubbed his stubbled face, going quiet for a moment. "What if the president takes orders from Supremalus?"

Stopping dead in his tracks, Charlie looked at Jim and raised an eyebrow. "That's some serious tinfoil hat bullshit."

Jim halted as well, thrusting his hands into his pockets. "After seeing what Nian was capable of, nothing would surprise me."

A glint of recognition crossed Charlie's eyes and he looked at the floor, his massive chest expanding and contracting with each breath. He was silent for some time.

"Charlie?" Jim said.

Charlie blinked and looked up, shaking his head. "Did Kraig have any other info?"

"Yeah, he gave me a location—some warehouses up north. I think we should check it out."

Charlie clenched a fist, causing his knuckles to crack. Then he opened his hand and frowned. "I hate having to trust that psychopath."

"I know what you mean," Jim said. "I get sick every time I talk to him. It takes everything I have not to puke all over the place. But he's our best chance." Jim shook his head. "Do you think we can snoop around the place and see if we find anything?"

Charlie scratched his head. "You're suggesting a covert operation consisting of a washed-up Navy SEAL and an office worker?"

"Accomplished ultramarathon runner," Jim said.

"Right," Charlie said. "It's still crazy."

"Lacy needs us, Charlie."

"I know," Charlie said. "Hell, I'd give my life for that girl. She's like a daughter to me. But you . . . ." Charlie paused. "You and Emily have a bright future ahead of you and—"

"We're not arguing about this anymore," Jim said, flashing a look at Charlie that startled him. "None of this would have even happened to Lacy if she hadn't helped me when I was in trouble." Jim breathed through his nose, calming himself down. "I am always going to be there when she needs me, got it?"

Charlie nodded.

"Now," Jim said, "let's start making a plan."

CHAPTER 10

C rouching in the brambles beneath the trees, Jim and Charlie watched the two warehouses for any sign of life. The area was abandoned and the structures looked old and weathered, sitting in the middle of a field full of tall weeds. The buildings were made of brick, now gray and crumbling, along with steel beams, which were a rusty red.

A cloudy mist hung low in the field surrounding the warehouses and it seemed to move around like hundreds of ghosts keeping watch as they constantly changed size and shape. The sight gave Jim a chilling sensation on the back of his neck. Though it seemed like it had been decades since there was activity in this place, the area still felt alive somehow.

Jim moved closer to Charlie, the cold hard ground crunching under his feet. "What do you think?"

"I think Kraig lied to us," Charlie said.

"Maybe. I don't know," Jim said. "Kraig's driving force is always to prove how superior he is. What better way to prove that than to out-hack this almighty Supremalus from his prison cell?"

"Or," Charlie said, "he could have made this whole Supremalus nonsense up, just to screw with us." Charlie reached down and grabbed a handful of snow from one of the few remaining white patches on the ground, where the sun never breached the shade of the trees. He squeezed the snow in his palm until water dripped down the sides of his hand.

Jim closed his eyes and massaged his forehead with his fingertips. "I don't think so," he said. "If an organization had Lacy, it would give them unimaginable power. The last thing Kraig wants is for someone else to gain power."

"Okay, fine," Charlie said. "Let's just focus on the task at hand then. We're going to stay along the edge of the woods until we get behind the compound. Then we'll climb the fence and sneak into the back door of the nearest warehouse."

"Got it," Jim said. He could feel his body trembling as his voice wavered.

Charlie noticed. "Just stay close to me."

They crept along the brush and Jim did his best to stay quiet. After moving along for a few minutes, Jim stepped on a fallen tree branch, making a startling crack, which caused Charlie to stop and glare back at him.

Jim mouthed a "sorry."

Charlie shook his head and turned back around, continuing to move through the brambles with ease. Jim followed, determined not to make another sound.

Finally, they were behind the warehouses, near the chain linked fence. Charlie started climbing first. As he neared the top, Jim came up after him. Jumping down to the ground on the other side, both men surveyed the area. Nothing in the field moved and the warehouse buildings stood silent in the misty sunlight. Charlie ran across the field of weeds, his thick legs knocking down the crisp stalks as Jim stayed close behind. Reaching the back door to the closest warehouse, Charlie grabbed the handle and turned—it was unlocked. He looked back at Jim and frowned. Jim nodded and jerked his head toward the door. They were going in, no doubt about it.

Charlie opened the door just enough for them to slip in, and Jim pulled it shut once they were inside. They were engulfed in complete darkness. Charlie clicked a small flashlight on, and shined it all around. The entire building was an open area with a cement floor. Ten feet above the floor, a loft circled all the way around the warehouse, with a railing made of steel bars that looked brown and rusted. Dust floated thick in the open space, making Charlie's flashlight beam look like a solid white shaft. The only sound was their breathing, which seemed almost amplified in the emptiness. The air was heavy and warm compared to the outside, with a musty smell so strong it was suffocating.

"Looks empty," Jim whispered.

"Let's make a sweep, just to be sure," Charlie said.

They walked along the wall as Charlie moved his flashlight beam side to side, up and down. Jim pulled out his phone, turned on its LED light, and shined it outward.

A click broke the silence, coming from the opposite wall. A door opened and long rectangle of light appeared on the floor of the warehouse. Hearing a whoosh of rustling clothing, Jim realized that Charlie had disappeared. The silhouette of a man appeared in the doorway, and then there was a whistle sound right next to him. The man in the doorway turned his head, and Jim saw the outline of his nose perfectly against the light, just before Charlie's forehead smashed into it. The man crumpled to the ground with a thud as his body hit the cement.

Charlie waited a moment and Jim held his breath. Nobody else came through the door. After recovering from the shock that they were not alone, Jim hurried toward the door. Charlie dragged the man across the floor.

"Close the door," Charlie whispered.

Jim reached the door and squinted, looking around in the sunlight. He didn't see anything but tall grass and the other building as he grabbed the knob and pulled the door shut.

"What do we do with him?" Jim said.

"We gag him, wait until he wakes up, and ask him some questions," Charlie said.

They sat in the corner, watching the unconscious man lying on the floor, with his shaved head, camo pants, and skin tight t-shirt. Charlie checked his gag to make sure it was tight, then pulled up the man's sleeves, looking at the tattoos on his arms.

"Devil Dog tat," Charlie said. "Pretty faded."

"What does that mean?" Jim said.

Charlie pulled the man's sleeve back down with a yank. "He was a Marine." Charlie reached down to his own ankle and pulled a gun out of a holster.

"What the hell?" Jim said. "You're not going to kill him are you?"

"I don't plan on it," Charlie said.

The man stirred. Charlie jumped to his feet and moved behind him, pressing the barrel of his gun against the back of the man's neck.

Realizing he was bound and gagged, the man's eyes widened and he tried to move.

"Hold still," Charlie whispered. "Or I'll have to shoot you."

Jim felt his skin tingle at the tone in Charlie's voice.

The man stopped struggling.

"My friend here is going to remove your gag," Charlie said. "You will only answer my questions, and make no other sounds." He pushed the gun harder against the man's neck. "Nod if you understand."

The man nodded.

Jim edged forward, reaching his hand out; he tried to keep it from shaking, but he couldn't. With a quick jerk, Jim pulled the handkerchief out of the man's mouth. The Marine sat there, silent, staring at the ground.

"Where is the girl?" Charlie said.

"You guys are as good as dead," the man said.

Charlie put his free hand on top of the man's head and

pressed the gun barrel into his neck so hard, Jim thought a vertebrae would snap. The man groaned, arching his neck.

"Where is she?" Charlie said through gritted teeth.

The Marine snarled. "We don't know."

"How many of you are there?" Charlie said.

The man said nothing.

A click of a switch broke the silence and light filled the entire warehouse. Jumping to his feet, Jim swung his head around and saw nothing but empty space and walls. Then he looked up, and the entire loft was filled with men pointing rifles down at them. Jim and Charlie were surrounded.

"Twenty two," the Marine said.

"Toss your weapon," one of the men in the loft shouted.

Charlie cursed, crouched down, and slid his gun across the cement. Then he put his hands behind his head.

~ ~ ~

"Where is she?" a man wearing a dark mask asked.

"You tell me." Jim shifted in the chair, trying to yank his hands free.

The man swung his fist around, smashing into Jim's cheekbone. Jim's face exploded with pain, and his head slumped down, hanging limp with his chin against his chest. Tasting iron in his mouth, Jim tried to look up, but the strength in his neck had left him.

The man paused, waiting. Then he said, "Lacy Chase. Tell me where she is hiding."

Jim gurgled and coughed. "I don't know . . . ." He took a painful breath. "We came here looking for her."

"Liar!" the man yelled, kicking Jim in the chest and knocking him backward on his chair. Jim tried to hold his head forward to prevent it from slamming against the floor, which helped, but his skull still thumped on the cement.

The man pulled a knife out of a sheath on his belt and took a step toward Jim. Then another masked man, wearing a gold chain necklace, pulled out a billy club and lifted it above his head. With a grunt, he swung the billy club in a downward arc, cracking the interrogator on the back of the skull. The interrogator went limp, collapsing on top of Jim.

The man with the billy club pulled off his ski mask.

Jim's heart jumped into his throat and he squinted, not trusting his blurred vision. "Jake?"

"Hey, Jimmy boy," Jake said.

Jim wheezed, his body trembling. "Are you going to kill me?"

Jake's eyes softened and he tossed his club to the side. "Jim, I'm not going to hurt you."

"You're not?"

"No, I came to help you."

"I don't understand."

"One of my guys got word that some big fish was looking for a gang to help with capturing a computer hacker. A huge bounty was offered."

Jim's cheek was bleeding all over his shirt, but he didn't notice. He just stared at Jake, still in shock.

"At first, I wasn't going to even consider the job, because usually those things are a wild goose chase. But this was a lot of money, so I got more info. Then I heard the name of one of the people of interest, Jim Wisendorf."

Jim tried to swallow and ended up choking on blood instead. Jake squatted down and grabbed Jim's shoulders, pulling him up with a grunt, so that his chair was upright again.

"So, I decided to join up and see what all the fuss was about," Jake said. "You seem to get into a lot of trouble, Jimmy."

"Are you going to turn me over to them?" Jim asked.

Jake shook his head. "No, I'm not."

"I thought you hated me," Jim said. "I ruined your life."

"You didn't ruin my life. I made my own choice. I don't blame you for kicking me out of your house, if that's what you're worried about. You did the right thing."

"But I thought—"

"Look, Jimmy, your world and my world are very different. You can never know about some of the things I've done. But you need my help." Jake pulled a key out of his pocket and unlocked the cuffs holding Jim to the chair.

When Jim's hands were free, he brought his fingers to his cheek, feeling the sticky blood coming from his beaten in face.

"Anyhow," Jake said. "Your friend that came with you, the big son of a bitch—"

"Charlie." Jim scrambled to his feet. "Where is he?"

"In the next room. They're trying to make him talk."

"He won't," Jim said.

"They'll kill him then."

"Not if we help him first." Jim looked around the small room, his gaze stopping at the closed door behind Jake.

Jake moved in front of Jim, blocking his view. "Jim, remember, he and I have history. And it's not pretty. I didn't exactly give him a warm welcome in St. Louis."

"I know, I'll handle it." Jim moved toward the door. "I'll tell him you saved me."

"I sure hope he listens to you." Jake pulled his ski mask back over his face. "Because that guy could snap my neck before you even finish a sentence."

"That's for sure," Jim said. He knew he would have even less time than that.

~ ~ ~

Charlie closed his eyes and forced himself to count while several hands held his head underwater. He was capable of holding his breath for five minutes, but these guys were not aware of that. They were pulling him up after one minute. The men yanked Charlie's head out of the steel tub by his shirt collar and spun him around. His back slammed against the tub, his handcuffs clanging against the metal. He sat there on the floor, gasping, pretending to be in a lot more pain than he really was.

"This guy's worthless," one of the men said, pulling out a silencer pistol and walking up to Charlie. He pointed it at Charlie's head.

Charlie marveled at how stupid the men were. They had to be no more than hired thugs. These warehouses were not the main headquarters of the organization, that much was obvious. This was the bottom of the totem pole.

The masked man with the pistol grunted as he touched the barrel to Charlie's forehead. His finger resting on the trigger, the man's pupils were dilated and small wrinkles appeared at the corners of his eyes. Experience told Charlie the man was about to pull the trigger, and that he was enjoying the thought of it for a moment before he actually did it.

As Charlie closed his eyes, the door to the room flew open and another masked thug came striding in. The three interrogators in the room spun around.

"Wait a second," said the new thug as he entered, "I know how to make him talk."

An angry groan escaped the man with the pistol.

"Step back," the new thug said.

The man with the pistol backed away from Charlie.

The new thug said, "I'll need your gun." He held out his hand.

The man with the pistol hesitated.

The new thug said, "I don't have all day. If I'm going to make him squeal, I'll need your gun."

The man handed the pistol over.

The new thug walked up to Charlie and crouched down next to him. He shoved the pistol into Charlie's crotch. Then he leaned in close, putting his mouth right next to Charlie's ear, and said, "I sure hope you're good." His left hand fumbled behind Charlie's back, finding the handcuffs.

Charlie felt one of the cuffs on his wrist loosen, then pop open.

The new thug spun around, aimed the silenced pistol at one of the interrogators, and pulled the trigger, sending him crumpling to the ground.

Charlie leapt to his feet, charging at the one who had put the gun to his forehead. The man tried to throw a punch, but Charlie blocked it with his forearm before unleashing an uppercut to the man's chin that snapped his head all the way back, knocking him out cold. A flash of metal caught Charlie's eye and he sidestepped as the third interrogator lunged at him with a knife. Charlie grabbed the man's wrist and twisted, sending the knife to the floor with a clang. At the same time, Charlie's other hand reached around the man's head, grabbing his chin and jerking it sideways with a crack. The man's body went limp, and Charlie let it fall to the floor.

Charlie stood still for a second, looking around at the carnage, making sure none of them were going to get up. The man who had unlocked his handcuffs was standing there, staring at him, his gun still in his hand, but pointed at the ground.

"Who are you?" Charlie said.

The man said nothing.

Charlie took a step forward. The man didn't budge.

"Why'd you help me?"

They stared at each other in silence.

Shrugging, the man tossed the gun across the room, causing a grating sound of metal on cement to echo against the walls. He cracked his knuckles and reached up, pulling his mask off.

Molten fire flooded into Charlie's veins. "You!" he said. In an instant, Charlie had his hands around the man's neck and had lifted him two feet off the ground. He took five steps and slammed the man against the wall, holding him there.

Jim burst in through the doorway. "Charlie, don't! He saved our lives!"

Jake held onto Charlie's wrists, turning his head and trying to breathe. "It's about time, Jim," Jake managed to gasp.

Running up to Charlie, Jim put his hand on his shoulder.

"Without his help," Jim said, "we won't get out of here alive."

Charlie took a deep breath, still holding Jake against the wall, but loosening his choking grip. "You remember what he did to me, Jim?"

Jake sucked in air, his chest heaving.

"We'll have to work that out later," Jim said.

Jake choked. "You were a soldier once, right, Charlie?"

Charlie nodded.

"You ever have to follow orders you didn't like?"

"Of course," Charlie said.

"That's what I was doing with you."

"You were ordered to torture me?"

Jake shook his head. "In my organization—" Jake gasped. "Showing any sign of weakness is a death sentence."

"Why are you in that organization?" Charlie said.

"It's a long story," Jake said. "And we need to get the hell out of here."

Charlie lowered Jake until his feet were on the ground. Jake sucked in deep breaths, but stood tall, staring Charlie in the eyes.

"And how do we do that?" Charlie said.

Jake pointed at the door. "Down the hallway and to the left, there is a room with a small window." He looked at Jim and pointed his thumb at Charlie. "I'm not sure if Rambo here will fit through, but it's the only option."

"What's keeping us from going out the front door?" Charlie said.

"We'd have to go through the main room," Jake said.

"About twenty men are hanging out there."

"Fine," Charlie said. "We'll follow your lead."

Jake nodded. "There is one guy in that room, Mack, the leader of this ragtag outfit." Jake walked over to the other side of the room and picked up the gun. Coming back toward Charlie, he twirled the pistol in his hand. "Stay hidden around the corner and give me two minutes to get Mack out of that room," Jake said, handing the weapon to Charlie. "If I haven't gotten him to leave by then, you can come in with guns blazing."

Charlie took the weapon.

"But be ready to fight for your life," Jake said. "The rest of the crew will be within earshot."

Charlie looked over at Jim and frowned. "I made peace with death a long time ago, but I'm worried about you. You going to be okay?"

Jim rubbed the back of his neck, his face going pale. He looked around at the lifeless bodies on the floor in silence. Straightening up, he set his jaw and nodded. "Yeah, I'll be fine."

"Okay," Jake said. "Let's go."

Charlie stood against the wall, peeking around the corner. Jim stayed crouched behind him. Gritting his teeth, Charlie watched as Jake opened the door to the room and walked in. Further down the hallway, the sound of talking voices echoed from the main room.

Charlie heard Jake speak.

"Hey, Mack," Jake said.

"What is it, Pike?"

"Hoosier wants to see you. He's in the main room."

"Why? He couldn't drag his lazy ass down here himself?"

"I don't know, but he said it's urgent," Jake said. "I can stay here and cover the phone in case an order comes in."

Mack grunted and his chair creaked, its wheels rolling on

the floor. "Fine."

Charlie tensed up as footsteps approached the door, then stopped. A shoe heel scraped the floor as it turned around.

"Hey, how's the interrogating going?" Mack said.

There was a slight pause.

"Uh, fine," Jake said. "We're working 'em over pretty good."

Charlie looked back at Jim and whispered, "Shit."

"The skinny one is Jim Wisendorf, right?" Mack said.

"Yeah, according to the photo they gave us," Jake said.

"Well, I sent the pictures we took to the bosses," Mack said. "They said they're coming out right away."

Jake cleared his throat. "They're coming out here?"

"Yep, they said to keep Jim alive until they get here," Mack said. "But if the big one won't talk, we can put him down."

"I think we might be able to get something out of him," Jake said. "Just need a little more time."

"Nah," Mack said. "I saw how tough that asshole looks. He ain't gonna give us anything."

Footsteps walked further back into the room. Then a drawer opened and something metal clanked against the side of it.

"In fact," Mack said, "I'll go take care him myself, right now."

"Sir, I'll do it," Jake said. "You'd better go see what Hoosier wants."

"Screw Hoosier, he can wait." The footsteps headed toward the door again. "I want to make sure this is done right."

Charlie pulled his head back from looking around the corner as Mack walked out into the hallway.

"Okay," Jake said, raising his voice. "Just a warning though, it's gotten pretty messy down there. I hope you can handle a little blood."

Mack gave a smoky laugh. "Remember who you're talking to, kid."

Standing up tight against the wall, Charlie reached his hand out and signaled for Jim to do the same. Jim's cheeks turned red as he held his breath and tried to become part of the sheet-rock he was leaning against.

A weathered looking man with a bald head strode around the corner. He flinched when he caught Charlie's looming shape out of the corner of his eye. Charlie's arms lashed out like striking cobras, one of his hands grabbing Mack's chin and the other hand cupping the back of his head. With a violent jerk, and a loud crack, Mack was nothing more than a sack of meat. Charlie caught him before he fell and lifted him onto his shoulder.

Jake hurried out the door, heading toward them. He stopped short when he saw Charlie walking with Mack thrown over his shoulder, like a lumberjack carrying a log. Jake nodded once and moved his hand in a circle, signaling for them to hurry up.

Charlie carried Mack into the room, as Jim and Jake scurried after him. Jake closed the door and locked it. With a grunt, Charlie plopped Mack down in his chair. As Charlie stepped back and looked at Mack, a recognition hit him and he drew in a deep breath. "What the hell?"

"What's wrong?" Jim's voice shook with adrenaline; his movements were jerky as he maneuvered around Charlie, taking a glance at Mack and then looking away. "Is he still alive?"

"No," Charlie said. "But I knew him."

"What do you mean, you knew him?" Jake said, coming up behind Charlie. "He didn't act like he knew you."

"I mean, I've seen him before." Charlie leaned against the desk, rubbing his eyes with his meaty hand. "At the Naval academy. He was a commander at the time." Charlie looked at Jake. "What did you know about him?"

"Not much," Jake said. "We're only told what we need to know here." He tilted his head up toward the ceiling and scratched the stubble on his neck. "I know he was in charge of everyone here, and that he got his orders from someone on that phone." Jake pointed to a touchtone telephone sitting on the desk. "I could tell he was a military type, as most of the guys are. But asking too many questions is a no-no around here. We do our job, take our money, and talk to nobody about what we've done."

"Lacy is the primary target?" Jim said.

Jake nodded. "The mission is to find her at all costs. And you and your wife are persons of interest. We're supposed to keep an eye on you."

A door opened down the hallway, and the voices from the main room grew louder, then quieter as the door shut again. They heard footfalls coming closer.

"Out the window, hurry." Jake ran over and pulled the glass pane upward—it went slow and made a loud moaning sound, but it moved. "Jim, you first."

Jim leaned over and stuck his head through the window.

"Run for the fence, don't wait for us," Jake said. "We'll be right behind you."

Someone tried to turn the door handle, rattling it when it did not open.

"Go, now!" Jake grabbed Jim's belt and shoved him the rest of the way through the window. Falling to the ground with a thud, Jim scrambled to his feet and took off into the open field.

A fist pounded on the door. "Mack, what's the deal?" A voice yelled.

Charlie squared up to the doorway. "Get out of here," he said to Jake over his shoulder. "I've got this."

Jake hesitated. "They'll kill you. There's way too many."

"If you don't jump through that window right now, I'll kill you first," Charlie said. He clenched and unclenched his fists, staring at the door as the pounding grew louder. "Get Jim somewhere safe, he'll need your help."

Jake shook his head. "I'm—"

"Go!" Charlie said through clenched teeth.

Jake turned and dove through the window as someone kicked the door open with a booming crash. Charlie growled, charging like a linebacker at the first man to come through the door. He wrapped his arms around the man's waist and lifted him into the air, plowing through the doorway and knocking down four other men in the hallway. Slamming the man he was carrying into the far wall, Charlie let him fall to the ground and spun around to face the other men that were closing in on him. Charlie swung his elbow around into someone's nose, causing them to holler in pain. Looking over his shoulder, he saw another man unholstering his gun and gave him a hard side-kick to the gut, doubling him over. A fist slammed into the side of Charlie's forehead, and he fell to his knees.

CHAPTER 11

J im sprinted for the fence, jumping onto it when he got close enough. He climbed to the top before he turned around to look. Jake was halfway across the field. He didn't see Charlie. Looking up as he ran, Jake saw that Jim was stopping at the top of the fence, straddling the barbed wire.

"Don't stop!" Jake yelled. "Get into the woods!"

Jim saw the silhouettes of several men coming out of the warehouse building. It was near dark now, and a cool, heavy mist hung over the grassy field. As Jake neared the fence, a gunshot rang out, and a chunk of ground exploded next to Jake's right foot. Jim stayed put on top of the fence, reaching down with his hand open. With a leap, Jake hit the fence halfway to the top. Jim grabbed his hand and yanked him up and over. They both fell to the ground on the other side.

Another shot pierced the air, ricocheting off the steel links next to Jim, as he scrambled to his feet.

"Where's Charlie?" Jim said.

Jake stood up and grabbed Jim's shirt collar, yanking him toward the thick brush of the forest.

"We're dead if we don't run," Jake said.

Jim wrenched free of Jake's grip and lunged back to the

fence, grabbing the metal wire and peering through the fog.

"He stayed back to buy us time," Jake said.

"No," Jim said. His eyes were burning as he choked back a sob. "I'm not leaving without him." He started climbing the fence, his face twisting as tears and sweat blinded his vision.

A gunshot sliced through the mist and Jim's thigh exploded in a splatter of tissue and blood. His fingers rattled the fence as he slid down to the ground. Crying out, Jim tried to get up. Jake hooked his hands under Jim's armpits, grunting and lifting him to his feet.

"Charlie told me to keep you safe, no matter what," Jake said. "I owe him that much." Jake grabbed Jim's wrist, crouched down, and lifted him up in a fireman's carry.

Then Jake Pike, Jim's estranged childhood friend, the one who had taken every wrong turn in life, the one who had become a crime boss and did unspeakable things, said, "Hold on, Jim. You're gonna be alright." He took a deep breath, adjusted Jim's body weight across his shoulders, and plunged into the woods.

Jim bounced and groaned as Jake's legs pumped up and down, barreling through leaves, branches, and shrubs. Stumbling once, Jake righted himself and kept going, his breathing raspy and desperate. As his leg bled out, Jim remembered the time he had to sneak out of a bathroom window and run ten miles to get home, because a party Jake had brought him to was raided by the cops for drugs. Then he pictured the moment Jake had come to his house, asking for money because he was indebted to gangsters who would kill him if he didn't pay up. Eventually, Jake had become one of those terrible men.

Snapping out of his thoughts, Jim realized that Jake was coughing, choking, and struggling to stand. Jim's leg was bleeding all over Jake's shoulder and chest, causing his soaked, sticky shirt to cling to his skin. Pain jolted through Jim's brain with every one of Jake's strides.

"Jake, you have to stop and rest," Jim said.

Jake could barely get a word out. "No," was all he said.

Jim could feel Jake's wiry frame underneath him, twitching as he continued stumbling forward.

"I think I can limp," Jim said.

"No." Jake's voice was nothing more than a whisper and he coughed with every breath. "We have to move faster."

Jake must have run two miles through the woods with Jim on his shoulders. With a desperate wheeze, Jake finally collapsed, and Jim held in a scream as they tumbled to the ground. They both lay on their backs, in the brown leaves and mossy dirt, trying to catch their breath.

"How's your leg?" Jake said. He rolled onto his stomach to get a closer look.

"Hurts like hell," Jim said, biting his lip as the shock wore off.

Jake pulled a folding knife out of his pocket, flipping it open. He cut Jim's jeans around the thigh, just above the bullet wound, and yanked the pants leg down. Blowing air out in a whistle through tightened lips, Jake shook his head.

"I've seen worse," Jake said. "Looks like it just took out a chunk of your muscle." He took a piece of denim and wiped the blood way.

Jim sucked in through gritted teeth.

"We'll need to take care of it, though," Jake said. "That sucker'll be infected."

Jim shivered. "We need to get out of here alive first."

Jake started wrapping the pants leg around Jim's wound. "How did you guys get here?" Jake said.

"We drove. Emily, my wife—"

Jake smiled and nodded when Jim mentioned Emily.

"—she parked on the main highway, to the south. She was going to wait for us. We told her if she saw anything strange, or we took longer than two hours, to just drive away. We'd meet up with her in Night Harbor." Jim raised his eyebrows and tried to push himself to his feet. "Oh, shoot. That was like—"

"Five hours ago," Jake said. "At least."

"I'd try to call her but they took my phone back there," Jim said.

"It wouldn't matter," Jake said. "There's no signal out here."

Jim managed to get up on one leg and looked around at the sky. The sun had begun to disappear behind the horizon, causing the woods to get dark. Pointing behind him, Jim said, "That way." He turned, trying to take a step, his foot dragging in the leaves. "If Emily's still waiting, she's parked about three miles that way."

A light flickered far off in the forest, barely visible through the trees. Jim froze, his heart thumping. Jake took two slow, careful steps toward Jim and leaned over so his mouth was right next to Jim's ear.

"They're searching the woods," Jake said.

"What do we do?"

"We can't move right now. We'll have to hunker down in the dark and wait." Jake's breath was hot and intense in Jim's ear. "It's too quiet out here. They'll hear us from a long ways away."

Jim thought about Emily sitting in the car, in the dark. He decided she had to be gone by now, that she would have left hours ago. He hoped that was the case. He didn't want to imagine her waiting, alone and in the dark—wondering, hour after hour, whether anyone was coming back. His stomach tightened as it churned up acid. Sitting against the tree, Jim rubbed his arms and looked at Jake, who was crouching next to him. The temperature had dropped as darkness came, causing them both to clench their arms around themselves.

"Do you think they'll search the woods all night?" Jim said.

"Maybe," Jake said. "But I doubt it. Most of those guys aren't that loyal to the cause." Jake's steamy breath billowed around them in the moonlight. "And now that Mack is dead, a lot of them will want to bail on the whole operation."

Jim nodded his head and started rocking back and forth to stay warm.

"There is something big going on, Jim. Even though I was low in the chain of command, I heard whisperings. Whoever's in charge of this has a lot of reach, like nothing I've ever seen. Military, police, gangs, mobs, and criminals. I wouldn't even dare take you to a hospital right now, cause there'd probably be someone there working for them."

The mention of military made Jim think about Charlie, and he fought back sobs that threatened to wrack through his body. Charlie deserved better. The man was a hero in every sense of the word. He had been asked to complete impossible missions for his country, missions that would give the rest of us nightmares if we even knew about them. Yet he completed them with steadfast determination.

"What I don't get," Jake said, "is why anyone would organize such a massive operation just to find some girl?"

"Lacy's not just some girl," Jim said. "She's a hacker."

Jake laughed, snorting through his nose. "She must be some hacker."

"You have no idea," Jim said.

Something rustled the leaves, a stone's throw away, startling Jim out of a daze. He lifted his head, surprised that he had dozed off with his leg in such pain and his body shivering from the cool night air. He shot a glance at Jake, who was staring into the dark in the direction of the noise. Flicking his knife open with his thumb, Jake looked over at Jim and put his finger to his lips. Jim leaned forward and tried to focus on the trees in the moonlight, searching for any sign of movement.

Jim gasped when a shape emerged from the thick brush. He couldn't see a face, it was too dark, but he would recognize the silhouette anywhere. Charlie was alive and had somehow found them in the middle of the dark woods. Jim leapt up onto his good leg and hobbled toward Charlie, abandoning all thoughts about staying quiet and hidden. When he got closer, the moonlight illuminated Charlie's face, stopping Jim in his tracks. Jake came up as well, and when he saw Charlie, a gasp rattled in his throat.

Charlie was a twisted, bloody mess, covered from head to toe in thick crimson. He looked like he had been through three wars before finally crawling through hell and back for good measure. There was a rifle in Charlie's hand, which slid out of his fingers and dropped to the ground. Wavering on his feet, Charlie lifted his heavy eyes to look at Jim, then fell forward, flat on his face with a giant thud on the forest floor.

Jim lunged toward Charlie, stumbling onto his knees and crawling the rest of the way. He grabbed Charlie's shoulder and yanked, flipping him over onto his back. Jim recoiled, pulling his hands away in horror, trying to ignore the dark pasty gunk that was now caked on his palms.

Jake knelt down and checked Charlie's pulse. "How can you still be alive after losing this much blood?"

Charlie's lips moved, but nothing came out at first. Then he mumbled, his eyes flickering open. "Most of it is not mine."

Jake's mouth opened, then it shut. He stared at Charlie in silence.

"I just kept killing," Charlie said, "until they stopped coming." He coughed again. "They had me down, beaten to a pulp, when one of them walked up with a rifle, intending to execute me." Charlie's body stayed limp, his arms at his sides, only his lips moving as he stared up at the stars. "The smug bastard put the muzzle right in my face. I managed to disarm him, and once I had a gun, it was pretty much paint by numbers from there."

"There's no more left?" Jim said.

Charlie shook his head. "A handful took off in a truck, and a few are searching the woods."

"Do you think we can make it back to the car?" Jim said. Charlie nodded and took a deep breath. "Just give me a few minutes to rest."

Jake leaned over and grabbed Charlie's shoulder, giving it a light squeeze. The moonlight reflected in Jake's eyes and his tough expression softened, his scars almost fading away.

"Take all the time you need, buddy," Jake said, patting Charlie on the arm. With a nod, Jake got up and walked over to a nearby tree. He stood tall and looked out at the dark woods, keeping a vigilant watch.

J. ARTHUR SQUIERS

CHAPTER 12

Emily sat up in her car with a jolt when something scratched on the windshield. She slapped her hand over her mouth, trying not to scream. A raccoon was on the hood, attempting to scurry up the glass, its paws slipping and going nowhere. Looking right into the animal's eyes, she gave a muffled cry. The creature's black eyes and white face looked like a grinning ghost in the pale moonlight. Emily closed her eyes and laid her head back, forcing herself to calm down. The scratching continued and she could not take it anymore. Emily yelled at the animal and pounded on the windshield with her fist, trying to scare it away. The raccoon stopped moving and sat still, watching her.

It had been eight hours since Jim and Charlie stepped out of her car and headed into the woods. The plan was that she would wait for two hours, and if they were not back by then, she would drive straight to Night Harbor, to her friend Susie's house. She was not to go to the police, nor anyone else. But as the hours had passed, she couldn't bring herself to leave. Knowing that the man she loved was out there, she was determined to stay and wait.

Exhaustion had taken over and after she had drifted into a

worried sleep, she woke up hours later, face to face with this ghastly raccoon. It was well into the night now. Her body was aching from sitting in the car for so long and she was freezing cold. Remembering that she had a sleeping bag in the trunk, Emily decided she would try to scare the raccoon away and go get it. She did not want to make too much noise, in case people were nearby, so she resisted the urge to honk the horn. Emily opened her door an inch and then pulled it shut, making a soft clank. The animal took off running, but it did not go far. The raccoon stood in the middle of the road, ten feet away, still watching her.

Emily reached down under her seat and popped the trunk. Taking two quick breaths, she opened the door, ran around to the back of the car, and grabbed the sleeping bag. She glanced up at the raccoon, still there and baring its teeth. A squeak escaped from Emily's lips as she slammed the trunk shut, darted around the car, and dove back inside. She yanked the door shut with a loud sigh.

Emily had considered going and looking for Jim and Charlie earlier, when she was squatting in the ditch to relieve herself. She had even started heading into woods; but as soon as she stepped into the thick grove of oak trees, she knew she would only get lost.

"That's what the dumb girls in movies do," Emily told herself. "The 'too stupid to live' girls, they go wandering into trouble."

No, it was better to stay put. Even if she had to stay in the car until morning, she was going to wait. If they were not back by sunrise, then she'd follow the plan and head back to Night Harbor.

In a final moment of hope, Emily decided to try using her phone one last time. The screen did not show any signal bars, but she thought she might get lucky. She dialed Jim's number and brought the phone up to her ear, but there was nothing, no ringing, no voicemail.

As Emily stuffed her phone back into her pocket, a pair of headlights reflected in her rearview mirror, shining into her eyes. The muscles in her stomach tightening, she slouched way down in her seat, hoping they would just drive by without seeing her in the car. It would be better if they thought it was just some abandoned vehicle on the side of the road.

Emily had been sitting out there for all those hours, reading books, listening to music, and manicuring her nails. In that entire time, not one car had driven past on the gravel road in the middle of nowhere. Why now? Who could possibly be out driving around at . . . . Emily looked at her watch . . . . three in the morning?

Sweat started rolling down Emily's forehead, and she tossed the sleeping bag off of herself. She slouched down even further, tucking her head between her knees. The lights kept coming closer and it looked like they were slowing down. Cursing, she reached over to the glove box and opened it, taking out the handgun that Charlie had left for her. Her hand trembled as she checked the action to make sure it was loaded.

Several months ago, Lacy had brought Emily to the shooting range. Emily had proven that she could not hit a target, even if it was ten feet in front of her. After Emily had unloaded an entire clip and missed with every shot, Lacy had looked at her with a serious expression. Lacy then told Emily if she ever got in trouble, she had better run. Kick them in the balls and run, that was Lacy's solemn advice.

The vehicle slowed way down and approached Emily's car at a coasting speed. She kept her eyes fixed on the floor, willing them to keep going. The headlights stopped and Emily glanced over to see a Humvee sitting on the road next to her. Two men were in the front of the monstrous vehicle. The passenger, wearing a black stocking cap, was looking at her and rolling his hand in a circle, signaling for her to roll down her window. Emily set the gun between her legs and opened the window a few inches.

"You need help?" said the passenger in the Hummer.

Emily's mind raced, trying to think of anything that would get them to keep moving. She found her angle. "I'm out here stargazing with my husband," she said. "He had to relieve himself, so he went into the woods."

The man in the truck glanced across the ditch at the woods. "He had to go all the way in there to take a piss?"

Emily felt her face turn red. She was so damn nervous, she couldn't think straight. "He had to go number two," she said, forcing a smile. "Needed leaves for . . . . you know."

Narrowing his eyes, the man in the truck turned and looked at the driver, then back at Emily. "We'll wait until he gets back." His eyes went to the backseat of Emily's car, then back to her. "Just want to make sure you're okay."

Blood rushed to Emily's head and she felt dizzy. "That's not necessary, I assure you."

The man grinned. "We insist."

Emily sat there for a minute, looking over at the forest, trying to decide what to do. The massive engine of the Humvee idling rumbled in her ears. She opened her door and stepped partway out, looking over the top of her car at the woods. Then she yelled, "Honey, everything okay?"

There was no sound except for the truck motor.

The passenger in the Humvee said, "I'd better go make sure a bear didn't get him." He opened his door.

When the interior lights of the truck came on, Emily saw the driver. He was a bald, beefy man, with a stern, chiseled face. The driver looked at Emily with a cold, emotionless stare. As the passenger with the stocking cap jumped out and slammed his door shut, Emily bent down and grabbed the gun from her seat. She turned around, pointing it at the man. He stopped and raised his hands to chest level, showing her his palms.

Emily tried to swallow the bile that was coming up in her

throat. "Just go," she said, trying to keep her voice steady. "Get back in your truck and drive away." Her words warbled with each beat of her thumping heart.

Squinting, the man eyed her gun. "Sweetie, you got the safety on."

When Emily looked at the side of the gun, the man grabbed her wrist with one hand and the top of the gun with his other, yanking it away from her.

Emily shifted her weight and swung her right foot up into the man's crotch, the toe of her shoe connecting with its target. The man groaned and dropped the gun. With a squeal, Emily turned and ran, her legs pumping fast and hard. She heard the driver open his door and shout as he ran after her in the dark.

As Emily bolted into the woods, kicking up twigs and brush, she could hear the heavy breathing of both men behind her. But Emily was fast. Even though she was a prissy, curvy woman, her hips and thighs were strong and full of power. There were not many people who could outsprint her.

~ ~ ~

Jim shuffled along with one arm over Charlie's shoulders and another arm around Jake. They were making steady progress toward the car, though they had to stop and adjust the dressing on Jim's wound a few times. Gritting his teeth as his foot struck a tree root, Jim perked his head up at the sound of a crashing noise in the distance.

"Wait," Jim said. "What's that?"

They stopped and listened.

"Maybe a deer," Jake said.

"No," Charlie said, "it's a person running." He turned his ear toward the noise, concentrating. "More than one person."

"They're coming fast," Jake said.

Charlie crouched down, unstrapping his rifle from his shoulder. Jake's body tensed as he supported Jim's weight.

Jim heard the person running out in front of the others; he heard her gasping and crying out in agony.

"It's Emily," Jim said. "They're chasing her."

Charlie looked up at Jim, keeping his ear facing the sounds. Nodding in agreement, Charlie said, "Don't stop her. Let her pass by."

Jim clenched his jaw and crouched down with Jake. Gritting his teeth, Jim tried to ignore the searing pain in his thigh.

Charlie crept along the ground to the left and waited. After a few seconds, Emily flew past them, her long hair floating behind her. Jim heard her gasp with each footstep and knew she could not go much further. Then Jim heard the heavy, lumbering sound of boots hitting the ground, and he could tell there were two men chasing her. Emily had gotten ahead of them by a decent margin, but they would have soon overtaken her.

Charlie popped up from the bushes and swung his rifle like a baseball bat, the butt of the gun smashing into a man's head with a sickening crack. The second man, realizing the ambush, shifted his course, trying to veer away from Charlie. There was a flash of steel in the moonlight, followed by a whistling sound through the air. The man gurgled and fell down with a knife in his neck.

Jim heard Emily stop running. She doubled over and sucked air in deep gasps.

"Emily," Jim said.

"Jim?"

"Don't worry, you're safe."

Emily let out a sob and dropped to her knees.

Charlie came stumbling back to Jim, his mouth hanging open, his eyes looking weary.

"I hate this," Charlie said, looking at his hands. "I'm taking so many lives."

"I know," Jim said. "I'm sorry."

Charlie shook his head. "I've slipped into a mode that scares me. It's become too automatic to kill."

Jim put a hand on each of Charlie's shoulders and looked him in the eyes.

"You protected your friends," Jim said. "We're being hunted by dangerous people, and there's nobody we can trust. I'm lost without you, Charlie . . . . Lacy has no chance without you."

Charlie nodded and straightened up, pushing his shoulders back. Jim felt a pang in his chest; he had never seen Charlie, the toughest man he had ever met, looking so vulnerable. At the same time, Charlie was right. He had killed a lot of people that night, many of whom were former soldiers just looking for some extra cash.

"We're almost to the car," Jim said. "We'll get out of here and find somewhere to regroup."

Charlie's face came back to life, his eyes becoming sharp and focused. He nodded. "Thank you," he said, clapping Jim on the shoulder. "I just needed a little pep talk to get over that hump."

"Well, I'm no four star general," Jim said.

Charlie smiled. "I didn't need a general, I needed a friend."

Emily walked up to them, still trying to catch her breath. Jim turned on his good leg, grabbing her in his arms. She pushed against him and he had to hop backwards to catch his balance. He sucked air through his teeth and grabbed his thigh in pain.

Emily gasped, her hand slapping over her mouth. "Jim, were you shot?"

"I'll be okay," Jim said.

She turned and looked at Charlie, her eyes opening wide as she shrieked at the sight of him covered in blood. Emily gagged as she tried to absorb what she was seeing. "What hap—"

"Let's get moving," Jake said.

Emily spun around to face Jake. When she saw him, her mouth opened wide and she looked like she was about to faint.

Jim caught her up in his arms. "He's right, we need to move," Jim said. "I'll explain in the car."

CHAPTER 13

J im welcomed the flood of relief that came over him as he stepped out of the forest and into the brown weeds of the ditch. Emily's car sat there, looking silent and frightened in the dark. A huge military truck was parked next to it on the road, its engine still running, its headlights cutting through the darkness far ahead.

"Man, let's take the truck," Jake said as he pushed a branch aside, striding into the open air ahead of the others. His breath trailed behind him like exhaust from a muffler in the night air.

"No," Charlie said. "It probably has a tracker somewhere in it, and we don't have time to find it."

"Dang." Jake grabbed a weed as he walked along, sticking the end in his mouth and chewing on it.

Emily hurried up behind Jim, grabbing his arm.

"Who is that guy?" Emily said.

Scratching the back of his head, Jim looked at Emily and said, "That's Jake."

Emily stopped walking, her grip on Jim's arm tightening. "Jake, as in your old friend Jake?" she whispered.

Jim halted, nodding as he glanced at Jake, who was almost to the car now, just out of earshot.

"Jake as in . . . . crime lord Jake?" Emily said.

Jim closed his eyes, shaking his head. "He saved my life back there, Emily."

Emily put her hands on top of her head, grabbing fistfuls of her hair. Jim could see the gears churning in her mind.

"You trust him?" she said.

"He came all the way up here to help me when he heard I was a target. He infiltrated them, for me."

"Infiltrated? How do you know he's not playing you?"

Jim took a deep breath. "I can just tell—the things he did back there. He's on our side."

"You told me he's probably killed people," Emily said.

"I don't think he had a choice," Jim said. "I think he doesn't want to be that guy anymore."

Emily frowned. "Keep an eye on him, Jim. Sometimes you're too trusting."

Jim was silent for a moment. After what had happened back there, he could not fathom the idea of Jake having bad intentions. "Okay," Jim said. "But try to give him a chance to prove himself. We would have never made it out of there alive without him."

"Dammit guys!" Charlie shouted. "Hurry up! There'll be more of 'em here any minute."

Jim grabbed Emily's hand and hobbled toward the car. Charlie climbed into the driver's seat, and Jake jumped in on the passenger side, as they waited for Jim and Emily to cross the ditch.

In the distance, the sound of an engine running at high speed reached Jim's ears, causing his stomach to flip flop. His pulse raced and each heartbeat jolted the bullet wound in his leg with throbbing pain.

"They're coming," Jim said.

Emily let go of Jim's hand and broke into a sprint for the car. Charlie fired up the engine while Emily pulled the rear door open and dove across the back seat to the other side. Jake waved Jim in with his arm out the window like a third base coach sending a runner home. A white glow appeared on the crest of the hill far behind the car as Jim jumped in and slammed the door. Charlie gave the car some gas, building up a little momentum to avoid a spin out. Once they were moving, Charlie punched it. Snapping his head around, Jim looked behind them and saw the lights above the hill getting brighter.

"You think you can outrun them?" Jake said.

"I'm hoping I don't have to," Charlie said. "The moon is bright enough, I can keep our headlights off. I'll make sure I don't tap the brakes and maybe they won't see us."

"Where will we go?" Emily said.

"I want to have another chat with Kraig," Jim said. "Give him a piece of my mind about sending us into that rat trap."

"I don't know," Charlie said. "I think I've used up my favors at that prison."

"You can't go back there anyway," Jake said. "You can't go anywhere."

"Anywhere?" Jim said.

"They'll have people watching for you at the prison by now," Jake said. "At the hospitals, the banks, the grocery stores." He ran his fingers through his greasy hair and shook his head. "These people, you have to understand. They are everywhere. They control everything."

Charlie kept an uneasy eye on the rearview mirror. "We have to go off the grid," Charlie said.

Jake nodded.

Emily's face was pale, her eyes getting rounder as the implications sank in. "Kind of like Lacy did," she said. "When she was running for her life."

Jim put an arm around Emily, trying to comfort her.

"Yeah," Charlie said. "Exactly like that."

J. ARTHUR SQUIERS

CHAPTER 14

Keep your head down the entire time," Charlie said. "Pull that baseball cap low and don't ever look up."

Glancing across the parking lot at the convenience store, Emily took a long, deep breath and let it out through tight lips. She tucked her hair under a Nike hat that Jim had given her and pulled down on the brim. "Are you sure it should be me? I'm not experienced with this."

"You're the only face they didn't see at the warehouse." Charlie turned around and looked at Emily in the back seat of the car. He gave her a reassuring smile. "It's our safest bet."

Jim reached over and grabbed Emily's hand.

"I'll go with her," Jim said. He brushed a lock of hair out of Emily's face and looked at her with concern. "I don't like you going in there alone."

"No," Emily said. "I can do this."

Jim nodded and kissed her on the forehead. "We'll be right here watching. If anything seems off, just run out the door."

Exhaling one more time, Emily pushed the car door open and walked across the parking lot. Jim watched as Emily fidgeted with her hat while she shuffled toward the store with stiff arms and jerky movements of her legs. He closed his eyes and willed her to stay calm.

Pushing the glass door open, Emily entered the store. She kept her face tilted toward the floor and looked side to side with quick glances. A middle aged woman with leathery skin stood behind the counter.

"Morning," the woman said, her voice rattling with a smoker's rasp.

Emily just forced a smile and nodded. She scanned the aisles; there was only one customer, a petite girl, with long hair. She was reaching for a carton of milk, her back facing Emily. Emily's heart was in her throat and a tingling sensation spread throughout her body.

"Lacy?" Emily whispered.

The girl turned around. Her cheeks were round, her eyes bright and big—the complete opposite of Lacy's sharp, intense features. Emily felt herself deflate, realizing how much she missed her friend in that moment. The girl hesitated for a second, and Emily looked away, cursing herself for staring.

As the girl carried her milk toward the counter, Emily strode across the store to the packaged sandwiches. She grabbed eight of them, then walked over to another aisle and picked up a gallon of spring water. Hearing the cashier ringing up the girl with the milk, Emily glanced around at the ceilings of the store. There was a camera in one corner, above the hallway to the restrooms, and another camera above the front door, pointing at the counter.

Emily's forehead glistened with sweat as she walked up to the cashier, placing the sandwiches and water on the counter.

"Find everything okay?" the cashier said.

Emily nodded once and tossed a twenty dollar bill onto the counter. The cashier punched buttons on the register and it opened with a ring. She grabbed the twenty and pulled out some ones and change, slapping it on the glass countertop. As Emily went to grab the change, the cashier bent down, fishing around for something under the counter. Emily's chest thumped and a loud fluttering sound filled her ears. Her first thought was that the cashier was one of them, and she was reaching for a gun. Or maybe she was pressing a button that signaled the police to come and get her. Emily was a millisecond away from bolting out the door and leaving her stuff behind, when the cashier came back up with a plastic bag and stuffed the sandwiches inside. Grabbing the bag and water, Emily turned, and rushed out the door as the bell dinged overhead. She speed-walked to the car, fighting the urge to run. Charlie started the engine as Emily approached.

Jumping inside and slamming the door shut, Emily let out a loud sigh.

"Everything go okay?" Jim said.

"I was so nervous," Emily said. She fought back tears as relief washed over her. "And paranoid as hell."

Reaching into the bag, Emily handed sandwiches to each of them.

"You did good," Charlie said. "I'm proud of you."

"Thanks," Emily said, giving him a half smile.

Charlie cracked his knuckles, gripped the steering wheel, and accelerated the car out onto the highway.

They drove down the road in silence for an hour. Jim stared out the window at the lush spring landscape flying past, a sea of green treetops sprawling all the way to the horizon. His leg still throbbed more than he was willing to let on. Every once in a while, he slid his finger under the dressing they had made from strips of Emily's blanket, taking a peek to make sure he was not bleeding again. Jim was grateful for the first-aid kit Emily kept in her trunk, not just for the antiseptic, but especially the aspirin. While the pills were little match for the gunshot wound, they took some of the edge off the pain. It was still a terrible, pounding ache, but he could deal with it.

Crinkling a plastic wrapper, Charlie stuffed a second sandwich into his mouth with one hand while spinning the steering wheel with his other hand.

Jake turned and looked at Charlie, the scar on his cheek looking red and prominent in the sunlight. "Hungry, big guy?"

Charlie mumbled through bread and processed lunch meat.

"We need to go somewhere remote," Jake said. "Set up a camp in the sticks and make plans."

"We need to find Lacy," Jim said.

"We'll do both," Charlie said.

"Suppose they haven't gotten her?" Emily said. "Do you think Lacy would go to the Boundary Waters again?"

"You'd better hope she didn't," Jake said. "Part of the mission they were hiring people for was to search that wilderness area, on foot and with drones. They knew she had hid there before."

"She's way too smart for that," Charlie said. "Let's just find a place to camp and try to figure things out."

CHAPTER 15

C harlie guided the car along a rough dirt road, with grass and weeds growing down the center. They had been driving for five hours and finally reached the deep wooded area that Jim had picked out on the map. The road became nothing more than a trail, and Charlie pulled off into an area of high weeds.

"We'll cover the car with branches and hike in from here," Charlie said.

"So, we'll build a shelter then?" Jim said.

"Yeah, after we walk for a few miles," Charlie said.

Emily slammed her door shut and walked over to a tree. She broke off some branches and laid them gently over the top of the car. "It'll be nice to sleep somewhere other than in the car," she said. "Even if it's the ground."

Jake pushed over a sapling, jumping on it to break it off at the bottom of the trunk.

"We just need time to think," Charlie said. "There has to be a way to figure all this out."

Leaning the big sapling, wide and full of leaves, against the car, Jake rubbed his hands together, trying to warm them up. "We're going to need a fire."

"We'll build one," Charlie said. "We're deep in the boonies, and they can't look everywhere. I think it's safe."

"I hope so," Jim said. He tossed a leafy branch on top of the car and stepped back, looking at the vehicle. "I really do hope so."

Sitting down on a log near the campfire, Emily snuggled next to Jim. Charlie stirred the coals with a stick, causing a burst of sparks to float up into trees above them. The night air was cool and silent, except for the crackling of burning logs and an occasional animal rustling in the trees.

Charlie had washed his shirt and pants in a nearby stream, trying to get the bloodstains out as best he could. He hung his wet clothes from a branch and sat down close to the fire, wearing only his boxer shorts. The flickering firelight glowed across Charlie's massive, ripped physique. The fibers of his muscles flexed and relaxed with each small movement, causing his shoulders, chest, and biceps to bounce and twitch without warning. Deep scratches, cuts, and bruises covered Charlie's skin like a roadmap.

Realizing that she was staring too long, Emily turned away, looking off into the woods. "Where'd Jake go?" she said.

Charlie looked up from the fire, turned, and glanced backward. "He went to get more firewood."

Emily frowned, shivering. "I'm still worried about him." She looked at Jim. "From everything you told me—you know, when you guys were younger. I'm just nervous about it."

Jim sighed. "He took a wrong turn when we were teenagers, got into drugs and then gambling. It was too much for me to deal with and I pretty much shut him out of my life."

"But he turned into a gang leader," Emily said.

"I think that started out because he owed them money," Jim said. "He probably had to earn it back by working for them, and then he just got deeper into it." Jim scratched the back of his neck and shook his head. "The thing is, I feel partly to blame. He came to me asking to borrow the money. He was in such deep trouble, but I turned him away. I sometimes feel responsible."

Charlie shook his head. "You were a kid and you had enough problems of your own. You can't feel guilty for that. Besides, if you had given him the money, he probably would have gambled that away too."

A raspy voice broke the air behind them. "He's right, I would have," Jake said.

Emily felt her face get hot and she wanted to shrink under the log. Jim spun around and his skin flushed as well. Charlie shrugged and went back to poking the embers in the fire. Jake rolled a rotted log up to the fire and sat down between Jim and Charlie. He looked at Jim with weary eyes and a half smile.

"You were right to turn me away," Jake said. "And I respect you for not giving in." He let out a rough laugh. "I still remember you booting my ass out the door when I tried to threaten you by saying I'd tell your dad about you running from the cops."

"You ran from the cops?" Emily said.

Jim opened his mouth. "I—"

"That was my fault too," Jake said. "Anyways, I made bad choices. Hell, let's not sugar coat it; I became a very bad person. We all know I've done horrible things."

Charlie sniffed, causing Jake to look over at him.

"Yeah, I even did a number on Hercules over here when he paid a visit to my bar." Jake leaned over, trying to pat Charlie on the shoulder.

Charlie regarded Jake with a stern look, his forehead wrinkling. "It's best for both of us if we just forget about that," Charlie said.

Jake withdrew his hand back, deciding not to touch Charlie after all. "You're right. Though, I do plan to make it up to you."

"You already did," Charlie said. "Just don't bring that up

again."

Jake nodded, looking up at the stars beyond the dark tree tops. He took a deep breath and gazed into the fire. "When I saw Jim's name on the Mercenary Board, something came over me. I had this feeling that I didn't want to be a monster anymore. I decided I wanted to change."

Charlie shifted on his log. "Mercenary board?"

Jake nodded. "It's a place on the internet where guys like me can be hired to do things. You know, things that straight-laced people aren't willing to do."

Jim looked at Jake with raised eyebrows. "So, they use a website to hire gangs?"

"And soldiers, dirty cops . . . . even doctors. Anyone who is willing to bend the rules and has the credentials for the job," Jake said.

"Could you get back on there?" Charlie said. "Maybe it would give us an idea of what this group is doing."

Jake tilted his head, staring at nothing for a moment. Then looking at the inside of his wrist, he traced his finger along a tattoo of the letter "D," written in a gothic script. Jake stared at the fire for a moment before speaking. "I have a son, you know," he said.

Jim perked up, his lips turning into a smile. "Really?" A small laugh of disbelief escaped his mouth. "How old is he?"

"He's three," Jake said, still moving his fingertip along the letter on his skin.

Emily tried to picture Jake, this rough and dangerous looking man, pushing a cute little boy on a swing. The visual was comical. "Where is he?" Emily said.

"I don't know," Jake said. "I haven't seen him since he was born."

"Oh," Emily said. Looking at Jake with concerned eyes, she waited, not sure if she should pry.

"His mother got a restraining order against me," Jake said.

Charlie threw a log onto the fire with a crash, then sat still, listening.

"She's a drug addict," Jake said. "But the judge knew my reputation and decided a crack whore was better than a crime boss."

"Did you . . . ." Emily took a deep breath, looking at Jake's tattoo and shivering.

Jim put his arm around Emily, rubbing her opposite shoulder.

"Did you hurt her?" Emily said.

Jake shook his head. "I may have said some things, but I was never violent with her." He looked at Emily, his eyes clear and shiny. "I've never hurt a woman."

Emily pressed her lips together, nodding.

"What's your son's name?" Jim said.

"Darrian," Jake said.

Everyone let the name hang in the air as they watched the crackling flames.

"From the Greek," Charlie said. "Darrian means gift."

They all turned and looked at Charlie, whose gaze was still fixated on the glowing coals.

Charlie glanced up, raising an eyebrow. "What?" He shrugged. "I happen to know some stuff."

"Well, I hope to see him someday," Jake said. "And because of that, I don't want to be a criminal anymore. I'm not going back to that life."

"What about your crew?" Charlie said. "They're such charming fellas."

Laughing, Jake picked up a twig from the ground, snapped it in half, and tossed it into the flames. "They were loyal to me because I earned their respect. I'm sure they'll be loyal to whoever takes my place." He looked at Jim. "I am never going back down there."

Jim nodded, rubbing the heel of his shoe in the dirt as he sat there, digging a small trench. "About the message board you mentioned, can you get back on there?"

"Using what?" Jake said.

"I still have a smartphone in the car," Jim said.

Charlie's head jerked up in alarm.

"Don't worry, I took the battery out just in case," Jim said. "It can't give us away."

"I probably could get on there," Jake said. "The web address always changes, but if I use the right search words, I think I can find it."

"You can't turn that phone on," Charlie said.

"We'll drive somewhere," Jim said. "Tomorrow, we'll drive for a few hours and get online long enough to gather some information. We need to gain some sort of advantage."

Charlie scratched his chin, thinking.

"Who's going?" Emily said.

"All of us," Jim said. "We need to stick together."

Jake got up and walked over to Jim, patting him on the shoulder. "I agree with you, Jim."

"Then that's our plan," Charlie said. "We'll go first thing in the morning." Charlie stood up and put his hands on his hips. "You guys get some sleep, I'll take first watch."

Opening his eyes, Jim sniffed as consciousness returned to him when the first rays of sunlight crept in between the trees, shining on his face. Emily slept next to him, her arm draped over his waist. The ground was firm and bumpy, but he had been so exhausted that he slept hard after finishing his turn to stand watch. They had laid blankets down, which Jim had fetched from the trunk of the car, yet the cold still penetrated through it and into his bones. The smell of dead leaves and soggy dirt filled Jim's nostrils as he inhaled and tried to scoot out from under Emily's arm without waking her. Charlie, a few feet away, snored on his back. Jake was on watch and nowhere to be seen, probably wandering around in the forest. The fire had died down to smoldering ashes, and there were no more branches in the pile. Perhaps Jake was gathering more firewood.

Forcing his achy body to stand, Jim crept down the hill to the river where Charlie had washed his clothes. His eyes felt crusty, his mind groggy and full of cobwebs. The gurgling water looked refreshing and cool. Jim decided to take a quick bath, so he slid his pants and shirt off, setting them in a pile next to the river. He stepped into the water and let out a gasp when the icy water hit his skin. After a few steps, he was in the river up to his waist. The cold water woke Jim up, jolting his senses like an electrical shock. As he got used to the temperature, he bent down, cupping handfuls and splashing it on his face. It felt good on his bullet wound, numbing the area and giving him relief from the constant throbbing pain.

A movement at the top of the hill caused Jim to jump backwards, sloshing water all around him. Emily was making her way down the slope with a gentle smile on her lips.

"That looks nice," Emily said. "I need to get clean too."

Jim tried to hide his smirk. "It's pretty cold."

"I think I can handle it," Emily said. She unsnapped her jeans and slid them down to her ankles. The skin of her smooth, bare legs stood out in contrast to the rough, brown leaves and brush all around her. Stepping out of her pants, Emily crossed her arms in front of her waist and pulled her shirt and sports bra up over her head. Her ample breasts bounced in the sunlight as they fell free from the garments. Stepping down into the current, Emily shrieked when her legs plunged into the cold water.

"Oh, dear, that's freezing." Emily said.

Jim laughed, watching her wade toward him. "I warned you."

When Emily got close, Jim put his arms around her waist. She looked up at him, kissing him and pressing her fingers into his back. Then she pulled her head back a little bit and looked him in the eyes. She brushed his cheek with her hand, then ran her fingers through his hair.

"You okay?" Emily said.

"I am now," Jim said.

"No, I mean with everything we're going through. Are you going to be alright?"

Jim looked up to the top of the hill. Sighing, he shook his head. "I don't know. Charlie and Jake, they're both very tough men."

"You are tough, Jim. Don't you dare think otherwise. I've seen you dig deeper than anyone I've known."

"I know," Jim said. "But those guys are on a different level. They've dealt with this kind of stuff before. Life and death, having to fight, to kill or be killed. I'm just a regular guy and this is terrifying." Jim took a deep breath and brushed Emily's long curls out of her face.

"Those two would not be on the same side if it weren't for you," Emily said. "They'd be at each other's throats." She reached around Jim's waist, pulling him closer. "They're working as a team because you keep them grounded, and they respect you. They are drawn to your good heart." She gave his lips a soft kiss. "People who have dealt with too much violence need someone around who hasn't been tainted; it keeps them sane."

Jim moved his hands below Emily's waist.

"You keep me sane," Jim said.

Emily put a hand behind Jim's head, pressing her mouth against his. As Emily became more forceful, Jim's pulse quickened and his breathing grew loud through his nose.

Out of the corner of his eye, Jim saw a figure appear on the hill. His head snapped around to face it.

"Gaaahhh!" Jake yelled from up above, throwing his arms up in front of his face.

Emily dropped down into the water with a splash so that only her head was poking above the surface.

"What the hell?" Jake said, backing away and shouting as he

disappeared over the crest of the hill. "Haven't you guys already been married for like, years? Seriously!"

"Three years," Jim said, looking down at Emily.

Smiling, she stood up from the cold water and pressed her wet skin against him.

CHAPTER 16

I think this is far enough," Jim said.

They had been driving for over three hours and were passing through a tiny farm town in the middle of northern Minnesota. Jim had driven for the last hour of the trip.

"I think so too," Jake said.

"Why don't you pull in where that sign says Blackrock Diner?" Charlie leaned forward from the back seat, pointing.

Jim signaled the blinker and steered the car into a crumbled old parking lot. The diner looked like an old church that had been converted into a backwoods restaurant. The wood siding had once been painted white, but was so weathered, it looked more like a dull gray.

"Is this place even in business anymore?" Emily said.

"Yep," Charlie said.

A plump man in dusty blue overalls, wearing a trucker hat perched high on top of his head, came out the door and shuffled down the street.

"It seems safe," Jim said. "I'm sure they don't have any security cameras."

"I'll be surprised if they have electricity," Jake said.

"At this point, I don't even care," Charlie said. "I just need a good, hot meal. It's been way too long."

"Okay," Jim said. "We'll eat first, and when we're done, we'll power up the phone and Jake can log on."

"Right," Charlie said. "We spend no more than twenty minutes online and then we shut it down and get the hell out of here."

The four of them got out of the car and walked inside the diner. Charlie held the door open as the others entered. Jim was limping on his bad leg as he passed by Charlie.

"Is it feeling any better?" Charlie asked, following Jim through the door.

"A little," Jim said. "I cleaned it out this morning and I don't think it's infected."

"Good," Charlie said, giving him slap on the back. "That's the last thing we need right now."

Jim sat back in his booth, rubbing his stomach, feeling the unfamiliar sensation of a full belly. He searched the room with his eyes, noting all of the deer and elk heads hanging on the walls around them. Finally he looked at Charlie, then Jake.

"Okay," Jake said. "Let's get this done."

Jim reached into his pocket and pulled out the smartphone, his hands starting to shake as he held it. From his other pocket, Jim pulled out the battery for the phone. He slid it into the back and powered up the device. When the phone booted up, Jim started up the web browser. His default search engine popped up and he squinted at it. "That's weird," he said.

"What's weird?" Charlie leaned over from across the table to look at the screen.

"There's a big red word under the search field. They never put anything on this page but the entry box," Jim said.

Emily looked over Jim's shoulder. She laughed. "Actwood," she said. "I love it."

"Actwood?" Jake said.

"It's a shoe brand," Emily said. "One of my favorites."

Jake shook his head. "Okay, type in these words: hero, validated, crusty, and bones."

Jim typed them in and pressed search. The first site popping up in the list was titled, "Special Skills Wanted." Jim clicked on it and was prompted for a username and password.

"Here you go." Jim handed the phone to Jake.

Jake took the device and started tapping the screen. After a moment, he frowned. "Shit." He typed his password again. "Dammit, I'm locked out. I think they disabled my account."

"Maybe the real site has moved," Jim said. "Try a different search engine to get there."

Jake nodded and tapped the screen. He snarled. "That word is on this search engine too. Actwood. Is it some kind of special thing today?" He looked at Emily.

"Not that I know of," she said. "But last week I—" She stopped, her eyes getting big. She stared at the table, thinking. Then she grabbed Jim's arm. "Last week I brought Lacy to Goldbrook's to get a pair of Actwood shoes."

Jim looked at Emily, the realization crashing over him like a wave.

"Did I miss something?" Jake said.

"It could be Lacy trying to send us a message," Jim said.

Jake smirked. "You think she could hack the two biggest search engines in the world to send you guys a message."

"Yes, she could," Charlie said. "In her sleep."

Jake sat back in his chair, his jaw hanging open. "Holy smokes," he said.

Staring at the word on the screen, Jim scratched the top of his head. "Where did you say you guys went to get the shoes?"

"Goldbrook's," Emily said.

Jake sniffed. "I'm going to go out on a limb here and say she's not hiding in Goldbrook's." He leaned back further, putting his hands behind his head.

Charlie rubbed the palm of his hand over his face, shaking

his head. "Imagine you could do anything to any website; the internet is your playground. How do you send a secret message to us that The Supremalus won't see."

"You hide it in plain view," Jim said.

"Go to the Goldbrook's website," Emily said.

Jim tapped the top of the browser and typed in the website. He examined the page. "I'm not seeing anything out of the ordinary."

"We're running out of time," Jake said. "A video feed from this phone is probably already raising flags on a server somewhere."

Emily rested her chin on her hand, closing her eyes. After a moment, she sat up. "Search for the shoes on the site. The Actwood shoes."

Jim typed in the word and brought up the page for the brand of shoes. His eyes moved back and forth, taking in all of the text. His neck was getting hot and he felt sweat seeping through the armpits of his shirt. "Damn, this is hopeless," he said. "I thought we had something. It just seemed like too much of a coincidence that you and Lacy had bought those shoes right before she disappeared."

Emily frowned. "Actually, we didn't end up buying them. She settled for a pair of Mishka's instead."

Jim's face lit up, his back straightening as he typed. He looked at the page for Mishka shoes on the website. Everything seemed normal as he read the text. His eyes went to a paragraph of lighter colored, fine print, at the bottom.

"Whoa," Jim said. "I think this is something."

"Well, what is it?" Charlie said. "Spit it out."

"Numbers," Jim said. "Two numbers. They look like coordinates."

Charlie tore off a chunk of paper from their receipt and picked up the pen that the waitress had left. "What are they?" he said.

"47.67 and -91.61," Jim said.

Charlie scribbled the numbers down.

"Okay, pop the battery out, Jim. Hurry," Jake said.

Jim flipped the phone over, slid the cover off, and flicked the battery out onto the table.

J. ARTHUR SQUIERS

CHAPTER 17

L acy had to pee, so she opened the door of the Winnebago camper and stepped outside into the dark. She looked up at the top of the ravine, a few hundred yards above her, where Tom's house and camping supply store sat nestled among the trees. A single light shined through one of the windows. Tom was still up, probably reading a book as usual. It must have been a good novel, he rarely stayed up this late.

Walking to a nearby oak tree, Lacy slipped her sweatpants off and held them in her hands while she squatted with a wide stance. She looked back up at the hill, feeling comforted by the glowing light far above. It was like a distant campfire in the night that makes you feel cozier just by looking at it. That warmth was doused with a sudden chill when she saw a shadow pass in front of the window. At first she hoped it was just Tom, checking on something outside the house, but her gut told her it was someone else.

Lacy thrust each leg into her pants and ran back into the RV. She grabbed the machete that she kept leaning against the wall just inside the door. Once she was back outside, Lacy crept up the side of the ravine, staying on the well-worn path to avoid shuffling the leaves.

Cresting the top of the ravine, Lacy tried to keep her breathing quiet, even though her lungs burned from the climb. She waited, crouching within the branches of a thick fir tree. A figure came around the corner of the house, tall and lanky. Lacy waited, holding her breath.

The figure walked up to the window, cupping his hands around his eyes, peering inside. Lacy placed one foot in front of the other, feeling the ground with her bare feet as she slinked across the yard. She had five more feet to go when she extended the machete in front of her, pressing the point of the blade against the person's back. The man froze.

"If you even flinch," Lacy said, "I'll gut you."

"Lacy?" the man said.

"Jim?" Lacy dropped the machete.

Jim turned around and looked at her, his eyes wide open in amazement. Lacy leapt forward, wrapping her arms around him, burying her face in his chest. Tears filled her eyes and relief flooded her mind. She squeezed him like a vice, trying to convince herself that he was real, that it was not one of her dreams taunting her.

"You colored your hair red?" Jim said.

"It's auburn," Lacy said. "I decided blue was too conspicuous."

"I like it," Jim said.

Lacy pulled back, studying Jim's face. "How did you find me?"

Jim squinted at her, deep lines appearing on his forehead. "We found your message . . . . the shoes."

"What shoes?" Lacy took a step back, shaking her head.

"The shoes you and Emily bought a few weeks ago." Jim reached behind him, grabbing the wall for support. "The coordinates for this place were on the website, next to those shoes."

Lacy's hands shook as she touched them to her cheeks. "I

wouldn't have taken that risk, Jim. Whoever those people are, they own the internet. They see everything."

"So you haven't gone online once?"

"No," Lacy said. "Not since I escaped from the airport."

Jim sank down to a knee as one of his legs seemed to buckle under him. "That means—"

"Someone else knows we're here," Lacy said. "Is anyone else with you?"

"Yeah," Jim said. "Emily, Charlie and . . . . my old friend Jake."

Lacy raised her eyebrows. "The crime boss?"

"I wouldn't be alive if he hadn't helped me," Jim said, scratching his head. "I guess he's turning over a new leaf."

Lacy frowned. "If you say so." She heard a noise and turned to see a huge man coming around the corner of the cabin. She started walking toward him. "Charlie, we have to leave right now."

"It's great to see you too," Charlie said.

Lacy strode up to Charlie, giving him a quick hug. "I'm really glad you're here, but I didn't put my location on that website. Someone else knows I'm here, which means they're coming."

"Dammit," Charlie said, his eyes darting back and forth, searching the woods. "How could they know?"

"I have no idea," Lacy said.

Jake ran around the corner, stopping short when he saw the group of them in the glowing light from the window. He looked at Lacy with wide eyes and a smirk. "Whoa," Jake said.

Lacy walked up to Jake, her hand outstretched. "Hey, I'm Lacy."

Jake stood frozen for a second, then blinked and lifted his hand, giving Lacy a slow shake. "They told me you were a genius," Jake said. "But they didn't warn me that you were so gorgeous."

Lacy smiled.

Charlie cleared his throat. "They could be here any minute. We'd better get to the car."

"No," Lacy said. "We'll have to take the RV. I'm not leaving Tom here if they're coming, and we'll need the room."

"Who's Tom?" Jim asked.

Lacy pointed her thumb toward the cabin. "This is his house and his store. He's been keeping me hidden." She took a few steps closer to the window, peering inside. "He's also a sound sleeper. You'd better let me go wake him up and explain things to him. He's old and I don't want you all piling into the house and giving him a heart attack."

"Where's this camper we'll be driving?" Charlie asked.

"It's down there, in the valley." Lacy pointed. "We can drive it between the marshes and get onto back roads."

Jim nodded. "We'll get our stuff out of the car and head down there while you get Tom."

Lacy started walking around the cabin. "Good," she said. "I'll meet you down there."

Jim stood outside the camper and saw Lacy coming down into the ravine with a round, gray bearded man. Jim strode up the hill to meet them. Tom was carrying two jugs of water and breathing heavy. Lacy had a huge green camping backpack strapped over her shoulders.

"Charlie's working on the engine," Jim said.

His forehead glistening with sweat, Tom looked at Jim with eyes that were both alert and afraid. "Well, that's good 'cause I haven't run it in a long time."

Jim put his hand on Tom's shoulder, feeling the need to comfort him. "Charlie's wondering if you've got any guns."

"Yeah." Tom put the water jugs down with a grunt. "My pistol's in that bag." He jerked his head toward the pack on Lacy's back. "But I got rifles in a gun safe, up in the shed." He sucked air in, trying to catch his breath. "I'll go get 'em." He fished a set of keys out of his pocket.

"No, I'll do it," Jim said. "They'll need your help getting the RV ready."

"There's six rifles and some ammo boxes," Tom said. "You can't carry it all."

Jim looked up at the steep ravine and back down at Tom's sweat drenched face. "I'll bring Jake."

Jim unlocked the door to the shed and opened it, feeling for a light switch with his hand. He found one and flicked it on.

"I still don't get why someone left us a clue to find her," Jake said. He followed Jim into the shed. "Or how anyone knew where she was. She was living completely rugged down there."

"I don't know." Jim made his way to the back of the shed, fumbling through the keys that Tom had given him. "We'll have time to figure that out once we get on the road." Jim found the key and opened a giant, steel gun safe. He started pulling guns out and handing them to Jake.

"Dang," Jake said. "Was old Tom waiting for the apocalypse to come to his doorstep?"

"Well, I'm glad he was prepared," Jim said. He lifted two giant ammunition boxes with handles and motioned toward the door with his head.

Jake walked out of the shed cradling a pile of guns in his arms. He stumbled back inside, slamming the door shut with his foot. There was a popping sound, like a champagne bottle being uncorked, and a hole appeared in the side of the shed.

"Shit!" Jim ducked down. "What the hell was that?"

Jake tossed the guns on the floor. "About twenty of 'em, with big military trucks." He fumbled with one of the ammo boxes, pulling it open and sifting through it. "We're fucked."

Jim scrambled on his knees, grabbing for one of the guns.

Jake pushed Jim away. "Forget those damn things, you're going to run when I tell you to. Run faster than you ever have and fly down that ravine to the RV."

Jim stopped and held Jake in his gaze as time stood still for a moment. "No," Jim said. "Hell no, there's got to be another way."

"There ain't," Jake said. He grabbed a handful of shotgun shells and started stuffing them into a pump action twelve gauge.

Jim's temples throbbed and he wanted to scream. "Charlie! We'll fire a warning shot and Charlie will hear it. He could get up here in a few minutes."

"We'll be dead in a few minutes and then Charlie will be cut to ribbons too," Jake said.

Jim tried to grab a gun again, and Jake shoved his shoulder hard, sending him backwards.

Jake clenched his teeth. "I know how good Charlie is; what he did back there. But this is different. I got a look at these guys and they ain't chumps—they're elite soldiers, just like him. They'll make swiss cheese out of him if he comes up here."

Jim cursed and shook his head. Jake started stuffing shells into a second shotgun, counting each one under his breath. A bullet busted through the shed door and nicked Jim in the shoulder, causing blood to spatter on his own cheek.

"Swear two things to me, Jimmy boy," Jake said, standing up with both shotguns, tucking one under his armpit.

"Jake, don't—"

"Fucking dammit, Jim, swear two things right now or I will shoot you myself."

Jim tried to swallow but it felt like there was a golf ball in his throat. "Okay, I'll swear it."

"Number one, you'll run your ass off as soon as I step out there, and you won't stop until you are in that camper."

Jim nodded, tears streaming down his face.

Jake breathed in deep through his nose. "And two." He choked. "Two . . . .someday, you find my son and tell him his daddy became a good man, even if it was for a short time."

Jim bit his lower lip hard, tasting blood, and nodded once.

Jake gave Jim a sad smile, turned, and opened the door just enough to poke one of the shotguns out. Fire exploded out the muzzle of Jake's shotgun, and Jim heard a windshield shatter across the yard. Then Jake kicked the door open and walked out, firing and pumping so fast that the shots seemed like one long thunderclap of noise. Jim slipped out, turned left, and bolted for the ravine, his arms pumping, his eyes blinded by tears. The sound of firing stopped for a heartbeat as Jake tossed one of the shotguns to the ground and started shooting the other one. Jim reached the edge of the ravine, and just before he descended it at breakneck speed, he cranked his head around for one brief look. Jake was on his knees, still firing. A bullet slammed into Jake's chest, sending a spray of liquid through the air that shimmered in the pale light of the moon. Jake fired one more shotgun blast before another bullet pierced through his head, and his lifeless body slumped to the ground.

It took everything Jim had to keep from screaming as he soared down the ravine, with vomit in his mouth, blood covering face, his bad leg threatening to give out. He saw Charlie coming up the hill and waved his arm, trying to signal Charlie to go back to the camper.

"Where's Jake?" Charlie said, his eyes bulging out in alarm at the sight of Jim.

"No time," Jim said, grabbing Charlie's shirt as he passed by, pulling him along. "Run or we're all dead. Please trust me."

Charlie turned and followed Jim without saying another word. Jim heard the Winnebago engine running and he put his chin to his chest, willing himself to go faster. Emily opened the door, her face stark white, her eyes opening wide at the sight of Jim and Charlie flying down the ravine.

Flailing his arms now, to keep his balance, Jim shouted to Emily. "Start driving, start driving!"

Emily ducked back inside and yelled something. The old Winnebago RV camper started to move, almost hesitating at first, then rolling out of its spot. Jim had to keep his pace to catch up to the vehicle, and he grabbed a handle next to the door, yanking himself inside. Turning around, Jim clasped Charlie's hand and helped him climb in. Lacy was driving, and Tom sat next to her in the passenger seat. Both of them looked back at the door, expecting Jake to jump in next. Then they looked to Jim. The twisted agony of Jim's face told the whole story.

Jim fought to breathe. Fought to speak. "There's an army up there," he said. "And they're coming to kill us." Sobbing, he turned and stumbled to the back of the RV, collapsing on a bed. Everyone was silent, only the sound of the engine could be heard. Emily went and sat near Jim, putting a hand on his shoulder. Tom's raspy voice broke the air from the front of the camper.

"We can lose them in the swamps," Tom said. "Hundreds of acres of marshland and I know where it's drivable."

Lacy punched the gas. "Just tell me where to go," she said.

CHAPTER 18

Jim's body bounced on the bed as the RV climbed out of the swamplands and onto a gravel road. His head ached and he kept his hands over his ears, as though he could shut out the sound of the gunshots that kept echoing over and over in his mind. Sobbing, he kept his face pressed into a pillow. Emily came back to check on him again.

"Jim, I think we're okay for now," she said.

Jim turned his head, looking at Emily with stinging, bloodshot eyes. "I can't get that image out of my head," he said.

Emily frowned, rubbing Jim's back.

"Jake was on his knees and they annihilated him," Jim said. "He did it so I could get away."

Emily let out a slow breath, shuddering.

"I feel like such a coward."

"You're not," Emily said. "You are the opposite of a coward because you're going to make his death count for something." She kissed him on the back of the head and ran her fingers through his gnarled hair.

Jim looked at her and blinked tears away. They held each other's gaze for a minute before Emily glanced toward the front of the camper.

"They need you," Emily said. "I know you're not a hacker or a special forces soldier, but you are a leader and you are their conscience. Jake believed in you. It's time you believed in yourself."

Jim felt a tingling sensation wash over him. He clenched and unclenched his fists, chewing over Emily's words. Then he rolled onto his back. "I need some time to pull myself together," he said.

Emily nodded, gripping his shoulder for a moment before leaving.

Forty minutes later, Jim walked to the front of the RV. Emily, sitting in a bench seat across from Charlie, looked up at Jim with concern. Lacy sat studying a map in the passenger seat while Tom drove.

"I've made a decision," Jim said. "But I want to know if you are all on board with it."

Lacy turned around at the sound of Jim's voice, her eyes looking sharp and serious.

"What is it, Jim?" Charlie said.

Jim pressed his hand on the ceiling of the camper for support as the RV rocked on the bumpy road. "I say we fight back."

Charlie slammed his fist down on the table in front of him, causing Emily to jump. "Now you're talking," Charlie said.

"Jim," Lacy said. "They have people everywhere. Armies of soldiers from all walks of life at their disposal. Fighting them is suicide."

Jim looked at Lacy, a slight smile showing briefly on his face.

"You can hack them," Jim said.

Lacy blinked. "It's too risky, I can't go online. They'll track me."

"There's a way, think about it," Jim said. "When you wrote the wildfire program—"

Lacy's eyes darted all around, paranoid that the mention of her program could be heard by someone.

"Remember what you said you did on Lake Superior?" Jim said.

"I accelerated the signal so I could hit towers farther away," Lacy said. "But I was surrounded by miles of water so I had more range, and these people hunting us could eventually pinpoint the location. It would only be a matter of time."

Jim glanced around the RV, causing Lacy to look around as well. Her face lit up and she popped out of her seat, lunging at Jim and grabbing him by the shoulders.

"Holy shit, Jim!" Lacy shouted. "You're a genius. You are a bonafide freaking genius!"

Jim shook his head, smiling. "Can it work?"

"You bet your ass it'll work," Lacy said.

Charlie cleared his throat. "Um, you two mind filling the rest of us in?"

Lacy turned and grabbed Charlie's arm, shaking it. "We keep driving. We randomly take backwoods roads, mountain roads, desert roads." Lacy's eyes, which had been dark and hopeless before, were now beaming. "We turn this old RV into a hardcore mobile hacking station, and as long as we never stop for more than ten minutes, they can't track us. We'll be hours ahead of any location they can pinpoint."

"I like it." Charlie wringed his hands, smiling. "Can we paint the RV camouflage?"

"Sorry," Jim said. "It has to look like a normal camper to people outside."

Lacy nodded.

Charlie groaned. "Can I put gun swivels on it, just in case?"

Lacy slapped Charlie on the back, laughing. "You can do whatever you want as long as you make it look like we're just a simple family driving an old beater Winnebago across the country." She went back up to her passenger seat and grabbed the map. "Come on, Charlie, let's figure out where to get the stuff we need."

Charlie walked up the aisle and leaned down over Lacy's seat, studying the roads on her map.

Emily stood up and put her arms around Jim's neck.

"You gave Lacy hope," Emily said. "She actually laughed—that was unbelievable. Do you think this will work?"

Jim looked up toward the front of the RV, where Lacy and Charlie were pointing to spots on the map and nodding to each other. "I hope so," Jim said with a half-smile.

Emily's brow furrowed. "Jim, how did you think of that idea?"

"I didn't," Jim said. "I just gave Lacy the confidence to figure it out. Showed her that someone believed in her."

"But, you were looking around at the RV, like it was obvious," Emily said.

Jim shook his head. "I was just looking around to see if there was anywhere to plug in a laptop."

Emily let out a loud laugh, causing Lacy and Charlie to lift their heads and look back at her. Emily shrugged and they went back to what they were doing. Still sitting at the wheel, Tom was talking to Lacy and Charlie, giving them his input on the roadways of northern Minnesota.

Jim looked down at the floor, then back at Emily, his eyes heavy.

"If we get through this," Jim said. "I mean, when it's over . . . . I'm going to need some time to grieve my friend."

Emily bit her lip and cradled Jim's head, placing it on her shoulder. Jim took a deep breath in through his nose, smelling her sweet scent.

"I know," Emily said.

CHAPTER 19

Where do we make our first stop for gear?" Jim said, sitting down at the table.

Emily had volunteered to take the wheel of the RV for a while, giving the others a chance to concentrate and make plans.

"We have to hit an electronics store, a smaller one," Lacy said. "Nothing huge. The bigger the store, the more sophisticated the security system."

Jim rubbed his temples and sighed, wishing his headache would go away. "We're going to rob some ma-and-pop stores of thousands of dollars?"

"There's no other way," Charlie said.

Jim shook his head and looked out the window at the darkness, pondering as the endless wall of trees zipped past in the night.

"Jim, this is life and death," Lacy said. She gestured at the window with her hand. "Anybody out there could be working for them. We have to have an attitude of us against the world, or we will not survive. You have to flip that switch in your mind, or we're all dead."

Tom had been watching Lacy through his thick glasses,

listening as she spoke. He turned to Jim and his gruff voice emerged from beneath his gray beard. "Jim, I respect your sentiment, believe me. I've been running that little camping store for twenty-five years, and I barely made enough to get by." Tom paused, his big round belly rising and falling. "But, if I knew that some people like you guys were trying to survive. That some horrible organization was trying to kill them, and their only hope was to steal from my store—I'd want you to have it all."

Jim regarded Tom, sensing a deep wisdom that he hadn't noticed before.

"Okay," Jim said. "We'll do what we need to do."

Tom leaned over the map and touched a spot with his big gnarled finger. "Right here," he said. "I believe there's a shop right here that has what you need. I've been through that town quite a few times."

Jim studied the roadways and nodded. "We'd get there in two hours, which puts us at 2:00 a.m. That would be a perfect time to get in and out."

Charlie traced a path on the map with his finger. "Okay, I'll drive from here," he said. "Emily could probably use a break anyhow." Getting up, Charlie went up to the front of the RV and mumbled a few words to Emily.

There was a groan of leather as Emily got up and Charlie slid into the driver's seat. Emily's voice murmured, then Charlie's. The divider wall blocked Jim from seeing them, but he assumed Charlie was explaining the plan.

Emily ambled back to the table and sat down next to Jim, her eyelids looking heavy.

Jim watched Emily with concern. "Did Charlie explain what we're doing?" he asked.

"Yeah," Emily said. "He did."

"Are you okay with it?" Jim said.

Emily shook her head, weary lines forming on her brow. "I don't think we have a choice."

Jim turned to Tom. "I'm sorry you got pulled into this," Jim said.

Tom looked at Jim, then at Lacy, who gave a light smile, then back at Jim.

"You know," Tom said, "when Lacy came into my store a few years ago, on her way up to the Boundary Waters, I knew something big was going to happen. I didn't know what, but I knew things were never going to be the same for me."

Lacy stared at the table, appearing to be deep in thought.

"When she came back, needing a place to hide, it gave me a sense of purpose I haven't had in a long time." Tom's gaze moved around the camper, stopping for a moment on each of them: Lacy, Jim, and Emily. Then Tom looked toward the front of the RV where Charlie was. "You're all giving me a purpose, and I'm glad I'm here."

Lacy put her thin hand on Tom's rough arm and squeezed.

"Look, I've traveled everywhere you can go in this old Winnebago, coast to coast. I used to drive all over with my wife and daughter—" Tom tried to swallow, but it seemed like something was stuck in his throat. His eyes became shiny and he glanced out the window for a minute before turning back to them. "I know the ins and outs of this country, all the nooks and crannies. I can help you stay hidden."

"Us," Emily corrected. "You're one of us."

Tom looked at Emily, his eyes clearing a bit, a faint smile appearing beneath his beard. He nodded. "I can help us stay hidden."

"Tom," Jim said. "What happened to your wife?"

Tom breathed air in through his nose and let it out with a whoosh. "Carol died twenty-five years ago, cancer."

"That's when you started the store?" Emily said.

Tom nodded.

"What about your daughter?" Emily said.

Tom pushed his lower lip out, glancing at the ceiling. "Ellie moved to New York right after her mother died. She's kind of a big shot on Wall Street now." Tom shook his head. "We haven't talked for quite a while. I did call her here and there at first, but it seemed like I was just bothering her. I think part of it was that she didn't want to be reminded of losing her mom, and that's what talking to me did."

Emily blinked and wiped her eyes with the back of her hand. Lacy kept her gaze focused on the table, and her hand on Tom's arm.

A silence hung in the air.

"You know," Tom said, wiping his face on his shirt sleeve, "I feel really guilty about this, but when you guys talked about driving this RV all over the country, I had an exhilarating feeling of excitement, deep down. I think it reminded me of all the adventures I had with Carol and Ellie in this thing. And I thought . . . ." Tom looked around at the faded white walls and at the tiny kitchen area. " . . . . I thought, this sure beats sitting in that camping store, all alone, for decades." Tom looked back at all of them, frowning. "But then I feel terrible, sick to my stomach about it. Your friend was killed, and the whole world is out to get you. I feel awful for thinking this was an adventure that I needed."

Tilting his head to the side, Jim regarded Tom for a moment. "Don't feel guilty," Jim said. "I think finding moments of joy in all this, however brief, is what is going to get us through it. That's how we'll survive."

Tom smiled and gleamed at Jim. "For a young man, such as yourself, you are pretty wise."

Jim let out a laugh. "I've come a long way." He shook his head and looked out the window. "A really long way." Jim was quiet for a bit, his mind flashing back on past memories as his words hung in the air. Then he said, "Tom, what did you do before you opened your store?"

"I was a mechanical engineer," Tom said.

Lacy's head snapped up to look at Tom. "You never told me that," Lacy said.

Tom let out a sigh. "It was a long time ago, almost a lifetime."

"You could help us modify the RV," Lacy said.

"Well, technology has advanced quite a bit since then," Tom said. "But yes, that's another reason I got excited."

CHAPTER 20

L acy stood outside the RV, watching the small technology store in the darkness of night, a misty rainfall spraying her face. She liked the cold moisture on her skin, it perked up her senses, keeping her alert. Jim came up next to her, holding his hand above his eyes to shield them from the rain. A neon sign towered above the shop, which was not lit but still readable from the flickering streetlamp a block away—it said, "Computer Land."

Lacy flinched when a dog barked far off in the distance.

"Do you think it'll have what you need?" Jim said.

"Enough to get started," Lacy said. "A laptop and parts to make an antenna." She wiped her wet face with the sleeve of her shirt. "We can get more stuff later on."

Jim pointed to the door of the store. "What about a security system?"

Lacy pulled out a pocket knife and flicked it open. "Minimal, I expect. I should be able to disarm it with this."

Jim turned and poked his head inside the RV. "You ready?"

"Yep," Charlie said, coming down the steps.

Emily followed after Charlie, her eyes big and alert. "I'll stand watch," she said. "Tom will keep the engine running. Try to be quick."

"We'll be in and out," Lacy said.

Jim nodded and headed toward the shop as Lacy and Charlie crept along behind him.

When they reached the door, Lacy pulled a wire out of her pocket and bent it in half, biting it in several places to make notches. She stuck both ends in the lock and put her ear close to the door, jiggling the wire back and forth. Jim and Charlie faced outward, their backs to Lacy, watching down the street.

Lacy turned the wire with a click and pulled on the door, opening it wide. A beeping sound started up and Charlie grabbed the door while Lacy rushed inside. She went up to a keypad with a blinking light, which was mounted on the wall, and shoved her knife blade behind the panel, prying it off. Her blade bowed for a moment before the plate popped off the wall. Using the point of her knife, Lacy fished a grouping of wires out. She cut two of them, stripping the ends between her thumb and the blade. The beeping grew louder as Lacy twisted two of the wires together and touched another end to a screw inside the panel. The sound stopped.

Lacy moved along the shelves, lifting laptops and examining them. She spotted a silver laptop down the aisle and ran up to it. Smiling with satisfaction, she tucked the laptop under her arm and squinted into the dark, searching for routers. She saw a stack of boxes in the corner of the store and strode across the room.

"Lacy," Jim hissed from the doorway. "We have a problem."

Lacy darted the rest of the way to the corner, grabbed two router boxes, and headed for the door. Then, out of the corner of her eye, she spotted a back room with a workbench. Changing course, Lacy hurried over and examined the tools on the bench. She swiped at them with her free hand, grabbing a soldering iron and screwdriver. Then she ran to the exit.

Charlie stopped Lacy with his arm before she got outside.

"Wait," Jim said.

Lacy looked at Jim with a furrowed brow, her arms full with her new treasures.

"Look." Charlie pointed outside.

Emily was talking to a man who appeared to have a small bulldog on a leash.

"Crap, who's that?" Lacy said.

"Some guy out walking his dog," Jim said. "He just came up and started talking to her."

"Who the hell walks their dog at two in the morning?" Lacy said.

"Him, apparently," Jim said.

Emily's voice echoed across the parking lot. "We're fine, really. We just got too tired to drive and stopped to rest."

The man rubbed his beard. "Why are you just standing outside?"

"I needed some fresh air," Emily said. "It gets stuffy in there."

The man's head turned and he squinted at the store, leaning forward. His dog barked.

"Dammit," Charlie said. "I've got to do something."

Jim grabbed Charlie's arm. "Don't hurt him."

Narrowing his eyes, Charlie looked at Jim. "I'm not a monster, Jim. I won't hurt him."

Jim sighed, shaking his head. "I'm sorry, Charlie. It's just . . . . everything we've been through, violence seems like the norm."

Charlie nodded. "Don't worry. I'll only do what's necessary to keep us safe." He strode out the door toward Emily and the man with the dog.

Jim looked at Lacy, shaking his head. "That's what I'm afraid of."

The man with the dog stepped backward when he saw Charlie emerge from the shadows of the store's doorway.

"Who's that?" he said, stumbling further back, bumping into Emily.

"A friend," Emily said.

"He was in the store," the man said. He sucked a quick breath into his chest and started to yell, "H—"

Emily grabbed the man from behind, wrapping one arm around his neck and clamping her hand over his mouth. Charlie sprinted the rest of the distance as the dog started barking and biting on Emily's pants leg at the ankle. Bursting out of the camper, Tom looked wide eyed at the dog, then at Charlie.

Charlie grabbed the dog around the waist, yanking it away from Emily and holding it in the air while it barked and snarled. The man's eyes bulged as he struggled to get away from Emily, but she tightened her grip around his neck.

"Don't move and you'll be okay," Emily said through clenched teeth. "I promise."

The man stopped struggling, either because he believed her, or because she had cut off his circulation enough to sap his strength.

"Tom, get the duct tape," Charlie said, pulling his head back away from the wiggling dog's snapping jaws.

Tom hesitated. "Don't hurt the dog."

"I'm not going to hurt the damn dog," Charlie said. "Just get the tape."

Tom jumped back into the RV and dove out with a roll of silver tape in his hand. Charlie walked over and tossed the dog into the RV, slamming the door shut. The dog continued to bark, but it was a muffled sound. Finally, Jim came running up to help.

Jim grabbed the duct tape from Tom and pulled out a length of it, making a loud ripping sound. He grabbed the man's wrists, pulling them together. The man tried to pull his hands away, but could not get them free from Jim's grip. Jim wrapped the tape around the man's wrists.

Charlie kicked his own shoe off and started yanking at his sock. A realization struck Emily and she felt a gag rising in her throat. Charlie stepped forward, his sock balled up in his fist, and Emily moved her hand away just enough for Charlie to shove the dirty ball of knitted cotton into the man's mouth. Jim stretched out another six inches of tape and placed it squarely over the man's mouth. The man was both sucking air in, and gagging, through his nose.

Jim got in front of him and looked him in the eyes. "I'm sorry we had to do this to you," Jim said. "You were just in the wrong place at the wrong time and I'm going to tell you the truth."

The man squinted at Jim, his brow furrowed in confusion and fear.

"We are being hunted by people," Jim said. "People so dangerous, you couldn't even comprehend it. They are very bad people, and they have eyes and ears everywhere, even in the police forces. When they find us, they will kill us. Actually, they'll torture us to get what they want, then they'll kill us."

Charlie took the roll of tape from Jim and started wrapping it around the man's ankles.

"Now you can report what happened here, that's fine. We'll be long gone before you get anywhere. But if you could just keep this to yourself, it'll buy us some time, and that would be much appreciated."

Charlie finished taping and stood up, patting Jim on the back.

"Let's go," Charlie said. "Where's Lacy?"

Lacy walked toward the commotion at the RV, looking all around her, studying everything. She knew they could handle the situation and she wanted to make sure nobody else saw what was going on. The closest house to the store was a block away, down the old crumbly street with high weeds growing on either side. The yard light was on at that house, but it had been on when they arrived. There was no reason to be concerned about it—at least there were no lights on inside the house. The misty air looked like smoke under the street lamps as Lacy watched and listened. Other than the muffled barking sound coming from the camper, and Jim giving a pep talk to the dog walker, everything was quiet. Yet something seemed strange, she could sense it. It wasn't that she believed in some kind of mystical ability to feel danger. She just knew that her eye had caught a glimpse of something that was not right.

Her head turned toward the empty lot next to the store. The area was overgrown with chest high grass and a few bushes. There were old newspapers that had been blown by the wind and were caught, hanging in some of the brambles, looking like pale faces watching her in the dark. Her eyes went to other pieces of garbage, such as plastic shopping bags that were strewn about in the empty lot. Then Lacy saw a figure standing there, watching her, unmoving. A tremor spread throughout her chest, like thousands of butterflies had escaped her heart and were now fluttering around. The figure was tall, thin, and dressed in all black clothes. A hood was pulled over its head, keeping its face dark like a gaping hole. The figure did not move, not even a flinch, though it seemed to be aware that she had spotted it.

"Who are you?" Lacy whispered into the dark.

It just stood there, its arms crossed. Lacy glanced over at her friends across the parking lot. Jim was talking to the man with the dog, trying to reason with him it seemed. She looked back to the figure in the vacant lot, its breath now billowing out from the hood and hanging in the air around its head like a halo. There was something familiar about the dark person standing there and it made Lacy's legs go weak. She wavered, sinking to one knee, almost dropping the laptop and boxes from her arms. Then she heard Jim's voice.

"Lacy, we gotta move, now!" Jim was looking at her. He noticed that she was struggling and came running toward her. Lacy tried to fight off her fear and stand up. She reached toward Jim. "Help me," she said, but her voice was too soft and weak for Jim to hear.

Finally, Jim got to Lacy's side and helped her up.

"What is it?" Jim said. "What happened?"

Lacy stood up as Jim lifted her by the arms. Her gaze went to the vacant lot and Jim's eyes followed.

The figure was gone.

"There was something there," Lacy said. "Someone was watching us."

Jim took a step toward the high weeds, peering into the night. "Are you sure?" Jim said.

Lacy shivered. "Very sure."

"Do you think there's more of them here?" Jim said. "Do you think it's a trap?"

Lacy shook her head. "Don't know." She looked over at the RV.

Charlie was waving his hands at them, signaling for them to hurry. The dog walker now sat on the pavement of the parking lot, his hands bound behind his back, his feet taped together, and his mouth gagged. Emily and Tom stood by the door of the RV, listening to the muffled sounds of the dog barking.

Holding her new laptop tight under her arm, Lacy handed the boxes of routers and tools to Jim.

"Let's go," Lacy said. "We can figure all this out on the road. The sooner I start hacking those assholes, the better."

"I agree," Jim said.

They both turned and sprinted for the RV.

Charlie held the door handle of the camper and waited until they were all ready. He yanked the door open and the barking dog came flying out, bolting at Jim's leg in full attack mode. The others rushed inside the camper while Jim kept the dog at bay with his foot. Finally, with a grunt, Jim jumped up into the camper and slammed the door shut before the dog could follow him inside.

"Gun it, Tom," Jim said.

They rocketed out of the parking lot, the RV tires screeching next to the bound man. The dog tried to chase the Winnebago down the street, but gave up after half a block.

CHAPTER 21

Emily gazed out the window of the RV as the bright red sunrise painted the rolling hills with a brilliant orange hue. She sighed and took a sip of coffee from her mug, trying not to burn her lip as the vehicle shook and bounced on the rough road. Lacy sat next to her in silence, staring at the ceiling as she often did when her mind was far away. Jim was sleeping in the back after a long night shift of driving. Meanwhile, Charlie was at the wheel, with Tom navigating in the passenger seat.

"Can I ask you something?" Emily said.

Lacy twitched, snapping out of her thoughts and seeming like she had forgotten where she was or that Emily was right next to her. She regarded Emily, but said nothing.

Emily shifted her weight side to side and fidgeted with her hands. "I don't really know how to word this . . . ."

Lacy's eyes narrowed. "What is it?"

"I just feel like there's this tension."

Lacy turned her body to face Emily, a deep crease forming on her brow. "Emily, we're best friends."

Emily nodded. "I know, it's just that, underneath, I get this feeling that you resent me."

Lacy's mouth opened to speak, but Emily continued before she could say anything.

"I don't think you mean to, but it's just . . . . so intense," Emily said.

Lacy closed her mouth and stared out toward the sunrise, the red glare reflecting on her face. She blinked and rubbed her eyes. Then Lacy nodded once and fixed Emily with her gaze. "Emily, my life has been bad. I mean really horrible, from the moment I was born."

"I know," Emily said.

"I do love you," Lacy said. "I think it's just difficult for me, sometimes, since you've had it so easy."

Emily blinked. Her jaw tensed and then her lower lip started to tremble. "You think I had it easy?"

Lacy raised her eyebrows, "Emily, I just mean—"

"You . . . . think my life was always rosy?"

Lacy tried to spit her words out fast. "No, it's just that you're so gorgeous and perfect, and I picture your happy childhood. But it's a good thing, Emily. This is just my own stupid—"

"Have you ever heard the term 'stage mom,' Lacy?"

Lacy frowned. "Yes, of course."

Emily nodded, turning her coffee mug around and around with her fingers.

A half smile started to appear on Lacy's face. "So, your mom entered you in pageants."

"Yes, and dance competitions. She was obsessed." Emily swallowed. "Though obsessed isn't really a strong enough word for it."

"I'm sorry to hear that." Lacy still had a half smile, though it had retreated a bit.

"It was so much pressure, and I was just a little girl, but I handled it okay, most of the time," Emily said.

Lacy put a hand on Emily's knee.

"But then I started blossoming early." Emily sighed. "And

when I say blossom, it was really more like exploding. All of the sudden, I had big boobs and a round butt."

Laughing through her nose, Lacy shook her head.

"My mom was furious."

Lacy's expression dropped.

"She put me on a diet. You can't win little girl pageants and be a prima ballerina when your body looks like that."

Lacy sat stiff, her cheeks looking red and blotchy.

"The diet didn't help," Emily said. "In fact, I went up another cup size and my hips got wider. So, my diet got stricter. I'd sit down at the dinner table and my plate would only have a few tiny bits of food on it. When I'd try to take another helping, my mother would click her fingernails rapidly on the table, and I would stop myself."

Lacy stared past Emily out at the trees. She didn't say anything, but her hand on Emily's knee squeezed tighter. Emily was taking deep breaths into her chest, heavy and labored. It was like her rib cage would not expand enough to take in any air.

"Then I became bulimic," Emily said.

Lacy blinked and a heavy tear rolled down her cheek. She brushed the tear away with her hand, and another one dropped from her eye straight to the ground, reflecting the sunlight on the way down. Tilting her face up to look at Emily, Lacy's mouth barely moved as she spoke. "Did your parents get you help?"

"No," Emily said. "My mom actually encouraged it."

Lacy's mouth dropped open. Emily's cheek twitched as she fought hard to maintain control of her expression.

"Mother would walk into the kitchen and see me eating a banana. She'd say, 'Are you sure that's a good idea?' " Emily's forehead was scrunched up, her face no longer pretty, but twisted in pain. "So I'd walk to the bathroom, toss it up, and when I'd come back, she'd say, 'Now do you feel better?' "

Lacy leaned over and put her hand behind Emily's head,

pulling her close and pressing her forehead against Emily's. A single sob shuttered through Emily's body like an electric jolt. "I fought that fucking disease for five years," Emily said. "I almost died." A few more sobs shook her, like a struggling car engine starting up after having sat idle for many years.

Lacy wrapped both of her arms around Emily and cradled her head against the side of her neck. Emily began to tremble, then she started to bawl. It was wet, messy, and terrible. Lacy squeezed Emily so tight that it seemed like she was trying to hold her together; as though she had just cracked a precious vase and was determined to keep it from falling apart.

CHAPTER 22

This place is creepy," Emily said, wrapping her arms around herself and shivering. "Where the heck are we anyhow?"

Jim stepped up behind Emily, placing his hands on her hips. "Somewhere deep in the heart of Montana," he said.

Emily sighed. "Well, I knew that, but why is this junkyard out in the middle of nowhere? I mean, we haven't seen anything or anyone for at least an hour."

Jim looked out at the huge monstrosity in front of him. It was at least thirty acres of beat up cars, old tractors, trashed mobile homes, and heaping piles of television sets.

"I don't think anyone wants to be near this place," Jim said.

"Yet, here we are," Emily said, laughing and fidgeting with her hands as she stood there.

The door to the RV opened and they both turned to see Lacy coming out.

"You guys ready?" Lacy said.

"Yeah," Jim said. "Is Charlie coming?"

Lacy shook her head. "He thought he should stay back with Tom, in case we have another problem, like that dog walker, or worse."

Emily looked from side to side in a mocking gesture. "I don't think anyone's walking their dog out here."

Lacy smirked. "I'm glad to see my sarcasm is rubbing off on you, Em. Soon I'll have you hacking computers."

Emily laughed. "Umm, I don't think so."

Jim pulled out a flashlight and moved the beam slowly in front of him, examining everything within sight. He shined the light at the thick woods, to the left of the junkyard, then along the chain link fence surrounding the entire place. The fence was not very high, and it didn't have any barbed wire at the top, so the owners did not seem too concerned about people trespassing. To the right of the junkyard, and extending far behind it, were vast fields of prairie grass. Way off on the horizon, mountains loomed, looking ominous and silent against the night sky.

Jim glanced over at Lacy and saw that she was examining every shadow in sight with intense focus.

"You never know," Jim said. "It's not a bad idea for Charlie to guard the RV while we're gone."

"Okay," Emily said. "So, what are we looking for in there, Lace?"

Lacy smiled at the nickname. "Mostly antennas; the bigger the better. And anything else that might be useful."

Jim nodded and led them toward the front of the junkyard. The gate was already open a few feet, and the chain that had locked it hung freely. Shaking his head, Jim lifted the chain in his hand and examined it. "That's odd, the padlock is just open and hooked here, but it's not broken. It's like someone just left and didn't bother to lock up."

A sound like metal cracking startled all three of them and they jumped, whipping around with hands raised. Charlie stood there, leaning against the RV, sipping a freshly opened can of beer.

Seeing that he had startled them, Charlie shrugged and smiled. "As you were, folks. I've got things covered here."

"Not funny," Lacy said. "Dammit, I'm skittish as hell."

"Sorry," Charlie said, flipping the back of his hand at them, shooing them toward the junkyard. "Just go on and get this done."

Jim turned, sidestepping through the gate and into the yard, Lacy and Emily following behind him. Shining his flashlight at the ground, Jim stopped and took a step to the side, examining the dirt.

"Look at this," Jim said. "There's two thick scrapes that lead through the gate and into the middle of this place. Like something was dragged."

Lacy knelt down, lightly touching the grooves. Her eyes followed them slowly, until she was gazing deep into the junkyard. With a gasp she sprang up and looked at Jim, her eyes wide with alarm.

Jim felt his stomach clench up. "What is it?"

Lacy seemed to be staring right through Jim. She didn't say anything.

"Lacy?" Jim said.

Lacy shook her head, appearing to shrug off her thoughts. "Nothing. It's nothing." She started walking toward a row of pickup trucks.

Emily glanced over at Jim.

"I really don't like this," Emily said.

"Me either." Jim pulled a pistol out of his belt, which Tom had stashed in the Winnebago long ago. He pulled the action back on the gun, loading a round. "I think our next stop will have to be somewhere we can get more firepower. I don't think this thing is nearly enough."

Emily nodded, her breathing ragged and shaky.

Lacy climbed on top of a diesel truck cab and started working at getting a CB antenna off the roof. Jim came over to stand near the truck.

"Need any help?" Jim said.

Lacy grunted. "I've almost got it."

Jim took a step toward the cab and something caught his foot. He stopped and shined his flashlight on the ground.

"What the?" Jim said. He crouched down to examine what looked like a shoe, sticking out of the dirt. Jim's skin started to tingle all over. Reaching down, Jim grabbed the toe of the shoe and squeezed, expecting it to be empty. It wasn't. Gasping, he yanked his hand back. Jim's breathing became loud and fast through his nostrils. He shined the flashlight at the ground surrounding the shoe.

"Oh, no," Jim said. "Lacy?"

Lacy worked her knife under one of the screws holding the antenna to the top of the truck. "Hold on," she said.

Jim moved his flashlight in a small circle, noticing how the dirt was a different color in one area. "Oh, shit, Lacy!"

Lacy's knife slipped and the blade skidded across metal. She grunted. "Dammit, what is it, Jim?"

Jim looked in the direction of the RV, barely able to see the dim light from one of the windows, far away on the other side of the massive junkyard. He wondered if he could signal Charlie somehow, or if they should go and get him. "There's a body buried here," Jim said.

Something clanged on the roof of the truck and Lacy's head appeared over the edge, looking down at Jim.

"How do you know?" Lacy said.

Jim shined his flashlight on the shoe, then he moved the beam around to outline the oval shape of the darker dirt, which mounded upward in the middle.

Lacy puffed her cheeks out and scratched her forehead with the blade of her knife. "Not our problem right now," she said. "Half of the gear I need is attached to this truck, just give me a few minutes."

Jim stood up, groaning. "I know, I just think we need to make this stop quicker than we had planned. I'll keep an eye out."

Lacy nodded. "I'll hurry."

"I'm going to get Emily over here too," Jim said. "She probably shouldn't get too far away from us." Jim gave a quick whistle. On the other side of the chain link fence, about fifty yards away, something rustled the brush within the woods. Jim stood frozen, listening for more noises, but it had stopped. He waited for a while, the only sound being Lacy twisting rusty screws on top of the semi cab. Then a shadow appeared across the open area, looking long and stretched from the low moon. Emily came around the corner of a row of cars, holding a roll of black cable in one hand, and a flat screen monitor under her arm. Jim swung his flashlight beam over at her, and she stopped, lifting her free arm in front of her face.

"Gah, you're blinding me," Emily said.

Jim moved the beam down. "Sorry, I was just worried about you."

"I'm right here," Emily said.

Jim didn't say anything. His flashlight beam started to shake as he stared at the ground by Emily's feet. Emily looked down, her brow crinkling.

"Jim?" Emily said.

Jim guided his light back and forth in slow, sweeping movements across the open area, which was the size of a football field. In a pattern that seemed not quite random, large ovals of dark dirt were scattered all over the place, an endless array that went on farther than Jim's flashlight could reach.

Jim staggered backward, his light now wavering all over the place. His back slammed into the door of the truck.

"I got it!" Lacy said, holding the antenna high above her head in triumph.

"This—" Jim's throat went dry, its sides sticking together like paste.

Lacy once again appeared over the edge of truck. "You okay?" she said.

"This isn't a junkyard," Jim said. "It's a graveyard."

Emily shrieked and covered the distance between her and Jim, turning her head left to right as she ran.

Lacy slid down onto the hood of the truck and leapt down to the ground, her eyes darting around. "It's both," she said. "It's a dump spot for someone."

"I don't want to find out who that someone is," Jim said.

"Me either," Lacy said.

Jim took the flat screen from Emily, as Lacy gave it a quick look and an approving nod.

"Let's hurry," Jim said. "I didn't think we had to worry about someone coming out here at night, but it appears I was wrong."

They ran through the junkyard, dodging random refrigerators, washing machines, and other appliances as the wind whistled in their ears. Just before the gate came into sight, Lacy picked up speed jumping ahead of Jim and Emily.

"Hurry," Lacy said, increasing her pace to a sprint.

Jim and Emily pumped their legs, catching back up to Lacy.

"What is it?" Jim said between gasps.

Lacy didn't look back at Jim. She kept staring straight ahead, running full bore as she spoke. "I saw something."

"What?" Emily said.

"I'll tell you later. Just run."

Charlie crushed another beer can in his hand, feeling thankful he had found Tom's secret stash in the back of the RV fridge. It was stale old beer, having been warm, then cold, then warm again several times over. Still, it was better than nothing—any beer is better than none.

A wild, bobbing flashlight caught Charlie's eye and he looked up to see Jim, Emily, and Lacy sprinting for the gate.

"Son of a bitch," Charlie muttered, tossing his beer can to the side. "Why do we always have to end our stops like this?"

He grabbed the handle of the RV door and waited. When the three of them were within earshot, Charlie pulled the door open, holding it like a chauffeur. "We in trouble?" Charlie said.

"Yep," Jim said, his footfalls thumping on the ground.

Charlie stuck his head inside the door. "Hey Tom, quick exit again."

A groan echoed inside the RV, followed by some ruckus as a metal pan clanged onto the floor of the camper. The engine fired up just as Emily's foot hit the first step leading up into the camper. Emily flew through the door, followed by Jim. Lacy stopped for a moment, guiding her long antenna inside before climbing in. Charlie stepped up into the doorway and slapped the side of the RV twice with his hand. The engine revved and they started rolling forward as Charlie shut the door.

J. ARTHUR SQUIERS

CHAPTER 23

A drop of water splattered onto Kraig's forehead. Looking up, he saw a rusty pipe hanging from the ceiling. Studying it, he realized there was some kind of green mold growing in splotches all the way along the pipe, from where it emerged on one side of the room and ran in a straight line across, before disappearing into the wall on the other side. Kraig wanted to wipe the water off his face, but the handcuffs holding him to the steel chair prevented it. It was a minor annoyance, but at the moment, it was all he could think about.

Kraig was surprised that he had once again been led to this secret, dank room, deep under the prison. He thought he was finished dealing with that profound idiot, Jim Wisendorf, forever. The notion that Jim could still be alive was preposterous.

The sound of metal sliding on metal echoed through the room, startling Kraig out of his thoughts. The door opened, grating on its rusted hinges. Kraig did not lift his head to look at the person who came through the door. "I didn't expect to see you again," Kraig said.

"I don't believe we've met," said a low, raspy voice. "My

name is Francis."

Kraig's head jerked up, his eyes wide. He saw a very thin man, with a gaunt face, at least eighty years old. The man was bald, with sunken eyes and deeply creased skin, like a wrinkled prune. Yet, his gaze was strong and alert, like a snake ready to strike its prey.

"Ah," Francis said. "You were expecting someone else."

Kraig felt a cold chill run throughout his body, something he had never felt before.

"Do you know who I am?" Francis said.

"I have a pretty good idea," Kraig said.

One corner of Francis' mouth stretched into a sly smile. "I know a lot about you, Mr. Freestone," Francis said. "I rarely perform this sort of grunt work myself, but I was intrigued to see you in person—such an interesting specimen."

Licking his dry lips, Kraig looked at Francis with intense awe. Francis glanced at Kraig's neck.

"I see that your pulse has quickened considerably," Francis said. "You are not capable of fear, yet you are extremely excited. Exhilarated I should say."

Francis took slow, deliberate steps toward Kraig, then leaned over, studying Kraig's eyes from inches away. Kraig could see hundreds of tiny red capillaries, just under the surface of the thin skin on Francis' face.

"Intelligence is the only trait you believe deserves respect," Francis said. "And you are aware, mostly through simple intuition, that I am the most ingenious man you will ever meet."

Kraig's mouth went dry, his heart thumping against his chest.

"You helped them," Francis said.

Kraig's breathing increased in rhythm and intensity.

"They offered you a sliver of freedom, and you helped them. They gave you a tool that, in your hands, equals immense power, and in return you gave them a location. You gave them the position of an operation that was working for me."

Keeping his eyes fixed on Francis, Kraig's mouth twitched as his breathing grew louder.

"Now, granted, you knew they would die if they went to that place, so it was a win-win. You get your revenge, and your access to cyberspace."

Kraig closed his eyes and breathed hard through his nose, in rapid gusts, his chest heaving.

"Of course, you also know that I cannot forgive this," Francis said, reaching his hand inside his suit coat as he walked in a circle around Kraig, stopping behind him. "You are fully aware I cannot allow anyone to live that has acted against me."

Moaning escaped Kraig's lips as oxytocin hormones gushed into his bloodstream.

"Yet the idea that I am the one to do this—that I personally came here for this purpose, fills you with an ecstasy that you have never experienced in your entire life."

Kraig looked at the wall in front of him, seeing Francis' shadow lifting a long, sharp object above his head.

"I am a god to you," Francis said.

His mouth opening in a giant smile, Kraig tossed his head back as the metal point pierced deep into the back of his neck.

J. ARTHUR SQUIERS

CHAPTER 24

L acy set her antenna down on the floor of the RV and went to the window, staring at the junkyard as they sped away. Jim put a hand on her shoulder, causing her to jump. Her eyes still remained fixed on the rows of old cars, deep inside, among the piles of salvage. Jim glanced up toward the front of the RV, where Emily and Charlie had gone to help Tom navigate the winding old road that led away from that dreadful place. He looked down at Lacy. Her body was shuddering, her fingers trembling as they rested against the window.

"It was him again, wasn't it?" Jim said.

Lacy nodded her head. She folded her arms and kept her eyes locked on the junkyard.

Jim put his hand up against the wall above the window to prevent himself from slamming into Lacy as the RV swerved around a curve in the road.

"What was he doing?" Jim said.

"Standing there," Lacy said. "Between two old Cadillacs. He just stood there as we passed by, ten feet away from him."

"I didn't see anyone," Jim said.

"I know, you and Emily were focusing straight ahead. I was

looking everywhere, because I sort of knew."

"You knew?"

"Knew he was there."

"I don't understand. You mean you sensed him?"

"Sort of."

Jim looked hard at Lacy, narrowing his eyes. "That's scary."

Lacy shook her head. "You know how people say they can feel someone's presence?" Lacy said.

"Yeah," Jim said. "But I think it's hooey."

"Well, it is and it isn't," Lacy said. "Your subconscious is very powerful. It might pick up on a subtle change in sound patterns, or a shadow being cast that just doesn't jive. It can figure things out, and start sending signals to your body, long before your conscious mind is aware of what's going on."

Jim scratched his head, considering the thought for a moment. He put his hand on Lacy's shoulder. "And your subconscious is extremely powerful, compared to everyone else's, I'm sure."

Lacy turned her head, looking up at Jim with sad, frightened eyes. "That's how I wrote the wildfire program. My subconscious was so terrified, it managed to piece together an infinite puzzle that no person or computer ever has. And now I need your help."

Jim's grip tightened on Lacy's shoulder, his lips pressing together. "We're going to get through this," he said. "We're all going to be okay."

Lacy blinked and a slight smile peeked through her sad expression. "You say that with so much earnest, that I'm going to choose to believe you. But I also need you to help me prove that I'm not going crazy."

"Lacy, you're not—"

"Jim, you and Emily have kept me from swirling into madness ever since . . . .Nian."

Jim's mouth opened, his brow furrowing.

Lacy continued before he could speak. "You don't realize

it, but you have. Only, now, I need just you. I need you to see him too, so that I know he's real." Her body turned and she grasped Jim's arm. "I can't tell any of them about this until I know for sure . . . ."

"That you're not seeing things," Jim said.

Lacy let out a sigh and looked down at the floor. "Yeah," she said.

Charlie yelled back from the front of the RV, "Jim, we got headlights coming this way."

Jim spun around in alarm. He looked back at Lacy, then rushed to the front of the camper.

"They're coming at us?" Jim said, bending down and peering ahead through the windshield.

"Yeah," Tom said. "Looks like they're heading for the junkyard."

"Oh my." Emily clutched at her chest. "What if they're bringing another body?"

Charlie and Tom both snapped their heads around to look at Emily.

"Another body?" Charlie said.

"There were people buried there," Jim said. "Like a hundred of them. We saw it."

"This is bad." Charlie shook his head. "This is why we need more guns."

"What should I do, folks?" Tom said.

Jim stared ahead at the approaching headlights. "We just keep going. There's no other choice."

Lacy came up behind Jim, watching in silence.

"You think they'll just pass by us?" Emily said.

"I hope so," Jim said. "Maybe they'll think we're just some tourists that took a wrong turn and we're heading back to the main road." He continued to watch as the headlights got closer.

"Why don't the rest of you go in the back?" Tom jabbed his thumb toward the rear of the RV. "It'll look better than them seeing all of you standing up here, mouths gaping as they drive by."

"You're right," Jim said.

They all hurried to the back of the RV, leaving Tom at the wheel, watching through his round spectacles as the floating headlights grew closer by the second.

Tom took a deep breath and held it in. When the car passed by, he let it out. Then Tom watched the mirror on the side of the RV, keeping an eye on the vehicle's tail lights. He pushed on the gas, gaining speed. The tail lights got smaller, and smaller, until they disappeared in the darkness. Tom tucked his head down to wipe the sweat off of his shiny forehead with his sleeve. When he looked back up, an elk stood in the middle of the road, its black eyes gleaming at him in bright light. Tom slammed his foot on the brake pedal, causing the RV tires to scream as they slid on pavement. Jim came barreling forward, grabbing onto the back of Tom's seat as the Winnebago struck the petrified animal. The RV slid sideways and squealed while Tom tried to maintain control. Switching his foot back to the gas, Tom tried to accelerate into the skid, but the vehicle just kept sliding until it went off the shoulder, plowed through the brush, and bumped up against a tree.

Tom put it in reverse and hit the gas; the wheels spun, but the RV didn't budge.

Jim swung the side door open and jumped out, with Charlie right on his tail. He ran around the front of the RV and crouched down to examine the damage. Jim's face cringed at the sight of the elk, wedged up inside the right wheel well. It looked like a mass of dark brown fur was bulging out all around the tire, while the back end of the animal was stuck under the frame of the RV, holding it off the ground.

Charlie cursed and kicked the front bumper. "You've got to be kidding me."

Jim went over to where the vehicle had struck the tree. There was a small dent in the hood, but nothing major. "How do we get this animal out of there?"

Charlie pushed on the furry carcass with his hand. "We'll have to jack it up and take the wheel off," Charlie said. "Then maybe we can pry it out of there." He stood up and shook his head. "Hopefully nothing's bent up or broken in there."

"That'll take some time," Jim said.

"Yeah, it will," Charlie said, looking down the road.

Jim thought about the car that had passed them and he pictured the endless rows of buried bodies in the junkyard. He rubbed his forehead, his temples pounding like drums. "Okay, let's hurry."

Charlie worked the jack, getting the front tire off the ground. Jim looked around for a stick or something else that could be used to pry at the elk. Lacy, Emily, and Tom stood near the back of the camper, watching the road.

Charlie grunted, yanking the wheel off the axle and tossing it on the ground. "Damn, that looks nasty," Charlie said, crouching down and looking at the head of the elk, wrapped around the axle. "I've never seen anything like it."

Jim came up behind him, holding a thick branch. He gagged. "Me either."

"Jim!" Emily's voice rang out from the other side of the camper. It sounded shrill and uneasy. "They're coming back."

Jim whirled around, while Charlie stood up and leaned out to see around the camper.

"Act normal," Jim said. "We're just a family that got lost and then hit an elk."

"Right," Charlie said. "I'll play along . . . . for as long as I can."

Jim gave Charlie a sideways look and Charlie shrugged.

The car came rolling along the road until its headlights swept over the RV, then it slowed to a stop—it was a shiny black town car. The passenger door opened up, and a short, stocky man stepped out. He appeared to be wearing a suit and tie. "You folks doing okay?" the man called to them.

Jim and Charlie walked up next to the others at the rear of the camper.

"We got lost," Jim replied. "Then we hit an elk on the way out. We've got it under control though."

The man in the suit nodded. "You sure you don't need a hand?" he said.

Jim glanced at Charlie, who was smiling and trying to look casual, but it didn't look natural—it looked like an irritated man trying to smile for a photograph.

"Nah," Jim said. He patted Charlie on the back. "We've got all the manpower we need."

Charlie looked at the ground and shrugged his shoulders. That was much better, Jim thought. Act sheepish, Charlie. Look shy, look dumb even. And Charlie did as he clumsily wiped his greasy hands on his t-shirt.

"Nonsense," the man in the suit said. "Besides, I'm trying to teach these boys to help their fellow man." He pounded on the top of the car and three other men, huge guys, opened their doors and stepped out of the car.

Charlie muttered something under his breath. Emily moved closer to Jim.

Jim took a step forward. "Guys, we don't want any trouble."

The man in the suit let out a laugh and shook his head. "Trouble? Friend, there isn't any trouble. I just can't leave some nice folks like you stranded out here." The short man started walking toward them and as he got a little closer, Jim realized the other men were wearing orange jumpsuits. Jim's eyes widened and he moved back a half step.

The man in the suit, seeing Jim's reaction, held his hands up in a reassuring gesture. "Whoa, don't worry, all three of these boys are months away from parole. They're just good men that made some mistakes long ago."

Charlie's torso straightened up and Jim feared he was going to make a run at them. Perhaps Charlie and Lacy could take them on, he was unsure. He could fight too, but these inmates were huge, each of them more massive than Charlie, and they looked like they could kill a man with one punch. The short guy in the suit also seemed very confident, which suggested that he was no slouch. Jim was determined to keep everyone alive; he could not handle losing another person. For now, that meant playing along.

So Jim nodded and shrugged. "Okay, if you insist."

The four men came down into the ditch.

Jim turned to Lacy and Emily, "Ladies, you want to go inside and find these gentlemen something to drink?"

Lacy gave Jim a tight lipped look, and he knew she did not want to leave her friends with these men.

"Nah," the man in the suit said. "We're good for now. Maybe afterwards." The man started unbuttoning his suit coat. "Now, let's take a look at the damage on this thing."

"Sure," Jim said. "Girls, why don't you just go get Charlie and I some beers then. We're parched."

Emily started heading for the camper door. The short man pulled two pistols out of holsters under his suit coat and pointed them at Jim's face. "Anyone moves, and your boy'll have two holes in his head," the man in the suit said in a firm, calm voice.

Freezing where he stood, Jim looked at the guns and swallowed hard. Out of the corner of his eye, he saw Charlie's muscles flex, his fists clenching.

Jim put his hands up in surrender. "You can take whatever you want, just don't hurt us."

The man cocked his head to the side. "Oh, we'll take what we want." He smiled. "And everyone will survive as long as no one decides to be a hero." He looked at Charlie and winked.

Charlie's jaw locked, his cheeks rippling.

"Chubs," the man in the suit said to the biggest inmate. "Go get the cuffs."

"Sure, Boss," Chubs said, nodding and jogging up to the car. The man in the suit moved his eyes to each person, then fixed his gaze on Lacy. His mouth curved into a grin.

Chubs jogged back down to them with a bunch of handcuffs in his hand and two shotguns over his shoulder.

"Pipes, here you go," Chubs said, tossing one of the shotguns to another inmate.

Pipes pointed the barrel at Charlie.

The man in the suit said, "Boomer, you cuff 'em up." He turned and looked at them. "Remember, everyone will be all right if you all cooperate."

Boomer walked over to Charlie and grabbed one of his wrists. Jim saw Charlie's eyes light up in a blaze and it seemed like he was going to attack. Closing his own eyes, Jim waited for the gun to go off. It didn't, he just heard handcuffs ratcheting open and shut. When he looked again, Charlie and Tom were both on their knees, handcuffed to the undercarriage of the camper. Boomer was cuffing Emily, and Jim bit into his lip, fighting the urge to grab for his own gun, which was tucked in the back of his belt under his t-shirt. Jim knew he would be dead before he even got his fingers on it.

Boss kept his pistols aimed at Jim's head while Boomer came up and slapped handcuffs on his wrists, then secured him to the camper. Finally, Boomer walked up to Lacy, who was staring back at Boomer with an intensity that made Jim's blood go cold. Boomer put a hand on Lacy's arm and Jim saw her other fist tense, ready to strike. Lacy gave each of her friends a glance, then her eyes flicked over at all the guns being pointed at them. She let out a resigned sigh and relaxed as Boomer cuffed both her hands behind her back.

"Okay," Jim said, staring into the barrels of the pistols as sweat ran down his face. "You can take everything we've got in the RV. It's all yours."

Boss chewed hard on a piece of gum. "Yeah? Well, you see folks, even though these men are almost rehabilitated, they still got some strong urges they need to get out of their system." He looked over at Lacy. "And you got just the flavor they like. The little girl type."

Jim felt his skin go burning hot, like it was doused with scalding water. Charlie tried to lunge at Boss, but the handcuff chain held him back.

"Oh, ho!" Boss said. "We've got ourselves a fighter!" He took a step toward Charlie. "I told you I wouldn't shoot anyone if you cooperated. But obviously, you didn't hear me. Pipes, put him down."

Pipes walked up and pressed the barrel of his shotgun against Charlie's forehead, while Charlie stared him in the eyes without blinking.

"Wait!" Lacy said. "I'll give you what you want!"

Boss's head slowly turned to Lacy.

"Just don't shoot him," Lacy said.

Boss raised an eyebrow. "I see." He looked at the inmates and shrugged. "It's a deal then."

Boomer smiled from ear to ear. Emily started to cry.

Chubs walked up to Lacy and grabbed her arm, pulling her along while Boomer got on her other side. Pipes, the biggest of them all, walked behind them with his shotgun.

Lacy tried to focus on her breathing and nothing else. She marched along into the woods, her body feeling numb all over. She could smell the big, nasty men around her and it took everything she had to keep from vomiting.

"Right here," Pipes said, his voice deep and rough.

Boomer stopped and grabbed the back of Lacy's shirt, pushing her hard to the ground while keeping a grip on the garment. Lacy fell, unable to reach out and break her fall with her hands cuffed behind her back. Her shirt ripped against her weight as Boomer held onto it, but it still kept her face from slamming against the ground. She hung there in the air, her nose a few inches away from the rocky dirt. Boomer gave a quick yank and her shirt tore off the rest of the way. He flung it into the bushes with a grunt. Lacy plopped onto her bare stomach and inhaled the sweet odor of earth and decay.

"I'm first," Pipes said. He was now breathing heavy and fast, his hands fumbling with cloth.

Lacy wanted them to shoot her. She did not care anymore, dying seemed far better than what they had planned. She could just flip onto her back and try to fight them off. Yes, they would kill her, but that was preferred at this point. Then after she was dead, she realized, they would go after Emily and take out their frustrations on her.

Lacy pressed her face into the ground, letting the dirt and grime block her breathing, hoping she would at least pass out. As her senses began to fade, she heard a pop, and Pipe's huge body fell on top of her, crushing her and forcing all of the air out of her lungs. Boomer and Chubs both spun around, gasping. Two more pops sounded, and Lacy felt the ground vibrate as the giant bodies crashed down. She could not see or breathe as she tried to push Pipes off of her. Grunting as adrenaline poured into her limbs, Lacy was able to push the massive man up enough to slide out from beneath him. She saw someone standing near a v-shaped oak tree, dressed in black, wearing a hood. Mixed feelings flooded her mind. She felt intense fear, because he was now pointing his gun at her, but she also felt relief, because she knew she was not crazy. The figure had killed three people; that was certainly real. It also looked like she was going to be next.

"Who are you?" Lacy said.

The dark hooded silhouette kept its pistol pointed at Lacy. It did not speak. Lacy got her legs under her and started to stand. She wobbled as fresh oxygen rushed to her brain, making her light headed. The dark figure lowered the gun, turned, and disappeared into the trees. Lacy heard soft footfalls on the ground that faded away. Groaning, she got to her feet and looked around at the carnage.

~ ~ ~

Jim pulled hard, trying to get his hand to slip through the handcuff. His wrist was bleeding, but he did not feel the pain. He was trying to get the bones in his hands to break, hoping that would allow him to get free. He gritted his teeth and dug his foot in the ground, pulling against the cuff with everything he had. The rusted undercarriage of the camper groaned with a loud creak, and Boss lifted his head up, looking at Jim.

"You trying to get away?" Boss said.

Jim looked at him with a defiant stare.

Boss shook his head and walked over to Jim. "I'm done giving warnings, son. You've left me no choice."

Emily started shrieking, her chain rattling and clanging in a relentless panic. Boss lifted his gun, pointing it at Jim's forehead.

The sound of a shotgun pumping came around the corner of the camper. They all spun around in surprise to see Lacy, standing there topless, holding a shotgun pointed at Boss. Still pointing his pistol at Jim's head, Boss's mouth dropped open, hanging there for a moment.

"Drop the gun you fucking piece of shit," Lacy said.

Boss's jaw came back to life and he regained his composure, even managing a smile.

"Where's my boys?" Boss said.

Lacy's eyes were ice cold. "Your gun, put it on the ground."

Boss hesitated for a moment, looking at Lacy in silence. His shoulders slumping, Boss lowered the gun and crouched down to set it on the ground. He held his other hand up in surrender. "Okay, okay, I'm putting it down, just don't shoot."

Lacy's eye started twitching, like a mosquito had flown into it, and she lifted her shoulder so she could rub it with her arm. Boss reacted by swinging the gun up to point it at Lacy. Her shotgun went off and Boss stumbled backward, holding a hole in his stomach. His hands were shiny with dark fluid. Lacy ran at him, slamming the butt of her shotgun into his face, knocking him onto his back as she stood over him. With a scream, Lacy shoved the barrel of her shotgun deep into Boss's mouth, causing him to choke, his eyes nearly bulging out of their sockets.

"You evil, sick motherfucker," she said. "I want you to think about what's going to happen next."

Boss gagged on the barrel, his breath rattling inside the steel pipe. Lacy pumped the shotgun.

"You ready? On the count of three."

Boss tried to shake his head side to side, but Lacy just pushed the barrel deeper into his throat, holding his head still.

"One . . . . two . . . . thr—"

"Lacy!"

Lacy stopped and looked up at Emily, hearing the sound of horror in her voice. Emily's eyes were wide and filled with tears, her chest heaving in and out as she looked at Lacy with sheer panic on her face. Lacy froze for a second. Then Lacy's body relaxed and she let out a sigh before looking back down at Boss. His face had gone pale, as white as a corpse, though he was still breathing. Bending down, Lacy picked his pistol up from the ground and tossed it to Charlie, who caught it with his free hand. Lacy turned back and watched Boss's eyes, waiting for the life to leave them as he bled out from his stomach. Then she yanked the shotgun from his mouth and tossed it onto the ground.

Reaching into her pocket, Lacy pulled out a key and went over to unlock Emily's handcuffs. When Emily was free, she stood up and threw her arms around Lacy. They held each other for a minute, crying together.

"I'm sorry you had to see that," Lacy said.

Emily released Lacy and looked at her. "I'm just glad you're alive." Emily's forehead creased. "Did they?" She choked. "Did they hurt you?"

Lacy shook her head.

"How'd you get away?" Jim said. "What happened?"

Lacy looked at Jim and said, "He killed them."

Jim felt weak, his head aching. "You mean?"

"Yeah," Lacy said. "The hooded man."

Lacy crouched down and unlocked Tom.

"Who are you talking about?" Charlie said.

Jim stood up, wiping his bleeding wrist on his pants. "Someone who has been watching us," Jim said.

"What?" Emily said. "You didn't tell us that someone was following us?"

Jim's cheeks grew hot and a flutter of guilt filled his gut. "Well, I—"

"I wasn't sure if he was real," Lacy said. "I'm the only one who's seen him, and I only told Jim because I didn't want everyone to think I was going crazy."

Emily cast her eyes down at the ground.

"But now I know he's real. And apparently he doesn't want me dead, at least not yet."

J. ARTHUR SQUIERS

CHAPTER 25

S tart her up," Jim said. **He stood outside the** passenger window, drenched in sweat, and gave a thumbs up to Tom.

Tom revved the engine to life and put the RV into reverse, backing it away from the tree.

"I think we're good," Charlie said, watching the newly attached tire roll.

Tom stopped the RV, letting Jim and Charlie come lumbering in.

Lacy was kneeling on the floor, patching together wiring with her laptop sitting on the table. The computer was on, with a command prompt blinking on the screen, waiting for its master. It had been some time since Jim had seen a computer of any sort, and even longer since he had seen Lacy using one. He remembered what a marvel it was to watch her do what she does best.

Emily sat slouched over the table, on the other side, sipping one of the remaining bottles of beer. Her gaze was distant, her lower lip trembling over whatever thoughts were going through her mind. Jim took a seat next to her, rubbing her back with his hand.

Plopping down into a cushioned chair, Charlie let out a deep sigh. "Well, I sure as hell ain't letting that happen again."

"I agree," Jim said.

Charlie gave Jim a stern look. "We are getting guns before we do anything else."

Jim nodded, his face grim.

Lacy got up without saying a word and sat down at her computer.

"I mean it," Charlie said. "That was bullshit. There's no way we should've been caught off guard by some lunatic prison warden and his thugs. We need to be a lot better than that if we're gonna survive this."

Jim's head pounded with rhythmic thuds. He pictured what almost happened to Lacy and thought about how lucky they were that some weirdo out there, following them around, had decided to kill the inmates and not her.

Lacy started typing commands on her keyboard, her fingers clicking away with speed and precision.

"I'll talk to Tom," Jim said. "We're almost to Colorado, and he's spent a lot of time there. He'll know where we can get plenty of weapons."

Charlie nodded, puckering his lips out with satisfaction.

"Guys," Lacy said, her focus still on her screen.

Jim, Charlie, and Emily all looked at Lacy, who had barely said a word since she had removed the shotgun barrel from Boss's mouth.

"I'm online," Lacy said.

Jim and Charlie looked at each other, both seeing the same realization in each other's eyes. Lacy Tabitha Chase was back on the internet; for better or worse, the whole game was about to change.

CHAPTER 26

I t turns out, there was no need for Jim to ask Tom where to get firearms in Colorado. Lacy had that information in a matter of seconds. In fact, just before they got to the gun shop, Lacy managed to disarm their security alarm from her laptop, making it easy for Charlie to run in, have a shopping spree in his own personal candy store, and walk out with a spring in his step. For good measure, Lacy even set off burglar alarms in high-end stores on the other side of town, just to make sure all of the police patrols would be elsewhere and not stumbling across their little gun heist.

Charlie smiled when he came bursting into the RV, shoulders loaded with big green canvas duffle bags. "You didn't tell me they had AK-47s here," Charlie said.

Lacy winked. "I wanted to surprise you."

Charlie took one of the assault rifles out of a bag and walked to the back of the camper. Sliding open a slot that he had cut out earlier, he mounted the gun on a pivot and moved it around, looking through the sights.

"Well, at least we know they can't get us from behind," Jim said. He was glad that everyone seemed to be in better spirits, having been worried they would not be able to shake off what had happened back in Montana. Lacy had refused to talk about it at all, though she was so engrossed in her hacking now that it was understandable.

"Now, more than ever, we need to drive on random routes and put distance behind us," Lacy said. "I'm covering my tracks on the servers as best I can, but these people, given enough time, can trace anyone."

"You hear that, Tom?" Jim yelled toward the front of the camper.

"Got it," Tom responded. "Don't worry, I know these mountains like my backyard. I've got some wild routes in mind."

Lacy clicked the keys on her keyboard so fast, it sounded like a downpour of rain on a tin roof. Jim became so used to the sound that it startled him when she suddenly stopped. He looked up at her and saw that her mouth was hanging wide open.

Jim felt his stomach tighten. "What is it, Lacy?"

"It's worse than I thought," Lacy said. "Every agency is on high alert to find me. Police, fire departments, special forces, FBI, mall security, mailmen—and it's all classified under national security. Who has that kind of power?"

"I don't know," Jim said. "Am I on there too?"

Lacy tapped the keyboard. "You are all listed as accomplices. All except Tom. He's not listed anywhere."

Charlie forced a laugh. "Good thing he's the one that fills the gas when we stop."

"Yeah," Lacy said, clicking her enter key a few times. "Damn, they've got facial recognition software running on feeds from every security camera in the country."

"But how did they find you before?" Charlie said. "Tom doesn't have cameras and you said you stayed down in the ravine the whole time? How'd they know you were hiding there?"

Lacy's brow furrowed and she tapped her finger on her

chin. Then her face lit up. "Give me a half hour, I think I might know how."

"This is insane," Lacy said.

Charlie put his hands behind his head. "You found something?"

Lacy jabbed her fingers into her thick hair and squeezed the long locks with a grimace. "This is so bad. So very, very bad."

"Lacy, what is it?" Jim said.

Looking at Jim, Lacy drummed her fingers on the table so loud it sounded like a stampede.

"They're using the ultra-satellites," Lacy said.

Charlie's head snapped up. "Nobody is even supposed to know about those," he said.

"I know," Lacy said.

Jim's forehead creased. "What are ultra-satellites?"

"They are satellites that have telescopes pointing at the earth," Lacy said. "Telescopes that can read the time off your watch from space."

Jim sat forward, leaning in toward Lacy as though he were going to whisper in her ear. "You mean our own government is behind this?"

"Maybe," Lacy said. "Or people who have a lot of pull at the highest level."

Jim's knee started bouncing up and down. He looked out the window and saw that they were near the top of the highest mountains. The sun glinted off the snow on the tall peaks in the distance. He was at a loss for words; all he could do was sit there and try to let the weight of the revelation sink in. Then he sat up straight and looked at Lacy. "Can you hack the satellites?"

"There's no way," Charlie said.

Jim stared at Lacy, his face grim and serious. "Lacy, I've seen you hack into the most secure government systems on the planet. Could you do this?"

"Maybe," Lacy said. "But it's going to take a lot of time and it will attract a lot of attention."

"I say we do it," Jim said. "How much more attention could we attract?"

Lacy drummed her fingers harder on the table, staring at the wall. Though, it seemed to Jim that she was looking through the wall to somewhere far beyond. He knew she was weighing every possible angle, playing out every scenario. He had some understanding about how her mind worked, and it was an amazing thing to behold. Soon, Lacy's hands began to tremble and her forehead glistened with sweat. Her chest expanded with a deep breath until it seemed her lungs would burst and then she let it out with a sharp exhale. With a final nod of decisiveness, Lacy tightened her fist into a ball and slammed it down on the table, causing Emily to stir in her sleep in the back of the RV.

"Screw it," Lacy said. "I'm going after those suckers."

"You're gonna hack the satellites?" Jim said.

"I'm going to try," Lacy replied. "Like Charlie said, it's quite impossible."

"You've done impossible before," Jim said.

"Not like this," Lacy said. "And it's going to take quite a while. You guys will have to buy me enough time."

Jim stood up and put his hand on Lacy's shoulder. "We'll give you all the time you need," Jim said. "It's the least we can do."

CHAPTER 27

Tom stepped out of the RV, keeping his baseball cap visor pulled low to hide most of his round race. Looking at the sun, which was starting to set behind the mountains, he walked back to the pump. The gas station, high in the mountains, seemed deserted. As the cold wind slammed against the side of the camper, Tom's huge gray beard blew over his shoulder and he shivered.

Feeling a strong urge to hurry, Tom held the pump handle tight, watching the number of gallons flip by. He was glad Lacy had given him a new credit card to use, one that she claimed could not be traced for at least a week. Now he could avoid having to run in and pay by cash, which had always been risky but necessary.

The pump handle clicked and Tom yanked it out of the RV, slamming it back into its slot. He looked up and saw a tall man, wearing all black clothes with a hood pulled over his head. Tom squinted into the wind, trying to focus on the person's face. The figure wore a ski mask and only the eyes were visible, white and narrow—they pierced Tom's soul with their gaze.

Tom's mind told him to move, but his body was frozen with fear. Finally, his mouth was able to move. "Who are you?"

Tom said.

The figure said nothing. It raised an arm, pointing a strange looking gun at Tom and pulling the trigger. A high pitched whistle broke the air and Tom felt a sharp pain in his chest. Looking down, Tom saw a small, hypodermic looking needle sticking out of his chest. Tom's hand reached up, trying to grasp the needle, but his arm felt weak and it fell back to his side. His vision went blurry, then everything became gray, then black.

~ ~ ~

Jim started to stir in his chair, a sense of panic forming in his stomach. Emily was watching Lacy type computer code at breakneck speed, both observing and listening in awe as though Bach were playing a masterpiece on the piano.

"How long has Tom been out there?" Jim said.

Emily blinked, shaking her head. She looked at her watch, her eyes growing wide. "He's been out there fifteen minutes."

Jim jumped out of his chair and looked out the window, his heart starting to thump fast. He saw nothing but an empty gas station lot. They were parked next to the pump that was farthest away from the store. The engine was running and exhaust plumed around the back of the RV.

"Do you see him?" Emily said.

Lacy had stopped typing, for the first time in hours. She looked up at Jim.

"No," Jim said, moving to the door. "I don't see anyone. I thought Charlie was going to keep watch when he fills up."

"Charlie's sleeping," Emily said. "Tom didn't want to wake him, and you were dozing in the chair, so he just said he'd make it quick."

Jim opened the door and leaned out, scanning the area.

"Maybe he decided to use the bathroom," Emily said.
Jim shook his head. "We agreed we'd only use the one in
the camper. He knew that would've been too risky." Jim
stepped down onto the pavement and walked around the RV,
peering down the road that wound around the mountain.
When he came back to the front of the camper, Lacy was
standing in the doorway, staring at the gas station windows,
which were dark. Nobody was on duty. The station had been
closed and locked up, with only the pay pumps left on.

"We're not going anywhere until we find him," Lacy said.

"Of course we're not leaving without him," Jim said.
"You'd better go wake Charlie up, we'll need his help."

Lacy disappeared into the RV and came back out a moment
later with Emily and Charlie behind her. Charlie went to the
gas pump and knelt down, examining the ground.

"There's no blood and no sign of struggle," Charlie said.

Lacy came up next to Charlie and looked over his shoulder
at the pavement. Then she scanned the area all around them,
studying the trees all the way out to the vast mountain range,
and peering down the long winding road. Her gaze came back
around and stopped on the gas station. Straightening up with
a jerk, Lacy strode toward the building.

"Lacy, what is it?" Jim said, hurrying to keep up with her.

Lacy didn't speak, she just sped up until she reached the
sidewalk in front of the door. She looked up, and Jim's gaze
followed.

"The security camera," Jim said. "It would have caught
what happened."

Lacy nodded and moved closer to examine the camera that
faced the gas pumps. "If the footage is stored on a server, I
can hack into it. But if it's just stored locally, we'll need to find
the tapes."

"How do we know which it is?" Jim said.

Lacy pulled a multi-tool out of her pocket. "We break in."

Jim let out a loud exhale and looked over his shoulder to

see Charlie, walking a wide circle around the parking lot. The cold, biting wind whipped across the open area, causing Jim to lean into it to keep his balance. When the howling wind died down, Jim heard a deep engine sound accelerating far below them, coming up the mountain. A tight feeling spread throughout his chest. The noise grew louder and he realized it sounded like trucks, not just one, but several.

Jim shouted to Charlie, "They're coming!"

Charlie's head snapped up and he turned his ear, listening to the sound for a second. His eyes growing big, Charlie looked at Jim. "Get to the RV!"

Lacy was working at the lock, her hands trembling. Jim grabbed her arm.

"Come on," Jim said. "They're coming for us."

"I need to know what happened," Lacy said, jiggling at the lock in frustration.

Jim pulled Lacy's arm around so she had to look at him.

"They're coming for you," Jim said.

Lacy looked at the road leading down the mountainside, then at Charlie running to the camper. She yanked her tool out of the door lock and broke into a sprint for the RV.

When they got inside, Charlie tossed an AK-47 to Jim. Looking at the gun thoughtfully, Jim shook his head and set it down on the table. His skin was covered with glistening sweat and he trembled at the thought of what he was about to do.

"I'm going to talk to them," Jim said.

"No! Please, Jim," Emily said.

"We need to know if they have Tom; I can't just run away," Jim said. "Charlie, just cover me from inside. If they start shooting, give me a chance to get in here."

Charlie nodded, a grave look on his face.

"I'm going out there with you," Lacy said.

Jim shook his head. "You're the one they want."

Lacy pressed her lips together hard, turning them white. She looked at Jim with eyes that cut through him like daggers, and

Jim knew this was one of those times there was no arguing with her.

Jim's shoulders dropped, weariness taking over. "If they get you, they'll do whatever it takes to make you create another wildfire program. They won't believe it was a fluke and they'll just keep torturing you."

The sound of the engines grew louder. They would be there in a matter of seconds.

"I know that," Lacy said. "And I'm still going with you."

Jim let out a defeated sigh, yet he felt a sense of relief come over him at the same time. "Stay right behind me," he said.

"If you're going out there without a rifle, at least bring something you can conceal," Charlie said. "I grabbed plenty of gear at the gun store."

"You got a good handgun?" Jim said.

Charlie nodded, a grim smile on this face.

Jim stepped out of the camper and walked around to the back, facing down the road toward the sound of the oncoming trucks. A row of camouflage Humvees came roaring up the hill and turned into the parking lot of the gas station. Jim held his hands up, signaling for the trucks to stop. He looked at his arms, and noticed they were shaking. Lacy stood right behind him, so close, he could feel her warm breath on the back of his neck.

Four trucks filled the parking lot, forming a wide line across it, fifty feet in front of Jim and the RV. Jim felt his throat tighten up and a thunderbolt of terror coursed through him— not just the fear that he might die, but that he would not even find the courage to speak. The gun he had tucked in the back of his pants dug into the skin of his lower back.

Men in full combat gear poured out of the trucks, pointing machine guns at Jim. Keeping his hands in the air, Jim stole a glance over at the security camera, hanging above the door to the gas station. He hoped that if he was gunned down with his hands in the air by soldiers, at the very least, the video would be captured, and that footage would be seen by people who could do some good with it.

A stern, stiff looking man in his early fifties stepped out of a truck and walked out in front of the line of trucks. He was dressed in camouflage, like the others, yet there was no question that he was their leader and carried a high rank. He had a megaphone in his hand.

The leader raised his megaphone to his mouth. "We're here for Lacy Chase," came the amplified voice. "Surrender her at once."

"And if we don't," Jim shouted, barely keeping his voice from cracking.

"We will use any force necessary to obtain her."

Jim felt Lacy's breath get heavier and hotter behind him.

"I assume you have a warrant for her arrest?"

The leader answered. "This is a matter of national security."

Jim put his hands around his mouth to shout louder. "Our friend was taken from us a moment ago; he's just an innocent old man. Give him back first."

The leader paused for a moment, his eyebrows furrowing, causing a deep line on his weathered forehead. He put the megaphone down and turned to say something to a man next to him. Nodding, he brought the megaphone back up and said, "That wasn't us, but if you turn Ms. Chase over we'll help you find him."

Lacy whispered to Jim, "I don't think they took Tom."

"Me either," Jim said. Then a realization struck him and his fists clenched into a ball. He became acutely aware of his gun, pressing against his skin. He cupped his hands around his mouth to yell as his own heartbeat thundered in his ears. Rage rumbled up from his gut and out of his throat, forming the words. "You cowards gunned down Jake Pike, in Minnesota. Twenty of you shot him up like an animal."

The leader paused again, then put the megaphone to his mouth and spoke. "We had nothing to do with that."

But Jim ignored the words, he was too busy looking at the smile that had crept onto the leader's face. It was a smirk that said, your friend was a worthless piece of shit, and we enjoyed using him for target practice.

Jim's hand darted behind his back, his fingers closing around the handle of the gun. Lacy gasped, and a machine gun next to the leader fired off four shots, all of which slammed into Jim's chest. Jim fell backwards, knocking Lacy to the ground along with him.

~ ~ ~

Emily dove out the door of the RV, her ear piercing screams echoing across the mountain tops. Charlie popped his AK-47 through the slot in the back of the camper and opened fire, his bullets spraying back and forth across the military trucks. His shots were not directed at anyone in particular, but it was excellent cover fire.

Emily and Lacy grabbed Jim under the armpits, their faces twisting as they lifted him. They carried him around to the side of the camper as machine gun fire pelted the metal siding next to Emily's head. Charlie was now firing two AK-47s at the same time, pummeling the trucks with bullets and sending broken glass and metal flying into the air. Emily tore the door open on the camper and gritted her teeth as they hoisted Jim inside. Lacy got up, rammed her hand inside one of the canvas bags holding the guns, and yanked out her own machine gun. Emily was on her knees, slouched over Jim's body, crying and pushing the palms of her hands against his chest in rhythmic thrusts.

"As soon as I stop firing," Charlie yelled over his gunfire.

"They're gonna turn this camper into Swiss cheese."

Lacy got up on the table and threw open a hatch in the ceiling of the RV. She popped out the top of the roof and started firing, but it was not wild cover fire like Charlie's. Lacy was focused on one person, the man who had shot Jim. She saw him, crouching like a weasel next to the front tire of a truck. Lacy lined up her sights and pulled the trigger. The first few bullets pelted the steel rim of the truck, next to the man, then she moved the gun a hair to the left, and he went down.

The leader of the soldiers yelled a command, and his men returned fire. Dozens of holes appeared in the back side of the RV, causing Charlie and Lacy to dive to the ground as parts of the table splintered and stuffing from the seats showered them like snow.

Lacy locked eyes with Charlie.

"I can't leave Tom behind," Lacy said. Rivers of tears flowed down her cheeks and she clenched her jaw as a bullet ricocheted off the metal table leg next to her head.

"We'll find him, I promise," Charlie said. "But if we all die here, we won't do him any good."

Lacy sucked in a shaky breath, closed her eyes, and nodded.

"Get us out of here, Lacy," Charlie said. "Drive this thing like a bat out of hell."

Lacy opened her eyes and looked at Charlie. He gave her a solemn nod. Jumping to her feet, Lacy scrambled to the front of the RV, while Charlie got up and rammed both of his guns out the back slot, unleashing a rainstorm of bullets.

Lacy punched the gas and the RV tore away from the gas station, across the ditch, and onto the road. The gunfire from the soldiers stopped, and Lacy glanced at the side mirror, seeing them getting into their trucks. Lacy realized that Charlie had started aiming at their tires, having already immobilized two of the trucks.

Cranking the wheel, Lacy screeched around a turn on the narrow mountain road. Her heart leapt into her throat when she saw the cliff just a few feet from the shoulder of the highway.

Jim coughed and gasped for air.

Turning her head for a brief moment, Lacy saw Jim getting up to his knees, looking around in a panic. Lacy's eyes went back to the road and she let out a long sigh of relief.

"Kevlar vest worked," Charlie said.

"Still felt like I got hit with a sledgehammer." Jim's voice sounded like he had been a chain smoker all his life.

"You were knocked out cold," Charlie said. "But you're still alive."

Three bullets pierced through the back wall of the camper, causing Charlie to leap to the floor. "For now," Charlie said.

Lacy accelerated into a straight stretch of road, getting up to sixty miles per hour. Charlie opened fire out the back and the windshield of the lead truck shattered, causing it to veer off the road and into the ditch.

"Still one on our tail," Charlie said. "Lacy, we gotta lose him."

Lacy came to a split in the road. The way to the left was a continuation of the paved street, while the way to the right was a steep, dirt route leading higher up the mountain. Lacy yanked the steering wheel to the right.

The RV revved as it climbed upward at a steep angle. Charlie fired at the remaining truck, which was hanging further back, but still following.

"They're just going to wait until I run out of ammo," Charlie said.

Lacy crested the top of the slope and her jaw dropped open. Ahead, she saw a wooden bridge, just wide enough for one vehicle, spanning a chasm that was at least half a mile across. At first she wondered if the bridge was only for people on foot, because the idea of it supporting a car seemed questionable. She gritted her teeth as the wheels of the RV clambered onto the wooden planks. Looking through the side window, she could not tell how far down it was to the ground. She saw no tree tops, only a foggy mist far below. Her hands gripped the steering wheel so hard, it seemed she might break it.

"Holy shit," Charlie said, now seeing the bridge they were on as he peered out the back of the camper. "This thing doesn't look useable."

Lacy shouted back, "If we stop, they'll kill us." Lacy swore she felt the camper drop a few inches, as though the bridge had sagged under their weight.

"Well, they're following us," Charlie said. "The second truck has caught up again."

Lacy leaned forward, pressing the gas, wanting to get off the bridge as soon as possible.

"I've got an idea," Charlie said. He turned around and grabbed one of his canvas bags, rummaging in the bottom.

When Charlie pulled his hand back out, Jim gasped.

"The store had grenades?" Jim said.

"There was a secret stash, for special customers," Charlie said. "I know about these things." Charlie yanked his shirt off over his head and wrapped it tight around the grenade. He glanced up at Jim. "That's so it doesn't bounce."

Jim squinted at Charlie for a moment, then the realization struck him like a bucket of ice water. Grabbing the chair next to him for support, Jim turned toward Emily. She looked at both of them, wide eyed.

"It's the only way we get out of this," Charlie said. "Our only chance. They have way more firepower than I do. I can't hold 'em off forever."

Jim nodded, sweat beads rolling down his forehead.

"Lacy," Charlie called. "Tell me when we're almost off the bridge."

"We've got fifty more yards," Lacy answered back.

Charlie thrust his hand with the wrapped grenade out the back of the camper and counted, "One . . . . two . . . " he pulled his empty hand back inside.

Lacy looked in the side mirror and saw a bundle of white cloth land with a plop, hopping forward a few times before coming to rest in the middle of the wooden planks. An explosion pushed the RV the rest of the way off the bridge—it turned sideways and to the right, skidding to a stop on the gravel road. As the RV sat there, its back tires a few feet from the mountain cliff, Lacy leaned toward the passenger side window to see what remained of the bridge. The half of the bridge closest to them was missing, having been blown away by the grenade. The other half hung out into the middle of the chasm, like a giant wooden arm reaching for them.

Charlie jumped out of the camper first, his assault rifle in hand. Jim and Emily followed close behind them. Lacy wanted to get the RV turned, ready for a getaway. Even though there was a quarter mile of deep mountain ravine between their pursuers and her, she did not feel safe at all. Making small, tedious maneuvers with the Winnebago, Lacy managed to get it straightened out—though she did come within inches of the back tire going over the edge of the cliff. She was too rattled to notice, however, while her frantic hands worked at the steering wheel. The enemy was still coming for her, and a canyon was not going to stop them.

Lacy kept the engine running and stepped out of the driver's door to watch. She stared at the long span of the remaining bridge, hanging there in silence. Hearing the distant sound of growling truck engines, Lacy felt her skin prickle all over with tiny bumps. Out of the fog, the first military truck rambled along the wooden planks, stopping with a squeaky brake five feet from the edge of the broken bridge. The second truck appeared behind it, coming much slower, and halting a short distance behind the first one. For a moment, which seemed like ages to Lacy, nothing happened. Then the leader opened the door of the truck and stepped out, standing tall and fierce in the relentless wind. He was too far away for Lacy to see his face, but his body language was full of fury and determination. The leader waved his hand and a soldier popped out of the truck, his rifle in hand. Walking to the edge of the bridge, the soldier got down on one knee and pulled his rifle up to aim.

"Get behind the RV," Charlie said, shuffling backward in retreat. "They've got a sniper."

Lacy scrambled around behind the grill of the RV, listening for a gunshot. Instead, she heard a groan from the other side of the chasm. It sounded like a person at first, but then it got louder and echoed against the side of the mountains. It was a haunting sound of wood and metal straining against too much weight. Then she heard a deafening sound of cracking and popping, like a tree that has been cut halfway by a logger, and the rest is breaking before it falls crashing to the ground. Lacy peeked around the hood of the RV to look. In that moment, the entire bridge dropped a few feet, paused, then plummeted down into the chasm. Screams reverberated through the valley as the two trucks fell end over end, looking like child's toys as they tumbled downward. Charlie, Jim, and Emily had stopped running toward the front of the RV, skidding to a halt and turning to look in horror. Emily cried out at the sight of it.

There was silence for a few seconds and then a soft crash, far below. The massive chasm stood empty, relishing in the open air. It was hard to believe that there had just been a bridge there, and that people had been out there a moment ago— people that were trying to kill them.

Lacy pressed her forehead against the steel hood of the RV, closing her eyes. She heard footsteps come up next to her and felt a warm hand touch her shoulder.

"They'll send more," Jim said.

"I know," Lacy said. "They'll keep sending more, and there will always be more people to send."

"We need to find them first," Jim said. "It's the only way."

Lacy looked up, her eyes burning. "We need to find Tom."

Jim nodded. "I think one will lead to the other, somehow."

Lacy rubbed her forehead with the palm of her hand. Her muscles felt achy and weak.

"How close were you to getting into those satellites?" Jim said.

Rolling her head around, noting a deep soreness in her neck that had been there for as long as she could remember, Lacy pondered the question. "I'll need at least another day," she said.

"Okay," Jim said. "In the meantime, I say we get out of these mountains."

Lacy laughed. "I couldn't agree more," she said. She felt way too trapped up there, and there was usually only one way they could go. That certainly did not fit with their plan of taking random routes to avoid being tracked. Looking out at the expanse where the bridge used to be, she shivered. Then she put a fingertip on her chin, cocking her head in thought. "It's a good thing Tom left some family photos in there." She pointed at the RV.

Creases appeared on Jim's forehead. "Why's that?"

"Cause we're going to need them," Lacy said.

CHAPTER 28

L et's get a bunch of full gas cans," Jim said. "We can store them underneath."

"You're thinking we'll cut through New Mexico and Texas without stopping?" Charlie said.

Jim nodded. "I want to give Lacy as much time as possible—uninterrupted time."

Charlie opened the door to step out of the RV, glancing up at the stars in the black sky. Then he looked back at Jim. "It does seem like something bad happens every time we stop somewhere."

Jim scratched his head and brushed his fingers through his scraggly hair, which had grown longer than he was used to. "They know more than we realize, I think. And they see more than we're willing to believe."

"On that, we agree," Charlie said, stepping down to the ground and closing the door behind him.

Lacy hammered on the keys of her laptop, sitting in the chair with her legs crossed underneath her. Jim and Charlie sat across from each other, both looking out the window, deep in thought.

"You ever see anything like this when you were a SEAL?" Jim said.

Charlie tipped his beer can back, his throat bobbing as he gulped. He set the can down on the table and let out a low burp. "What do you mean?"

"I mean, were you ever given orders to hunt down a civilian? Track them across the country if necessary."

Charlie shook his head. "All of my missions were overseas. And technically, I'm never supposed to talk about any of them."

"It's just that, most of the people after us seem to be from our own military. Granted, at the compound in Minnesota, it was a rag tag of all sorts, mercenaries for hire. But those guys back there?"

"They were active U.S. armed forces," Charlie said.

"It doesn't make any sense," Jim said.

"I'm as confused about it as you are, but I will say this . . . ." Charlie paused, taking another swig of beer and looking out the window, like he was watching something far off in the distance. "When some of my orders came through, I just got this weird feeling." He shook his head. "I tried to brush it off at the time."

Lacy stopped typing and looked up at Charlie, her eyes curious and unblinking.

"What was it?" Jim said.

"It felt like the orders weren't coming from our own government. It was almost like someone else was telling our leaders what to do. Some of the stuff just didn't really make sense for our country, but nobody would dare question it."

Jim sat back in his seat, trying to breathe. The air was thick and he felt like he was suffocating. "How are we ever going to get out of this alive?"

Charlie's eyes shifted over to Lacy, who had gone back to typing on her laptop. Without saying anything, Charlie had relayed the message loud and clear. Right now, everything depended on Lacy.

~ ~ ~

The wind and sand hit the side of the RV so hard, Jim thought it would tip over. He brushed the stiff curtain aside to look out the window. Squinting his eyes, he could only see thick clouds of sand swirling all around them.

"We drove right into a damn dust storm," Charlie said, pushing a glob of putty into one of the bullet holes in the back of the camper. "The stuff's blowing inside."

Jim shuffled up to the front of the RV. He put his hand on Emily's shoulder. "You doing okay?"

Emily had a death grip on the steering wheel. She jerked it side to side, trying to fight against the gusts as they slammed into the side of the camper. "I've got this," Emily said through a clenched jaw. She grinded her teeth together so loud it sounded like she was chewing gravel.

"You sure?" Jim said.

Emily looked up at him for a moment, her face tense and determined. "Go check on Lacy."

Sighing, Jim walked back and sat at the table across from Lacy. Seeing the concentration on her face as she worked her keyboard, Jim didn't say anything. He closed his eyes and leaned his head back, listening to the hypnotic clicking of the keys.

The clicking stopped.

"I think I'm getting somewhere," Lacy said.

Jim opened his groggy eyes and sat up straight. "Really?"

"Yeah, I found the computer that controls the satellites. I went through three demilitarized zones and eight firewalls.

Now I'm trying to break into the back door of the system."

Jim let out a triumphant laugh and slapped his hand on the table. "I can't believe it, you're going to do it. You're unbelievable."

Shaking her head, Lacy looked up at Jim with sad eyes. "That's the reason we're in this mess," she said.

Jim's posture deflated and he slid the palm of his hand down his face, from his forehead to his chin. "I'm sorry, Lacy."

Lacy shrugged her shoulders. "I'm here now, I might as well go for it."

Jim nodded. "This is the only way we can find Tom. I know you can do this."

Lacy bit her lower lip and tucked her head down close to the laptop. "Well, here we go then. I've got to be fast. Once I start, it will only be a matter of time before the firewalls figure out what I'm trying to do."

"I won't interrupt," Jim said.

Lacy started typing in a way that Jim wasn't used to hearing; it was beyond fast and seemed more random and chaotic, much different from the smooth rhythm she usually had. Jim folded his hands and watched, not wanting to even budge and risk distracting her in some way. Her typing got louder and it seemed like she was going to break the keyboard. Then she stopped.

"Wait, no!" Lacy said.

Jim raised his eyebrows. "What? What's wrong?"

"No, no, no!" Lacy was tapping one key over and over, so hard, Jim thought her finger would go right through the laptop.

Charlie's head snapped around and he hustled over behind Lacy to see her screen.

"What is it, Lace?" Charlie said.

"Someone's trying to boot me out," Lacy said.

"They found you?" Jim said. "They know you're in there?"

"I don't know how," Lacy said. "I'm going to scan the outer servers and see what programs are running."

Jim fidgeted his feet under the table. He felt so helpless he could hardly stand it.

"Oh shit, they are coming after me," Lacy said. "Whoever it is, they're tracing back through all the layers, all my hops, trying to find my laptop."

"Can you shut the laptop off?" Jim said.

"It's too late for that," Lacy said. "They made it so my footprints are appearing in the logs. I have to get rid of them or they'll be able to locate me."

Jim could only watch Lacy, her face gleaming with sweat, her eyes darting from side to side.

Lacy's eyes bulged out and she gasped. "This code," she said. A low wheezing sound started in her throat. "It can't be."

"Lacy?" Jim said.

The wheezing grew louder and Lacy's breaths became short and quick. Her mouth opening in alarm, Lacy tried to get air into her lungs, but she could not seem to inhale.

"Lacy," Jim said. "Look at me!"

Lacy's eyes darted to Jim's face, her chest spasming in and out.

"What color is my shirt?" Jim said.

"White," Lacy said. She shrieked for air.

"Okay, touch it," Jim said. "What does it feel like?"

Lacy leaned forward, reaching for Jim's arm. Pinching the fabric between her fingers, she felt the texture of the shirt. "Cotton, it's made of cotton."

Jim nodded and pointed at the wall of the camper. "What does that feel like?"

Lacy reached over and ran her fingers along the surface. "Like metal," Lacy said. Then she slapped her hand onto the table and dug her fingernails into the wood. As she pulled her hand toward her, making scratches in the table, her breathing slowed and her face started to relax. She took a deep breath and let it out, shaking her head. "I've never hyperventilated like that before."

"What set you off?" Jim asked. "You said something about the code."

With a weary look, Lacy nodded, cracking her knuckles and spreading her fingers over the keyboard. "There are only two people who could have used the code I saw. Nian or—"

"Kraig," Jim said.

CHAPTER 29

Kraig slouched over his keyboard, looking at the three huge computer displays on the table in front of him with a smile. By instinct, Kraig's left hand went to the back of his neck, feeling the deep, scabbing hole with his fingertips. Francis had told him, as he awoke in this very same clean, white room, that a tiny control pod had been injected into his spinal cord. The pod had two functions, which could be activated by Francis alone, using a wristwatch. The first function was to release a chemical that would render Kraig unconscious, and that one had already been used. Francis had grinned as he stood over Kraig and explained the situation, while Kraig lay still on the bed in the corner of the room. The second function was to release a chemical into Kraig's spine that would kill him. Actually, it would paralyze him for a few seconds, and then he would die.

Looking around, Kraig watched himself in the giant mirrors that were on each of the walls. He knew they were one-way windows, and he did not mind that at all. In fact, he loved that he was being observed for the genius he was. Kraig's fingers fluttered over his keyboard, the sound blending in with the soft Mozart music coming out of the speakers.

"She's trying to get control of the satellites," Kraig said.

"Good," came Francis' voice over the speakers, intertwining with the classical music. "Let her get in just far enough so that you can find her computer and hack into it."

Kraig's lips spread into a tight grin. That would be no problem.

~ ~ ~

Lacy shook her head. "I can't beat him. I've never been able to beat him."

"Yes you did," Jim said. "Remember, you found him for me. You created the wildfire program and you—"

Lacy slammed her laptop shut and flung it off the table, sending it flying into the wall with a crash. "Can't you see that's what they want!"

Jim sat there, silent. Charlie looked away, seeming like an awkward pile of muscle sitting in the corner.

Lacy sighed, her eyes looking wet and shiny. "Creating the wildfire program was a million-to-one miracle, and it happened because I was driven to insanity by Kraig. Do you know how long it took me to get my mind halfway back to normal after that?" She glanced over at Charlie. "You think those countless hours of martial arts training were just so that I could whoop some ass?"

Charlie blinked as blotches of red appeared on his cheeks. He shook his head.

"It was a physical distraction. Something intense to focus on," Lacy said. She plopped her face into her hands, mumbling. "And if I did create it again, someone would get ahold of it—the wrong people would get ahold of it." She looked at Jim with eyes that made his heart sink down to his feet.

"The power shift it would cause," Lacy said. "Millions of people would die. Can you imagine if someone like Hitler would have gotten his hands on a tool that could bring the world's economy to a complete halt, at the press of a button? That's what this is."

Jim sat frozen; he was unsure if he could not breathe or dare not breathe. His vision blurred and he blinked, trying to regain his sight.

"I would give my life to get Tom back safe," Lacy said. "But I can't do that."

They all sat in silence. An immense gust of wind shook the camper, rattling the windows. Emily grunted, but held the RV steady on the road.

Jim shook his head hard, like he was coming out of a dream. He looked at Lacy, his jaw muscles clenching. "You can beat Kraig without wildfire."

Lacy slouched down further. "Jim, I can't, I—"

"How did he beat you in the past? At the contests?"

Lacy's eyebrows scrunched together; she looked down at the table. "He played dirty."

"Think about what he did," Jim said.

Lacy was squinting now. "He'd bait me." She squeezed her hand shut, her knuckles cracking, then she opened it. "He would actually pave a path for me, leading into the system. Unlock a door for me and then set off the alarms." She looked at Jim. "He's a slimy asshole."

Jim held her gaze. "Can you do that to him?"

A slow grin crept onto Lacy's face. She bent down and picked her laptop up from the floor, setting it on the table in front of her. Then she opened it and pressed the power button. "I can do it better," she said.

~ ~ ~

"I'm almost into her system," Kraig said.

"Good," Francis' voice echoed in the room.

Kraig's hands shook with excitement as he typed. He saw the firewall that Lacy had put up to guard her computer and smirked. He knew he could break it. She still fell for the same old tricks. Lacy was still beneath him. Sure, she had amazing talent, even Kraig's ego could not deny that. Yet it was her girlish innocence that held her back and made her inferior to him.

A laugh escaped Kraig's lips; he was almost there. He gained root access to Lacy's laptop and was getting ready to run his own personal Trojan horse, which would give him everything—all the information he wanted about where she was and what she had been doing. It almost felt easy. Kraig's eyebrow twitched. Easy. Why had it been so easy? There should have been more of a fight from her.

Droplets of sweat appeared on Kraig's forehead as he scrambled on the keyboard. It was obvious to him now that she had set a trap, and he had fallen for it. Kraig balled his hand into a fist and punched one of the LCD monitors, knocking it over. His other hand still typed at a frantic pace.

Lacy had created a virtual machine, running inside her own laptop. It was an innocent looking environment that was fully contained and isolated from Lacy's real operating system. It was as though Kraig had invaded a lush meadow that he thought was Lacy's land, a green field filled with furry bunnies and chirping bluebirds. Only, once Kraig had arrived, standing in the middle of the meadow with a wide grin, wringing his hands in triumph, he realized it was not real. The sky turned black with smoke and the grass in the field wilted and died in seconds. The ground split open and Kraig had to run for his life to avoid falling into the earthquake.

Kraig was now unwillingly downloading Lacy's own special Trojan horse, and there was nothing he could do about it. Soon she would know everything he had been doing, and worst of all, she would know where he was.

"What is happening?" Francis' voice crackled into the speakers.

"Just give me a minute," Kraig said, his keyboard rattling from his frantic keystrokes. "I can stop this."

But he could not. His computer was already fully compromised, and soon the other systems within whatever building Kraig was sitting in would be taken over as well.

"She beat you," Francis said.

Kraig jumped to his feet, grabbed the table with his hands, and heaved upward, flipping it over. The monitors crashed to the ground and the keyboard slid along the floor. He let out a terrible howl and ran across the room, cocking his arm back and punching his fist into the wall. Plaster gave way before his knuckles struck unrelenting steel. Kraig pulled his hand back and stared at it with a snarl as several bloodied fingers hung limp and broken. There was a loud click and the lights went off. Someone had killed the power.

~ ~ ~

"I know where they are," Lacy said, sitting back and lifting her hands, letting them hover over the keyboard. "They've shut everything down, but not before I found out where they are."

Jim lifted his eyebrows. "Where?"

"The Florida Keys," Lacy said.

"Do you think Tom is there?" Jim said.

Lacy shook her head. "I'm not sure."

"What about the satellites?" Jim said.

"I don't think we can go after them again," Lacy said. "Now they know I was trying to take them over. They'd be expecting it."

"Then we go down to the Keys and figure out what's going on there?" Jim said.

Lacy nodded. "We have no other choice."

CHAPTER 30

Tyler Samsteen stood tall in the doorway of the Slippery Whistle bar, looking as out of place as a nun in a whorehouse. Several patrons turned and looked at him with interest as he brushed a fleck of lint off the sleeve of his impeccable suit. He scanned the room, first glancing at each of the dining patrons, then looking over at the bar where a few men on tall stools were slouched over mugs of beer. It was early in the afternoon, so the place was not packed with people. Tyler was able to give each one of them a curious look. Though, nobody seemed to care that he was there, other than giving him an amused smirk before biting into their greasy burger or chugging their frothy drinks.

A waitress came around the corner and stopped short when she saw Tyler. She was wearing a jean skirt and a plunging black blouse. Her hair was golden blonde and her eyes were crystal blue. Tyler's first thought was that she must have been gorgeous at one time, yet countless late nights of drinking and smoking had given her a rough, leathery look. She smiled at Tyler, her face lighting up as soon as she saw him.

"You looking for someone?" the waitress said.

"Detective Langston," Tyler said.

The waitress raised her eyebrow. "You?" She looked Tyler up and down. "You're looking for Hank?"

Tyler nodded, trying to remain polite.

Shrugging, the waitress pointed to the door in the back of the bar, which led to another room.

"Thanks," Tyler said. He strode across the hardwood floor, cringing at the sticky feeling under his shoes, and ducked through the door, where he stopped to take in the scene.

Topless women strutted around on an oval stage, which was in the middle of the room. Several men were sitting on stools at the edge of the oval platform, with drinks in front of them. Tyler saw Hank on the opposite side of the stage, facing him as he came through the door. Hank perked up when he saw Tyler and waved to him. Tyler nodded in response and circled around the platform, while the erotic dancers noticed him and made eye contact. He pulled up a stool next to Hank and sat down.

"Hello, Detective Langston," Tyler said.

Hank groaned. "Actually, I'm retired now." He lifted his glass in a salute to one of the girls on stage and tossed the remaining whiskey down his throat. "Just call me Hank."

"Well, Hank, I hope this is worth the trip from Seattle, seeing as you left no details in your message—just meet you here. That was a rather vague request."

"Couldn't have been that hard," Hank said. "You've got a private jet now, right?"

"Yes, that is true." Tyler gave a single nod. "At least this is under better circumstances. Last time I saw you, you were—"

"Crouched over a dead cop that was barely old enough to grow facial hair," Hank said.

The waitress that had greeted Tyler at the door came up behind him, placing a hand on his shoulder.

"Get you anything?" she said.

"Uh, bourbon please." Tyler smiled at her.

"You got it," she said and darted away.

"Actually," Hank said, "this might be worse circum-stances."

Tyler shifted his body, squaring up to Hank. "How so?"

"Have you heard from your friend Jim?"

Tyler's forehead wrinkled. "Not for a few weeks, I assumed he was busy."

Hank grunted, bobbing his head. "I tried to contact him."

"Why?" Tyler said.

"Because Kraig Freestone is gone."

Tyler's foot slipped off the lower rung on his stool, forcing him to grab the stage to catch himself. "He's dead?"

"Well, that's the official status," Hank said. "But I'm not so sure. Something is very wrong and there wasn't anyone else I thought I could trust. I tried to get ahold of Charlie Prentice, with no luck. Lacy Chase, also unreachable."

"And I was the last person on your list," Tyler said.

"Yeah," Hank said.

"Okay," Tyler said. "Tell me what you know."

"First, I'm going to need another drink for this," Hank said. He pounded his hand on the stage three times and a groan arose from across the bar. The waitress disappeared into the other room for a spell and came ambling back with a fresh drink for Hank. She also set a glass of bourbon in front of Tyler.

"Thanks, Sharline," Hank said.

"Mmm....hmm," the waitress said before she dashed away again.

Hank took a long swig from his new glass and stared ahead. "I still have a few friends on the force and I often stop by to shoot the breeze with them. When one of them mentioned that Kraig's status in prison had changed to deceased that morning, the hairs on my neck perked up. His arrest was the event that haunts me every time I close my eyes to go to sleep, so naturally, I was interested."

Tyler nodded, acknowledging that terrible day.

"So I decided to take a trip down to the coroner's office and get the details. I figured, what the hell? I've got nothing else to do. Only, when I got there, the coroner started stone walling me. Said no information could be given out. I asked if I could see the body and he said absolutely not."

"Is that normal?" Tyler asked.

Hank shook his head. "I've known that coroner for twenty years, he would have always given me leeway with something like that. But then I noticed the look in his eyes—it was a look of fear." Hank glanced around the room. "Before I go further, I'm going to need you to take out your phone. Remove the battery and set them both up here." Hank tapped the top of the polished stage.

Tyler slid his smartphone out of his suit coat pocket, removed the battery, and slid both items over so they sat in front of Hank.

Poking the phone, and then the battery, with his finger, Hank nodded his approval and continued. "I was confused at first by the coroner's actions and demeanor, when a thought occurred to me. I said, 'TS orders?' and he just blinked. But it told me all I needed to know."

"What's TS orders?" Tyler said.

Hank sighed and took another drink from his glass. "I only had it happen to me three times during my entire career, but when it does, you never forget it. All of the sudden a strange order will come through the top level of command. Something like, go detain this person at all costs, or make a certain piece of evidence disappear. The person giving you the order tells you it's 'TS orders' and the understanding is that you just do it, no questions asked."

Tyler's brow furrowed and he took a long pull from his own drink. "No matter what it is? That's hard for me to believe."

"I know it sounds terrible, and it is," Hank said. "Even the most die-hard, straight laced officers will just follow the order, get it done, then try to forget they ever did it."

"Hasn't anyone refused on principle, gone to a judge with it, something?"

Hank nodded. "A few have . . . . and they always disappear a day or two later. I mean, gone without a trace. Not one has ever been found. No dead body, no nothing. It's like an alien spaceship came down and beamed them up."

Tyler reached for his tie and loosened it until it was barely hanging on his neck. Yet he still had a hard time breathing.

"Anyways, I knew I was getting nowhere at the coroner's, so I decided to go up to the prison and see if there was any scuttlebutt going on there. I have a couple of buddies that work there too."

"Let me guess," Tyler said as he stared at his glass while turning it in a circle with his fingers. "They clammed up too? TS orders?"

"Yeah," Hank said. "They were shaken up too. But what they did tell me was that Jim Wisendorf had visited Kraig twice, a few weeks ago."

Tyler's head jerked up and he looked at Hank with an open mouth. "I thought Kraig wasn't allowed visitors."

"Apparently, Charlie got him a meeting in the 'off the books' room. I'm not the only one with connections."

"Off the books meeting room?" Tyler said. "Man, what the hell kind of operation is going on around here?"

"People are people," Hank said. "Sure, most of us are in it for the right reasons—we want to uphold the law and keep people safe. But no matter where you go, even the best people will trade favors. You know, scratch my back and I'll scratch yours. Look the other way. Isn't that how it is in business?"

"Yeah, but—"

"Look, I didn't ask you here to have a debate about integrity. I invited you here because I have information I thought you would be interested in and . . . ." Hank paused.

"And?" Tyler said.

"And I'm scared," Hank said. "Scared shitless."

Tyler took a deep breath. "Tell me the rest," he said. "I won't interrupt."

Hank nodded. "So I decided to go snoop around the area where the off-the-books meetings occur. There is a back door where you can get in there, if you know the right people. It comes out of the back of the prison. You have to drive into the fenced in area and through a back alley, where they take the garbage out, but I can get right up to the door. I was driving toward the spot, when I saw a shiny black limo parked right next to the door. There was one man standing there next to the limo. He held a briefcase in his hand and was dressed in a damn fine suit." Hank gestured toward Tyler. "A lot like yours."

Tyler took a swig of his bourbon and wiped his forehead on his sleeve.

"So I parked nearby and walked casually up to him. The man moved in front of the door, with his hand resting on a gun in his belt, but otherwise he seemed relaxed. I told him I was there because I had a special meeting, and he told me I would have to reschedule, because the room was being used. I shrugged and turned to leave, but the door opened and a guy poked his head out. He just looked at the man I had been talking to and said, 'He needs you right now.' Then he looked at me, and I said, 'I was just leaving.' I walked away and the man I had been talking to darted inside the door. I waited for a minute and then went up to the door while searching for a key on my keychain that I hadn't used in years. I unlocked the door and went inside. Then I crept down the hallway until I came to the second door, but I heard voices and didn't dare go in. What struck me as odd was that the man had set his briefcase down outside of that second door. So, you know, my son had once given me these tracking devices to find your keys. And you see, on instinct, I pulled it off my keyring and tucked it inside a pocket on the briefcase. Then I got the hell out of there as fast as I could."

Hank reached into his pocket and pulled out a crumpled piece of paper. "Here's the login for the website that shows you the location of that tracker. I figured you might want it, seeing as how your friend was the last person known to visit Kraig from the outside. And those weird guys were there on the day that Kraig disappeared."

"Have you looked for yourself?" Tyler asked. "Do you know where the briefcase is?"

"Yep," Hank said. "It's in the Florida Keys."

CHAPTER 31

W e'll have to ditch the RV," Jim said. "As soon as we get to Arkansas."

Charlie reached his hand out and rubbed one of the bullet holes in the metal with his fingers. "But I just got her all patched up."

Jim shook his head, forcing a laugh.

Smiling, Charlie shrugged. "Yeah, you're right. This thing is on its last leg."

Lacy looked around the camper, her gaze stopping on an old tea kettle, sitting on the small stove. Her eyes became glassy and Jim touched her arm.

"I know, Lacy. I'm sad about it too. All of Tom's old stuff is here. It'll be hard to just ditch it somewhere."

Lacy wiped her hand across her eyes and frowned. "Well, it's what we have to do to find him. That's what's important."

Glancing out the window, Jim saw that they were entering a wooded area. He was glad to have gotten out of the sandy desert. The lush green forests and shrubs comforted him, reminding him of home. He watched the bright green leaves fly by and his mind churned, trying to come up with a plan.

"Jim, I think we have a problem," Emily said from up in the driver's seat.

"What is it?" Jim said.

"I think it's a drone."

Jim and Charlie scrambled to their feet, rushing up to the front of the RV. When Jim looked up, he swallowed hard. It was indeed a drone, flying toward them, and it looked like the one Kraig had used—like a miniature bomber plane.

"Emily, get ready to turn hard to the left," Charlie said.

Emily looked to her left. There was nothing but weeds and trees.

"What? Why?" Emily said.

Charlie was staring up at the drone, which was closing in fast. "Just be ready when I tell you. Don't hesitate."

Emily's arms flexed, her tendons popping out at her elbows as she gripped the steering wheel and set her jaw. She kept her eyes fixed on the road ahead. The drone looked much bigger now, and it was less than a mile away.

Charlie shouted to the back of the camper, "Lacy, brace yourself."

Lacy slid onto the floor and wrapped her arms around a table leg. Jim squinted at the sky and saw something glimmer in the sunlight as it dropped from the drone. Then a blaze of flame lit up behind the shiny dropping object.

"Now!" Charlie said.

Emily cranked the wheel and the RV leapt sideways off the road. An explosion of fire hit the highway where they had been and chunks of pavement slammed into the side of the camper as they flew through the air. The nose of the Winnebago plunged into the ground and the entire vehicle slid deeper into the woods while flipping onto its side. The RV came to a stop when it slid into a marsh. The swamp started to pour into the camper, and they were all lying in water that had risen to a foot high before anyone could process the situation.

Charlie caught his breath as Jim scrambled to get off of him. "Get out now!" Charlie said.

Emily, still buckled into the driver's seat, pushed her door open with her legs and crawled out like she was shimmying out of a tank. Jim went out right behind Emily, holding her arm as they hopped into the waist deep swamp water and sloshed their way to dry land.

Charlie looked further back into the camper. "Lacy?" he called out. Then he saw her, toward the rear, floating face down in the water.

"No," Charlie said. His legs churned through the water as he made his way around a floating chair and seat cushions. "Please, no."

Scooping Lacy's body up in his arms, Charlie dashed through the camper and up to the driver's door. As he hoisted Lacy over his shoulder and pushed himself out through the door, he heard her start to cough. A burst of relief spread through him and he set her down on top of the Winnebago. She lifted her head and looked at him with heavy eyes.

"It's coming back!" Jim said.

Charlie wrapped his arm around Lacy's waist and they slid down into the pond. A high pitched squeal deafened them from up above as Charlie and Lacy sloshed through the water and leapt onto the mushy bog. The RV exploded into flames behind them and Charlie tucked his head down into the mud, feeling an inferno of heat roar over his back. When the heat disappeared, Charlie yanked Lacy to her feet and they both stumbled toward Jim and Emily.

"Get into the woods," Charlie said, his face covered in black muck, along with the rest of his body.

Jim and Emily turned and started running. Lacy hesitated, looking at Charlie, who was pulling his pistol out of its holster.

"Go," Charlie said. "I got this."

Lacy turned and darted for the woods.

Planting his feet in a wide stance, Charlie held the gun in

both hands and raised it toward the sky. He heard the buzzing sound. It was coming back. Charlie watched the tree line in front of him, keeping a keen eye on the blue skyline as the sound grew louder. He aimed his gun at where he thought the drone would appear.

Charlie's mouth dropped open as five drones came soaring into view. He turned and bolted the other direction, listening for the distinct sound that would tell him he was about to die. Just as he reached the thick grove of trees, he heard the screech he was waiting for—five screeches actually, and he zagged sharply to the right. Diving and rolling into a mass of shrubs, Charlie saw giant oak trees blow apart behind him. He clawed the ground, scrambling to his feet, and took off running again. Charlie heard Jim's voice calling for him, but wasn't sure which direction it came from; his ears were ringing so loud it made his head throb.

Pumping his arms, Charlie slammed through branches and leaves, dodging left and right as the foliage grew thicker. Then the bushes gave way to more open ground, as the tree canopy above was thick enough to block out the sunlight, allowing minimal vegetation growth below. Charlie heard Jim's voice again, and spun around, his eyes searching, but he saw no one.

Then Charlie heard a sound again, a terrible buzzing high above him. Looking up, he searched the canopy of thick, oak leaves for an opening—anywhere the drones would be able to see him. The blue sky wasn't visible and it seemed dark, almost like twilight, while under the trees. The buzzing grew louder and Charlie knew the drones were not going away. He took off running again, his boots kicking up crisp brown leaves. Charlie smelled the rotting scent of bog and swamp, thick in the air. It was humid and sticky, his sweat stinging his eyes. Gritting his teeth, Charlie pumped hard with his legs, his knees coming up high as he flew across the forest floor. His massive muscles contracted and rippled as his velocity continued to increase.

Up ahead, Jim peaked out from behind a huge cluster of

thick tree trunks. Charlie tucked his chin down and sprinted toward Jim. As he got closer, Jim stuck his arm out to help yank Charlie behind the solid oaks. Charlie's boots skidded to a halt, leaving long grooves in the dirt.

Lacy and Emily sat huddled behind the mossy trunks, though Lacy was barely recognizable, since she was covered from head to toe in dark mud. Charlie realized he looked the same, as he was caked with thick grime.

Again, a high pitched squeal screamed through the air, and they all dove to the dirt. On the other side of the oak trees, dirt and leaves erupted as rocks and twigs pounded against the trunks next to them. Looking up, Charlie saw that everyone seemed unharmed. The hum of the drones had changed, growing quieter.

"They're circling around," Jim said, searching the canopy of tree tops. "I don't get how they can still see us."

Lacy's eyes grew big, looking like white ping pong balls on her mud covered face. "They have infrared," she said. "That's how Nian found me in the wilderness."

Charlie spit mud and dirt out of his mouth. "Dammit." He started raking his fingers into the dirt, heaving giant fistfuls of leaves and moss behind him.

Lacy started digging as well, with a determined fury. "Do you think it'll work?" she said.

"Maybe," Charlie said. "But we can't take a chance on running again. We got lucky, but the next time they'll blow us apart."

Jim and Emily joined in on the digging, and within less than a minute, they already had a wide hole in the earth, about a foot deep.

"Lie on your backs," Charlie said.

Jim, Emily, and Lacy got into the hole and nudged tight together, side by side, looking up toward the treetops. The buzzing was getting close again, and Charlie became frantic as he plowed dirt, along with leaves and moss, over them with his hands. When only their eyes and noses were visible, Charlie scooted next to Jim and started covering his legs and torso. He could hear the drones getting closer and hoped they hadn't spotted him yet. Lying down on his back, Charlie covered his torso and slid a pile of moss over his face before pushing his arms down under the dirt.

Charlie could now hear the drones flying overhead and the deep hum was all around them. He closed his eyes, waiting for the screech of missiles to come. Waiting for his friends and himself to be blown up into nothing but a thirty foot wide crater. But the screech did not come, and the sound of the drones passed by. They waited until it was quiet.

"Don't move," Charlie said. "They'll probably make another pass."

And sure enough, they did.

They lay in the hole, covered with dirt, for half an hour before the drones stopped buzzing over them.

"There'll be people on foot soon, searching for us," Jim said.

"I'll take people on foot over those drones any day," Charlie said, turning his head just enough to see the others. Charlie noticed Emily's eyes, blinking at the sky. She was one tough girl, though he never would have guessed it a few weeks ago. They had all been through so much, and who knew how much more they had to endure. A feeling of hopelessness grabbed Charlie, as though it were trying to pull him deeper into the ground. The thought of what they were up against was too much to handle. Charlie's mouth twisted at the irony that they had all just dug a shallow grave for themselves, and were lying in it, waiting for the inevitable.

With a grunt, Charlie shook his head and booted those thoughts out of his mind. His friends were depending on his strength, and if Jim could remain unwavering and optimistic, so could he. Charlie made up his mind that they had to run.

They were sitting ducks if they stayed any longer.

"We've got to cover as much distance as possible, right now," Charlie said, getting up. "This is the last place we were detected, and soldiers will be coming for us."

Jim sat up, brushing leaves and grime off his face and arms. "I don't think I could stay like that any longer, anyhow," he said. "I could feel the bugs and worms crawling all over my skin."

Emily sprang to her feet, followed by Lacy.

Jim looked at Charlie. "Which direction?"

Charlie glanced around at the tree tops. "I think the drones split off into all directions, so we'd only have to deal with one, unless we're spotted—then they'll all come after us."

Jim pointed through the trees. "The road was that way, so when they come to search for us, that's probably where they'll come from."

Charlie nodded. "Then we go that way." He pointed in the opposite direction.

Lacy whirled around. "My laptop. They can't have my laptop. I have to go get it." She started heading back toward the RV, when Charlie stepped in front of her.

"Lacy, we can't, that's the first place they'll be searching," Charlie said.

"Then I'm going by myself," Lacy said. "Some of my best code was on that laptop, top secret stuff that I've been using for years. If they get ahold of that computer, there'll be security patches released to protect against it by tomorrow. I'll have to start over from square one."

Lacy tried to push past Charlie, but he grabbed her shoulders and held her tight.

"Let me go, Charlie." Lacy fought against his grip.

"No," Charlie said. "Not this time."

Lacy tried to spin her body away from Charlie, her teeth gritting in a growl. "Let! Me! Go!"

Charlie held her firm, his biceps contracting into hard

cannon balls as he blinked tears at her. He shook his head.

Jim walked up behind Charlie and looked Lacy in the eyes.

"Lacy, you have to let it go and start over," Jim said. "Your life is more important than your hacking."

Lacy shook her head, jerking it side to side, her bright auburn hair whirling around her. "You don't understand, hacking is all I have. It is my life. I'm all alone without it." Lacy took another hard look at Jim and a single tear rolled down her cheek. She slouched forward, falling, and Charlie caught her up in his arms. "I have nothing," Lacy mumbled.

Jim moved closer, and Emily came up behind Charlie.

"You have us," Emily said. "You'll always have us. You will never be alone."

Lacy let out a deep sigh, stepping away from Charlie. Then she looked around, biting her lip and pushing her hair out of her face.

They stood there for a moment, in the quiet woods, with only the sounds of their breathing filling the silence.

"Let's get out of here," Charlie said, giving Lacy a pleading look.

Lacy nodded. Then all four of them broke into a run, weaving in and out of the trees.

Charlie was the first to stop, his drenched shirt clinging to his torso. "Man, it's humid out here. Like a giant sauna." He put his hands on his knees and hung his head. It was dark now, but the temperature had not let up when night fell.

Jim came to a halt next to him, panting.

"Listen," Lacy said, slowing to a jog before she reached them.

They all stood silent, hearing millions of frogs croaking in the swamps that surrounded them. Then Charlie picked out the other sound, a drone in the distance. No one moved, no one breathed. The buzzing sound traveled across the treetops, causing Charlie to shiver despite the stifling heat. After a few seconds, the sound of the drone faded away and was gone. Exhaling with exasperation, Charlie waved his hand for them to run again. But Emily gasped, pointing into the darkness. Two bright flashlight beams were floating in the far distance, deeper in the forest.

"If we move, they'll hear us," Jim said.

Charlie agreed. "Stay still and keep close."

They waited, watching the eerie lights move through the trees, getting closer and closer. A slight rustle could be heard here and there, but otherwise, whoever had the lights was able to move without making much noise. Charlie reached for the holster under his arm, grabbed his pistol, and slid it out, cringing at the sound of steel scraping on leather. The lights split apart, each going separate ways, and then they disappeared. Charlie strained his ears, trying to block out the croaking of frogs, and the swarm of mosquitos around his head. Every few seconds he heard a crinkle of leaves, but it echoed around the trees, making it impossible to pinpoint a location.

After a few minutes, Charlie felt certain whomever it was out in the woods with them had wandered off in a different direction. He shifted his weight to move, when a flashlight flicked on, shining him right in the face. The other flashlight clicked on a second later. A tall boy, around seventeen years old, his face covered with a patchy attempt at a beard, was aiming a double barreled shotgun at Charlie's chest. The other kid was no more than fourteen, shirtless and skinny, with intense dark eyes, pointing a revolver at Jim.

"Y'all ain't aliens?" said the older boy.

Charlie squinted his eyes, turning his head away from the light. "Aliens?"

"Yeah," said the younger boy. "We seen UFOs in the sky, and then heard you's coming through the woods. Figured it was aliens."

Charlie looked at the younger boy, who was holding his

pistol with a shaky hand. The kid's eyes were wide with both fear and excitement. Charlie's gun was still tucked under his arm and he contemplated his next move. But these were just kids.

"Those weren't UFOs," Jim said. "They were drones."

The younger kid gave the older boy a nervous glance. "Drones?"

"Yes," Jim said. "Drones."

The older one, with the peach fuzz beard, scrunched his eyebrows together, his large forehead shiny and dirty. "They yours?" he said.

"No, not ours," Charlie said.

"They from the government?" the younger one said, his eye twitching. "We don't trust any of them people."

Jim held his hands in the air. "We don't know whose drones they are, but we are definitely not from the government."

The older boy spit a stream of tobacco juice onto the ground. "Why y'all out here in the woods. Yer ten miles from the nearest road."

"Those drones almost blew us up," Emily said. "We were running from them."

The older one moved his flashlight over to Emily, his eyes getting big as they gazed up and down her curves where her drenched t-shirt clung tight to her body.

Jim cleared his throat. "What are you guys doing out here?"

The younger one looked at the older boy, who shrugged and nodded.

"We live nearby," the younger one said.

"And your parents let you wander the woods in the middle of the night, looking for UFOs?" Jim said.

The older boy looked at the younger kid, shaking his head in warning. They both said nothing.

Jim took a step forward and the younger kid straightened his arms further outward, pointing his gun at Jim. Jim lifted his hands even higher in the air.

"Look, I know we're in your woods, but we mean you no harm. You can trust us."

The younger kid bit his lip and moved his eyes back and forth between Jim and the older boy. The older boy kept his gaze locked on Charlie. Moving slow, Charlie slid his gun back into the holster and lifted his hands as well.

Jim pointed a finger. "This is my wife, Emily."

Emily lifted a hand and tried to smile.

Jim gestured to his other side. "This is my friend, Lacy."

The older boy relaxed his shoulders and looked at Lacy, who nodded to him and waved. Finally, Jim slapped Charlie on the shoulder. "This big guy here is Charlie. While he might look mean, I assure you, he's a good man. He was in the military long ago, special forces actually, and he's protected our country many times."

The younger boy's face brightened and he started to lower his revolver, but he tensed up when the sound of buzzing echoed across the sky. Jim's head jerked up toward the treetops, then toward the older boy.

"Look, we're pretty desperate here. Do you think your parents would allow us to hide out at your house until these drones go away? I know it's a lot to ask, but we're out of options."

The older boy lowered his shotgun. "I'm Curt, and this here is my little brother, Robby." Curt looked at the ground while using his tongue to push his golf ball sized wad of tobacco from one cheek to the other. "Our parents are gone."

"Okay, will they be back soon?" Jim said.

Robby lowered his revolver. "Daddy left when we was tiny. I never seen him." Pausing, Robby looked at the sky, his throat working but seeming unable to speak.

"Momma died a year ago," Curt said.

Jim's mouth opened, but he did not speak.

"How'd your momma die," Emily said, her voice soft.

Robby was gulping, but he still stayed silent.

"Momma's mind wasn't right," Curt said. "Then she got worse."

Robby's cheek twitched and he wiped his forearm across his eyes.

"Robby found mamma hanging in the shed when he went out to get chicken eggs," Curt said.

Charlie tried to swallow, but a huge lump had gotten in the way. They all stood there looking at each other with dumbfounded expressions on their faces. The sound of the drone in the distance became louder.

Curt spoke up. "Our house is two miles from here. We best be moving fast." He turned and gestured into the woods with his hand. "Follow us."

CHAPTER 32

I t seemed to Charlie that no real home could be so deep in the swampy woods they trudged through. He was startled when Curt pulled a thick wall of bushes aside and they almost bumped right into a run-down shack that looked like it was once a house.

They walked sideways between foliage and the shabby gray siding until they came around to the front. Charlie glanced around the small yard and saw a shed that was barely standing and an old rusty pickup truck parked in the middle of the grassy area. There was no real driveway, just two worn down tire tracks leading away through the woods. It was getting close to sunrise, and Charlie wanted to get under cover before it was too light out.

Emily eyed the house with a blank stare. "You two live here alone?" she said.

Curt nodded, resting his shotgun on his shoulder. "Yup, but we get by."

Emily gave Jim a wide eyed look, and he put his arm around her shoulders.

"We should get inside," Curt said.

Charlie listened to the night air, not hearing any drones, but not wanting to wait around for them. Curt went up the steps to the front door, pulling it open as a hefty spring groaned and threatened to pull it shut with a slam. Curt and Robby stepped inside, while Jim and Emily followed after them. Lacy came up behind Charlie, putting her hand on his shoulder.

"I don't like this," Lacy whispered in Charlie's ear. "Do you buy their story?"

Charlie paused, watching the boys disappear into the house. "They're just kids," he said. "They seem more scared than we are."

"What if it's a trap?" Lacy said.

Charlie nodded. "Be ready for anything." He opened his hands and closed them, his knuckles cracking. "Either way, we've got to get indoors. The drones will be back."

"Fine," Lacy said. "But if I hear dueling banjos start playing, I'm outta here. I'll take my chances with the drones."

Smiling, Charlie shook his head and looked up to see Jim and Emily entering the house.

"You do know some drones can see through walls, right?" Lacy said.

"Yeah, I know. But this is still our best chance," Charlie said. He hustled up behind Emily and grabbed the door, motioning for Lacy to enter while he held it open for her.

Charlie found himself standing in a dim kitchen with the others. Curt hung his shotgun on the wall, resting it on two deer hooves that were protruding from the unpainted sheetrock. The irony was not lost on Charlie that the deer was holding the same gun that had probably killed it. As he expected, the kitchen was trashed. Unwashed dishes were piled so high in the sink, it seemed they would topple over at any moment. The smell of rotting food from the dirty plates made Charlie's nose wrinkle. He felt the wall next to the door for a light switch. When he found the switch, he flipped it, but nothing happened.

"Ain't got no electricity," Curt said.

"But you did at one time?" Jim said.

Robby said, "We've got a generator, but we ran out of gas."

"What about the truck out there?" Charlie said. "You take that into town?"

Curt shook his head. "It don't start. About once a month we walk ten miles to the road. Then we hitchhike into town and trade pelts for supplies."

"Pelts?" Emily said.

"Yeah," Robby said, puffing his chest out a bit. "From the critters we kill in the woods."

Curt nodded. "Like I said, we get by." He led them through the kitchen, back to a living area. A single couch sat in the middle of the room with deer, squirrel, and rabbit hides draped over the back of it. On the other side of the room, a small tube style television set was perched on a table. It had dials on the front and looked like it had been a pretty nice TV back in the seventies. A stack of VHS tapes sat on top of the television, and a VCR was on the floor, next to the table.

"Y'all welcome to stay as long as you want," Curt said. "But you'll probably want to sleep on the floor in the living room."

Curt pointed to a pair of doors on the right side of the living room. "We got two bedrooms, but we keep the door shut on the one. There's a shitload of mice living in the walls in there, and ya gotta have nerves of steel to sleep through the noise. One or two mice, you can ignore. But fifty of 'em scratching the walls all night—it's too distracting."

Emily let out a squeaky yelp.

Though it was the middle of the day, Emily fell asleep on the floor in the living room. Jim grabbed a dusty pillow from the couch and went down to the floor, snuggling next to her and dozing off within seconds. Charlie sat down on the couch and glanced around the house; it was filthy and smelly, but so were they. And it was still a real roof, something they had not slept under in weeks.

Lacy walked over to the opposite side of the room and sat down on the floor, leaning her back against the wall. She glanced at Charlie and he could tell what she was thinking by the look in her eyes—they'd better stay awake.

Robby sat on a stool, whittling a piece of pine with his pocket knife, sending thin slivers of wood onto the floor. Coming out of the kitchen and into the living room, Curt broke the silence by spitting tobacco into a tin can he held in his hand.

"Y'all hungry?" Curt said.

Charlie nodded, he was starving. Lacy just looked at him but said nothing.

"Okay, I'm gonna go out and check the rabbit snares," Curt said.

Charlie saw Lacy flinch, as though a disturbing memory had crossed her mind.

"Robby, you comin'?"

Robby looked up and his eyes shifted from Lacy to Charlie, then to Jim and Emily sleeping on the floor. It seemed that Robby sensed the awkwardness of leaving four strangers alone in their house, even though that feeling was apparently lost on his older brother.

"Nah, I'll stay back," Robby said.

Curt scratched his head and paused, staring at the floor for a moment. Then he said, "Okay, I'll be back soon and we'll make stew."

"Thank you," Charlie said. "And thanks for letting us come here."

Curt nodded and gave him a tobacco filled smile. Then he turned and headed into the kitchen. Plucking his shotgun off the deer-leg gun rack, Curt opened the door and headed outside.

Almost an hour had gone by since Curt left and he had not returned. Charlie looked at Robby, noticing that the wood he was carving was starting to resemble a bear. The boy had talent, he thought.

"Does your brother usually take this long to check the traps?" Charlie said.

Robby shrugged, not looking up from his carving. "Only if he sees a deer or something, then he'll go off tracking it."

Charlie nodded and rubbed his forehead, trying to shake off a sluggish feeling in his mind. He realized he must have dozed off for a moment while sitting there, or at least zoned out a bit, it was hard to tell. The same thing must have happened with Lacy, as her eyelids were almost closed, leaving just slits to show she was still aware of what was going on. Then Charlie thought he heard something, far off, and a tingling sensation spread throughout his chest. It sounded like a car engine, and then it stopped.

"How far did you say we are from the road?" Charlie said.

The sound of metal scraping on wood halted. Robby turned on his stool, looking toward the front of the house. "Bout ten miles on the path. Maybe eight as the crow flies." He went back to carving.

Charlie tried to replay the sound again in his mind, starting to wonder if he had imagined it. He strained his ears, hearing only the rhythmic sound of Robby's knife shucking slivers of pine, and horseflies clicking against the window. Charlie got up and walked to the front door, peeked out, then slid the bolt lock shut on the door, just in case. He walked back to the sofa and sank into it with a sigh. After a few minutes, Charlie's eyes started to blur and he laid his head back against the couch.

A booming knock startled Charlie awake, making him jump to his feet. He looked at Lacy, whose hand had gone to her chest as though her heart had just exploded. Robby's head jerked around, his eyes narrowing toward the door. Someone pounded on the door three more times. Jim and Emily both sat up, looking groggy and confused. Outside, two muffled voices spoke to each other on the doorstep. Robby got up, setting his knife on his stool, and started walking toward the door.

Charlie caught Robby by the arm as he walked by. "Does anyone ever come here?" Charlie said.

Robby's brow wrinkled as he looked at Charlie. "No, never. Nobody's ever come here."

"Don't go to the door," Charlie said. "They're looking for us."

"I'll just tell them nobody's here," Robby said, "and send them away."

Charlie shook his head. "They won't take your word for it. They'll shoot you dead and search the place."

Robby opened his mouth, paused, then shut it.

"Do you have any other guns in the house?" Charlie said.

"Yeah, in that room." Robby pointed to the bedroom with the closed door. "A couple of hunting rifles."

Charlie nodded and looked at Jim. "All of you get into the other bedroom, I'll get the guns."

Robby led the way, with the rest of them hurrying behind. They closed the bedroom door on the left as Charlie opened the door on the right. He gritted his teeth as hundreds of mice shrieked, scurrying away from him toward the opposite wall. The room was in shambles, with junk and newspapers all over the floor. The bed itself was torn apart and Charlie heard a chorus of squeaks coming from inside the mattress, as the whole thing shook. Trying to control his nerves, Charlie looked across the room to the closet on the other side, deciding that was where the guns were. He clenched his jaw, preparing to run over the swarm of rodents, when he heard the crashing sound of the front door being kicked in. There was no time to get to the closet.

Charlie pulled his handgun out and stood just inside the room, trying to listen. He heard voices talking, at least two people, maybe more. It was difficult to tell over the squealing mice. The sea of rodents was getting braver, starting to creep closer to him. The men walked further into the house, and Charlie began to understand what they were saying.

"Check the bedrooms," a man whispered. "Kill anyone who isn't Lacy Chase. No loose ends."

"You got it," said another man.

Boots clunked on the floorboards, coming closer. Charlie took one step back and then dove forward, out of the bedroom, landing on one knee, his gun aimed toward the kitchen. A man in green cargo pants and a gray t-shirt flinched as he stepped into the living room. Charlie fired his gun and the man flopped to the ground. Another man, still in the kitchen, had been pointing his gun to the left, and before he could turn and aim, Charlie fired again. That man stumbled backward out the door, holding his bleeding neck.

Charlie ran through the house, looking left and right. When he got to the smashed in front door, he peered out at the ground and saw the guy he had shot in the neck, lying there dead, having bled out already. The door frame exploded next to Charlie's head, with splinters of wood cutting into the side of his face. Charlie ducked back inside and waited. The other bedroom door opened and Jim came out first. Charlie put his hand up, and Jim halted in the doorway, looking around at the carnage. Robby's head appeared, his face pale and gaunt as he tried to the see what was happening from behind Jim.

Hearing soft footsteps approaching in the grass, Charlie moved close enough to see just outside the door. A shadow appeared on the ground and Charlie knew the shooter was to the right. Tensing his leg, Charlie pushed off the floor, sending his body flying sideways in front of the doorway, until his shoulder slammed into the frame on the opposite side. His eyes found the target right away and his finger pulled the trigger. The third man was dead before he hit the ground.

Charlie jumped out into the yard, spinning around, looking

everywhere. Nobody else was in sight, and there were no new vehicles in the area. The men must have parked where they thought their car was still out of earshot and came in on foot.

The others came running out of the house. Robby was holding a rifle in each hand, and after seeing the bodies outside, he handed one of the rifles to Jim without taking his eyes off of Charlie.

"How'd you do that?" Robby said.

Charlie turned and looked at Robby, seeing his slack jawed stare.

"It's what I'm good at," Charlie said. Then he walked up to Robby and stood in front of him, towering over the boy like a giant hulk.

Robby was looking up at Charlie like a kid who had just met his rockstar idol.

"But let me tell you this, kid," Charlie said. "Every time I have to kill someone, I convince myself it's the last time I'll ever have to do it."

Robby blinked and looked down at the ground.

"Robby," Jim said, pointing across the yard. "When was the last time that truck started."

Robby looked up. "About five months ago."

Jim walked toward the truck, looking over his shoulder at Charlie.

"You think you can get this thing running, big guy?" Jim said.

Charlie strode up to the rusty Ford and leaned his head inside the open driver's side window, pulling a lever. The hood of the truck popped up and a squirrel scampered out of the engine with a squeak. Shaking his head, Charlie moved around to the front of the truck and looked under the hood.

"I'll give it a try," Charlie said. He turned to Robby. "You got any tools?"

Robby motioned over to a small barn. "In there," he said, looking away. "But I don't go in there."

"I'll go get them," Jim said, raising his eyebrows at Charlie. Charlie nodded.

"Robby, keep an eye out for your brother," Jim said. "They know we're here now, or at least they will when those men don't report back."

Jim tossed his rifle to Lacy, who caught it and headed for the tire worn path.

"Emily and I will keep watch," Lacy said.

Jim nodded and hurried toward the barn.

When Jim came back to the truck, carrying a red toolbox in his hands, his face was stark white.

"You okay?" Charlie said.

Jim leaned forward to whisper to Charlie. "There's still a rope hanging in there," Jim said.

Charlie dropped a set of cables on the engine and faced Jim. "You serious?"

Jim nodded. "It was cut about three feet down from the beam. I think they had to get their own mom down and bury her."

Charlie lifted his shoulder, wiping his sweaty face on his shirt. He looked across the yard at Robby, who was walking along the edge of the woods, calling Curt's name every once in a while.

"You know we have to take them with us," Jim said.

"Yeah, I know," Charlie said.

"We can't just leave them here."

Charlie shook his head and gave an exasperated laugh. "Not only are we up against every operative in the country, but we get to open a roaming orphanage."

"It's our fault those men came to this house," Jim said.

Charlie sighed and took the tool box from Jim. "I know."

Dropping a wrench into the toolbox with a clang, Charlie walked around to the side of the truck and reached in, turning the key. The engine did nothing for a second, then lurched once, then paused, and lurched again, shaking the whole truck with each turnover. Charlie released the key and waited, then turned it forward again. Finally, the engine chugged three more times before starting up as a huge cloud of black smoke plumed out of the exhaust pipe.

Robby came running. "I can't believe you fixed it!"

Jim had just finished carrying the bodies inside the house and was shutting the door. Seeing Robby jogging by, Jim hustled up next to him.

"I'm worried about your brother," Jim said as they came to a stop at the idling truck.

Robby said, "I can't leave without him."

"We won't," Jim said.

Just then they heard a voice yelling from the woods. Both Jim and Robby peered into the trees. For a minute there was nothing, then they saw Curt running toward them, ducking under branches. Curt was yelling, and at first it seemed like he was hurt, but then Charlie realized he was cheering.

Robby had a big smile on his face and was waving Curt toward them.

"Hurry up," Robby yelled. "We gotta leave!"

"You got the truck running?" Curt hollered. "I got a big buck way back there and—"

Curt stopped and turned around to look at the sky. With a sinking heart, Charlie lifted his hand to his ear to listen and instantly recognized the humming sound.

Robby heard it as well and screamed. "Run, Curt! Run!"

Curt turned back toward them, his face filled with panic. Bolting into a sprint, Curt's knees pumped up and down. He almost made it to the edge of the woods when a screech pierced the air. Curt gave one last look over his shoulder before his body blew into hundreds of pieces, leaving nothing but a smoking crater in the ground. The drone rocketed past them overhead.

Robby let out a horrified shriek that pierced Charlie's soul like a knife. Before Charlie or Jim could grab him, Robby started running toward the spot where Curt had been. A blur flashed past Charlie and he saw Lacy charging at Robby, tackling him from behind. Robby crumpled to the ground, and Lacy scooped him up over her shoulder, wincing under the weight as she struggled to carry him back.

Robby wriggled and wailed. "No! Let me die with him!"

"Jim, get ready to drive!" Charlie said, running out to help Lacy.

Jim hopped into the driver's seat and revved the engine as Emily jumped in the passenger side. Charlie grabbed Robby off of Lacy and hoisted him over his own shoulder. He ran to the truck, stepped on the back bumper, and leaped into the pickup bed, while carrying Robby like a sack of wheat.

Charlie saw Lacy sprinting toward the tire path she and Emily had been guarding.

"Go," Charlie said. "Pick Lacy up on the way."

Jim hit the gas and the truck took off. Lacy bent down to scoop up her rifle, then moved to the left so Jim could drive past. Running along with the truck, Lacy tossed her rifle to Charlie and made a leap, lifting one leg over the side and tumbling into the box next to Robby. As soon as Lacy was on board, Jim sped up, winding along the path.

"Hold him down," Charlie said.

Lacy put her knee on Robby's back, as Robby screamed and tried to roll Lacy off of him. Hooking her arms under Robby's elbows to keep him from pushing himself up, Lacy looked at Charlie, her eyes brimming with tears.

Charlie looked up and saw the drone in the open blue sky, coming back at them. He pounded on the back window of the cab and yelled to Jim. "Stop the truck."

Emily looked through the window at Charlie as if he were insane.

"Stop the truck, now," Charlie said, putting his hand on the cab for support.

Jim eased on the brake and the truck slowed to a stop. Charlie looked down at the rifle in his hands, a .30-06, bolt action. He'd have to make it count. Charlie leaned over the top of the truck, squinting his eye in the scope of the gun. He hoped the rifle was accurate. If those kids had been surviving for a year by hunting wild game, it seemed likely they would at least take good care of their guns.

The drone was coming fast, and Charlie tried to estimate the range of its missiles. If he shot too soon, it would be impossible to hit. But wait too long, and the drone would blow them to pieces. Exhaling all of his breath, Charlie moved the crosshairs over the drone, holding steady and counting to four. He squeezed the trigger and the gun fired, kicking hard into his shoulder. But the drone kept coming, unfazed. He had missed and he knew they were all dead. Out of frustration and panic, Charlie slammed the bolt of the rifle back and then forward, getting a new shell in the chamber. Swinging the gun up as he stood tall, Charlie said, "Bite me," deciding those were fitting last words. He pulled the trigger and the drone exploded into a ball of fire.

CHAPTER 33

J im saw the drone blow up, then turned around to see the look of shock on Charlie's face. Charlie raised his arms in triumph and let out a primal howl. Jim knew that shot had been nothing short of a miracle. He swallowed and looked at Emily, meeting her gaze; she had shiny eyes and a somber frown.

"That boy back there," Emily said. "He just saw his own brother, all he had left in the world—"

Jim put his hand behind Emily's head, trying to comfort her by kneading her tight neck muscles with his fingertips.

"I know," Jim said, looking in the back of the truck where Lacy still held onto the kid. The boy had gone quiet now, just lying there limp. "We'll help him the best we can."

Charlie pounded on the top of the truck and sat down in the bed. "Go Jim! Drive like hell!"

Jim punched it and the old truck grumbled loudly as they picked up speed. A rapping knock on the back window made Jim flinch, and Emily turned around, stretching across the back seat to open the window. Charlie poked his head through the opening, his face having gone from elated to grim.

"More drones will come after us," Charlie said.

Jim continued to speed up. "Can we outrun them?"

Charlie pushed his lower lip out, looking to the side as he thought about it. Then he pulled his head outside and said something to Lacy; she shook her head.

"They can go one-hundred and forty miles per hour," Charlie said. "There's no way we can outrun them."

All feelings of hope were emptying out of Jim as though someone had pulled the plug out of a drain. "You can't keep shooting them down?" Jim said.

Charlie shook his head. "It was a fluke that I hit the one. Imagine three of them coming at us, or worse. These guys have an unlimited arsenal."

Jim envisioned an entire fleet of military drones flying toward him, missiles ready. His heart thumped like a bass drum. He felt suffocated by the fact that no matter what they did, or where they went, they could never hide. Whether it was cameras, satellites, or drones—it was just a matter of time before they were found, and killed.

The satellites, Jim thought. He remembered Lacy hacking from her laptop and her face off with Kraig. He thought about her desperation to get her computer back. Now, Lacy had nothing to use. Jim shook his head, glancing at the dashboard of the old truck; the old clunker had nothing even close to a computer. Just an old AM radio. He looked down at the floor and saw a big old CB radio, with a receiver that reminded him of The Dukes of Hazzard. With a sigh, Jim scoffed at the ancient technology. The weight of despair grew heavier and he accepted the fact that there was nothing he could do but keep on driving until the other drones caught up with him. He slammed his hand against the steering wheel, when an idea struck him, and his back straightened up.

"Emily, get Lacy's attention," Jim said.

Turning around, Emily called out the window to Lacy, who poked her head in.

"Lacy, we have a CB unit in here," Jim said.

Jim saw a flicker of realization appear in Lacy's eyes, just what he had hoped for.

"Do you think you can do it?" Jim said. "Can you jam the drone signals?"

Lacy looked down at the floor, her eyes darting back and forth as she examined invisible pictures and diagrams in her mind; images that Jim dared not even try to imagine. Finally, Lacy blinked and looked up at Jim.

"Yes," Lacy said. "I'll need some time though."

"I expected that," Jim said. He pressed the gas pedal down further, nodding. "I'll do the best I can."

Lacy sat in the front seat of the truck with the window open to keep her fingers dry while she worked on the CB unit. The lack of air conditioning in the truck had caused her hands to get slick with sweat, and her pocket knife kept slipping out of her grip. She had found an old John Deere baseball cap under the seat, and wore it to keep her hair from blowing in her face while she worked.

Emily sat in the rear seat, watching out the window for any sign of drones in the sky. Meanwhile, Charlie remained in the bed of the truck, sitting with his back against the cab. Robby had hoisted himself up so that he had his arm hanging over the side of truck, his hand dangling in the wind, his head lying limp on his shoulder. Jim frequently glanced in the rearview mirror, sometimes seeing Charlie mouth a few words and pat Robby on the back. From what Jim could tell, Robby never said anything in response.

Lacy worked on the inside of the circuit board with the point of her knife, bracing herself against the door for support whenever Jim had to speed around a corner. Jim was afraid to slow down at all, thinking a drone would catch up to them at any minute. Lacy had also pried the AM radio out of the dashboard and yanked its circuit board out to use as part of her contraption. She also used the cigarette lighter often, to heat up the blade of her knife.

Jim scratched the stubble on his cheek and squinted at the mess of wires Lacy had coming out of the box.

"It seems like you've done this before," Jim said.

"Something similar," Lacy said. "But I had less to work with then." She sniffed. "And I didn't have a whole fricking car battery for power."

Jim breathed a sigh. "Well, that's good then."

"Yeah," Lacy said. "But I don't know exactly what kind of drones they're using. I need to make this thing into a sophisticated jammer, not just your average home grown variety."

"Well, if anyone can do it, it's you."

Lacy wiped her face on her shirt sleeve. "Thanks," she said, as a stream of smoke spiraled up from where she was soldering a wire.

CHAPTER 34

C harlie knelt in the back of the pickup truck as they flew down the rural Arkansas highway. His nerves were raw, both from lack of sleep, and from the fact that he had two immediate worries. His first concern was that Robby's shock was beginning to wear off, and now Charlie began to think the kid might just leap out of the truck, at ninety miles per hour. Robby's leg had already moved in a way that suggested he was considering it, a few times. Each time, Charlie had reached out to grab him, trying to give him words of encouragement.

While Charlie was a hardened soldier who had seen immeasurable pain and death in his life, Robby's suffering was something that struck a chord deep in Charlie's heart. Charlie swallowed hard as he remembered the overwhelming despair that had engulfed him when his own older brother died. With a deep exhale, Charlie shook his head, thinking about how long ago it had been; he was seventeen at the time and now he was forty-five.

The worst thing about his brother Trevor's death had been that it was simply a matter of being in the wrong place at the wrong time. Trevor was nineteen when he decided to stop at a convenience store for a sandwich, just before an armed robber came barreling in. Later on, the store clerk, a young girl with curly blonde hair, had said Trevor tried to tackle the gunman. She said the robber threatened to shoot her if she did not open the safe, a safe which she had no way of opening.

When he found out that Trevor was dead, Charlie felt like he had been pushed down a deep, dark well, hundreds of feet under the ground. The sides of the well were hard and slippery, and the opening at the top looked like a tiny speck of light, miles away. There was no way out and so Charlie had resolved to crumple up in the bottom of the well and waste away. Eventually, Charlie had joined the military and, over time, he found some sort of meaning and purpose in his life.

Yet Charlie knew how far away that tiny light must seem to Robby right now, and it was hard to tell what he would do next. Charlie's other concern was that drones were coming for them, and if Lacy could not pull off a miracle of her own, he was going to be blown up in the middle of some obscure Arkansas road. Charlie supposed there could be worse ways to go out. Better to take your last breath out in the open, fighting back, than die chained up in some prison camp cell—which had almost been his fate, several times. Maybe they would make it to Mississippi before the drones caught them. That would be preferable, since it was the state in which he was born. He found it ironic that he had not been back to his childhood town in decades, yet at this moment of certain death, he was heading right for it.

Sure enough, that whimsical thought was short lived. Charlie's muscles tightened up as he squinted at the horizon far behind them. He could not be sure yet, but he thought he saw four tiny dots in the sky. Charlie knocked on the back window of the cab and Emily slid it open.

"I see them," Charlie said.

Emily jerked her head around, trying to look through the window.

"Shit, it's not ready yet," Lacy said.

"I think we've got about five minutes before they get within range," Charlie said.

"Dammit," Lacy said. "I'll have to cut some corners and just hope this works."

"Charlie," Jim said. "Get ready with the rifle."

"There's four of them," Charlie said.

Jim pounded his hand on top of the steering wheel multiple times and cursed. The truck growled and sped up as he gave it more gas.

Charlie turned around and faced the back, bringing his rifle to his shoulder. Robby lifted his head, looking on with mild interest.

"Come on, Lacy," Charlie muttered under his breath. "You've got this, girl."

The drones were getting closer. As Charlie peered into the scope to get a good look, he saw a police car scream past them, going the other direction. A wry smile formed on Charlie's face as he watched the red lights flick on, both the flashing ones on top of the car, and the brake lights down low. Oh, nothing to see here, officer, Charlie thought. Just an ancient hillbilly truck doing ninety miles an hour, with a lunatic in the back holding a hunting rifle. No big deal here in Arkansas.

Charlie wondered if the cop would be able to catch up to them in time to see the show. Highly unlikely, he decided. The drones were now close enough for Charlie to make out their wings and their v-shaped fins in the back. Twisting the end of his scope, Charlie increased its power and brought it up to his eye. He could see missiles hanging from three of the drones, the fourth one having already used up its firepower.

Charlie shouted out of the corner of his mouth. "Lacy? How're we doing?"

"Need more time," Lacy shouted.

Charlie bowed his head. Go down fighting, he thought. With a sigh, he brought the rifle up and tried to center one of the drones in his scope. The sound of his gunshot cracked the air, and he watched the sky. They kept coming. He had missed. He fired again, and missed. A third time, missed. The drones would be in range within seconds. Charlie got the drone furthest on the left within the crosshairs and pulled the trigger. The butt of the gun had not been in the ideal position, and the recoil of the rifle slammed into his shoulder. Charlie hesitated before looking up, but when he did, all four drones were still coming at them.

The chamber of Charlie's rifle hung open and empty. He was out of bullets. Tossing the gun down hard against the floor of the truck bed, he sat down and slumped against the back of the cab. Closing his eyes, Charlie waited for the screeching sound of the missiles. Then he felt movement next to him and opened his eyes to see Robby getting up and walking to the back of the pickup truck. Robby was looking up at the oncoming drones, oblivious to the speed at which the truck was moving. As he reached the tailgate, Robby lifted his arms, standing tall and holding his hands outstretched as far as they would go. Robby's face was tipped upward, looking straight at the imminent death coming for him. Charlie sat watching, deciding not to stop him; if they were all going to be vaporized, let the kid go the way he wants.

The drones were so close, Charlie could see every detail. He wondered why they had not fired yet. What were they waiting for? Then the drones floated overhead, seeming like they were barely moving, given the speed the truck was traveling. Lacy's excited cry of joy came bellowing out of the cab. Charlie stuck his head in the window, as Jim started to slow down.

"They didn't fire," Charlie said.

Lacy had a huge smile on her face as she held up a metal box with wires and cable coming out of it like spaghetti. "I did it!" she said. "I blocked their signal . . . . blocked every signal within at least five miles! That's why they didn't fire!"

Jim grabbed Lacy's shoulder, shaking her. Emily leaned

forward and kissed Lacy on the cheek.

"But they're still flying," Charlie said.

"They were still following the last command they received," Lacy said.

Charlie laughed and slumped down against the truck. After a moment, Charlie's head jerked up. He turned and saw Robby, now standing with his shoulders slumped, looking over the tailgate at the road beneath him. Jumping up, Charlie grabbed Robby by his shirt and pulled him down, holding onto him with his beefy arms. Robby let out a moan and then his body shook with violent sobs, as he cried out.

Charlie closed his eyes and a single tear rolled down his cheek. "You're gonna be alright, buddy," Charlie said. "You'll be okay."

CHAPTER 35

A far off siren jolted Charlie out of his dazed relief. The police car that had turned its lights on when it passed them—it was catching up. Robby was slumped in the bed of the truck next him, his face buried in his arms, motionless and oblivious to the world.

Charlie rapped his knuckles on the back window of the cab and poked his head in. "We're not out of the woods yet."

"What do you mean?" Lacy said, still twisting wires together on her signal jammer.

"A cop car is catching up to us," Charlie said. "It's got its siren on."

Emily turned around, squinting through the back window. Cursing, Jim tried to give the truck more gas, but they were at top speed. Shaking her head, Lacy set her contraption up on the dashboard and twisted around to look behind them.

"It just never ends," Jim said. He shook his head and straightened out his fingers before squeezing the steering wheel again.

A bright blue "Welcome to Mississippi" sign flew past them on the right side of the road.

"Jim, get off on the next exit," Charlie said. "I'll tell you exactly what to do from there." Charlie swallowed, glancing up at the road ahead as he considered what he was about to do. "I've got a place we can go, but it's going to take a while to get there. We can evade him long enough if you follow my directions."

"You know this area?" Jim said.

"Yeah," Charlie said. "I grew up here."

~ ~ ~

Charlie jumped out of the back of the truck as they pulled into the driveway of a white two-story house with an attached garage. Sprinting up to the garage, Charlie flipped open the plastic cover of a keypad that was mounted on the outside wall. He tapped four numbers and the garage door started to open. Jim pulled the truck into the garage and Charlie pressed the button on the pad for the door to close, before ducking inside himself.

Flipping a light switch on in the garage, Charlie went up to the truck to take a look at Robby. He was lying on his back in the truck bed, looking up at the rafters, his eyes glazed and comatose. Charlie sighed. Being on the run and fighting for your life was no way to deal with what Robby had just been through. The kid's mind was refusing to process both of those things at the same time.

Jim stepped out of the truck, and a police siren screamed past on the road outside, causing him to crouch down on instinct. He straightened up after the sound faded. "You know the people who live here?"

"I know who they are," Charlie said. "But I've never met them."

Lacy opened the passenger door and slid out of the truck, followed by Emily.

"You knew the code for the garage," Lacy said. "How?"

"This was my childhood home," Charlie said. "I guess they never bothered to change it."

"And you knew they wouldn't be home?" Emily said.

Charlie nodded and leaned against the side of the truck, exhaustion overtaking him as the feeling of immediate danger ebbed away. "They've left by now to stay at their other place in Michigan for the summer. They have family up there."

"You've never met them and you know all this?" Lacy said. "Charlie, that's kind of creepy."

Charlie rubbed his eyes and shook his head. "No, it's just sad."

"Why did you bring us here, Charlie?" Emily said.

Charlie looked up, his eyelids feeling heavy. "We needed a place to sleep," Charlie said. "If we're going to even stand a chance at rescuing Tom, we can't go barging into the Florida Keys barely able to stand on our feet."

"You intend to spend the night here?" Lacy said. "We can't waste that kind of time."

"Lacy, look at us," Charlie said. "Most of us haven't slept in weeks."

Lacy took a step forward. "Charlie, you've done that before. I've heard about some of your missions—spending days in the freezing water."

Charlie slammed his hands down on the steel pickup truck and straightened up tall. Lacy took a step backward as Charlie towered over her, his massive chest heaving with each breath.

"Yeah, I did do that," Charlie spat. "And that's when people got killed. Good men that made mistakes because they were too exhausted to think clearly. Brothers that I went to war with—dead, because they thought they were invincible."

Lacy's eyes dropped to the floor.

Jim came up and put a hand on both Lacy and Charlie's shoulders. "Charlie's right," Jim said. "We should get some rest here." He turned to Lacy. "Are you okay with that."

Lacy nodded and walked up to a window in the garage, peering outside with a sigh.

Charlie walked up the stairs to the bedroom level of the house as memories flooded into his mind, causing his skin to prickle all over. He knew the next step was the one that creaked, and sure enough, as he placed his foot on it, the wood let out a familiar squeak. When Charlie reached the top, Jim and Emily came up behind him.

"When did your parents sell this place?" Emily said.

"Right after my brother died," Charlie said. "They couldn't handle being here anymore."

"Are they still alive?" Jim said.

"My mother died of a heart attack years ago," Charlie said. "My father is in a nursing home in Massachusetts. He has late stage Alzheimer's and doesn't know who I am anymore."

"I'm sorry," Emily said.

Charlie shrugged. "They were never the same after my brother was killed. Especially Mom."

"Your brother that was shot trying to stop a robbery?" Jim said.

"Yeah, Trevor," Charlie said. "It broke her."

Jim looked down the hallway. "Are you sure you're okay staying here?"

Charlie nodded. "I'll be fine. You two take the master bedroom." He pointed inside a room with a large bed covered by a plush white comforter.

"Okay," Jim said. "Lacy wanted to stay downstairs by the garage, so she could check on Robby and keep watch."

"We found some blankets and pillows in the linen closet," Emily said. "All Robby said was, 'I'm not leaving my family's truck,' so we made him as comfortable as we could. I hope he'll be alright."

"I think he will be, eventually," Charlie said. "But he's going to need time."

Emily nodded and looked in at the bedroom, her eyes looking so heavy they were almost closed.

"Go get some sleep," Charlie said.

Jim nodded and he and Emily went into their room.

Charlie continued down the hall and stopped to look in the room which had been his. It had been turned into a study. There was an oak desk with a black leather chair in front of it. A bookshelf now stood where his bed had once been pushed against the wall. In the far corner, a grandfather clock ticked away. Most of the floor was covered by a giant fur throw rug. Charlie stood there for a few minutes, picturing where everything of his had been. His chest felt tight and his throat felt like he had swallowed a marble that got stuck halfway down. With a sigh, he continued down the hallway.

Trevor's old room was now a guest bedroom. The dark wood dresser that had been Trevor's was still there. Charlie's mother could not bring herself to get rid of it, so she had just left it there when they sold the house. It seemed the new owners liked it enough to keep it, and so it stayed. The bed was new, however—a simple steel framed twin size.

Charlie's legs started to buckle and he swayed to the side. He ambled forward and allowed himself to fall, turning on his way down so that he was facing the ceiling when he landed on the bed with a bounce. Closing his eyes, Charlie felt streams of tears run out of the outside corners of his eyes and down into his ears. He let it happen for a minute, let a few sobs come up from his belly and shake him. Then he lifted his arm up to his face and wiped it dry on his sleeve.

Charlie lay on the bed with his hands behind his head, staring up at the ceiling. He tried to distract himself from the far off sounds coming from Jim and Emily's room, the squeaking bedsprings and whispering that cut through the pin-drop silence of the house like butter. He laughed to himself at how embarrassed Emily would be if she knew that every sound she made could be heard throughout the house, clear as a bell.

As the house finally went quiet, Charlie found himself counting the cracks in the plaster ceiling. He was starting to drift off to sleep when his gaze stopped at the air return vent above him. He studied it with interest, then realized that the paint around the screws had been worn away. Squinting up at the vent, he sat up and then stood on the mattress for a closer look. Someone had unscrewed the vent quite a few times.

Charlie reached up with his hand and stuck his thumbnail in the groove of one of the screws, giving it a turn. The screw had not been tightened all the way and turned easily. He worked the first screw out and then moved on to the second one. After removing the vent cover, he stretched as tall as he could and put his hand in the opening, feeling around. A tremor ran through him as his hand touched something solid. He grabbed it and pulled down a brown cardboard box. It felt surprisingly heavy.

His heart thumping, Charlie opened the box and gasped. It was Trevor's secret stash. On top were several Playboy magazines, which Charlie smirked at with a shake of his head. He tossed them aside, as well as a stack of old baseball cards. Then Charlie saw a beautiful teenage girl staring up at him. It was a picture of Trevor's girlfriend—she had been with him for almost two years when he was killed. She had a sweet smile and jet black hair, cut in a short pixie cut. Charlie turned the picture over and read the note scribbled on the back: "Trevor, you will always have my heart. Love, Jessica." Charlie shook his head as his eyes started to sting. Last he had heard, Jessica had married a neurosurgeon in Connecticut and had five children.

As he set the picture aside on the bed, Charlie leaned over the box and saw what had been so heavy; it was Trevor's throwing knife. Charlie lifted it out, holding his breath as he examined it. It was the throwing knife that he and Trevor had spent many days practicing with in the backyard after school.

They would have contests using a target or run around pretending they were assassins while throwing it at trees.

Trevor had saved up his money for a long time after seeing the throwing knife in a cutlery shop at the mall. It was a beautiful blade with a black handle. Trevor even had his name engraved in large, calligraphy letters on the handle. Charlie slid the knife out of its leather ankle sheath and rubbed his thumb across the edge of the blade, noting that it was still razor sharp. Trevor had always been a stickler about maintaining its edge.

With a deep sigh, Charlie put the blade in its sheath and lay down on his back, clutching it to his chest. He took a shuddering breath, closed his eyes, and fell asleep.

Charlie woke with a start to see Lacy standing over him.

"Lacy, what time is it?" Charlie said.

"It's seven in the evening," Lacy said.

Charlie sprang out of the bed, looking around in a daze. "We've been asleep for a full day?"

"I guess we needed it, like you said. We hadn't slept for weeks. But that's the least of our problems right now."

"Why?" Charlie said, rushing over to the window and looking outside to see the setting sun.

"Robby's gone," Lacy said.

"What? He's gone?"

"I fell asleep on the couch," Lacy said. "I just woke up now, so I went out to check on him and he was gone."

"Dammit," Charlie said. He stumbled out into the hallway, heading for the stairs.

Jim and Emily were climbing out of bed, looking alarmed and confused. Charlie flew down the stairs and across the kitchen to the garage. He opened the door and looked in the back of the truck. It was empty. He turned around and saw Lacy standing there.

"Did you check the house?" Charlie said.

"I searched everywhere," Lacy said.

Charlie clenched his hands and stormed into the kitchen. "Crap, we don't need this right now, we've already stayed way too long."

Just then, the knob on the front door started to turn. They spun around in time to see the door open and Robby come walking in.

"Robby!" Lacy said.

Robby's looked up, his eyes wide.

"Where'd you go?" Charlie said.

"I . . . ." Robby's cheeks turned red. "I had to take a pee."

"Oh." Charlie relaxed. "There are bathrooms in here you could have used."

"I know," Robby said. "I didn't want to wake you guys up. So I went out in the trees."

Lacy's eyes softened and she gave Robby a warm smile. "It's okay, we were just worried about you, that's all."

Robby looked at Charlie, then back to Lacy.

"Are we leaving soon?" Robby said.

"Yeah, we're leaving right now," Lacy said. "Will you ride up in the cab with us? We've got a long way to go."

Robby looked at the floor, his brow creasing. "You guys don't mind?"

"Of course not," Lacy said. "We want you with us."

"Okay," Robby said. "I'll be out in the truck." Robby walked across the foyer and through the door leading into the garage.

Jim and Emily came tromping down the stairs.

"Everything alright?" Jim said.

"Everything is fine," Charlie said. "Robby's out in his truck waiting for us."

Jim scratched the back of his neck, shaking his head. "We're going to have to ditch that truck before morning. A description of it will have been widely broadcast, and where we're going, we can't take that risk."

"You want to be the one to tell Robby that?" Charlie said.

"He clings to that thing like it's the only thing he has left of his family."

"That's because it is," Emily said.

"I'll do it," Lacy said. "I'll tell him." Then she turned on her heel and walked out the door.

J. ARTHUR SQUIERS

CHAPTER 36

L acy flicked on the headlights as she steered a brand new, silver Chevy crew cab pickup truck out of the car dealership near Brewton, Alabama. She coasted a half a mile down the road before pulling the hood down off her head.

Charlie's face lit up when Lacy squeaked the factory fresh brakes, bringing the truck to a stop next to him. She jumped out and tossed him the keys.

"Dang girl, you really know how to pick out a nice ride," Charlie said.

Jim and Emily came walking up, looking at each other and shaking their heads.

"What's going on?" Lacy said. "Are we ready to head out?"

Jim gave Lacy a sullen look and sighed.

Lacy squinted into the dark. "Where's Robby?"

Jim pointed down the road. "He won't talk to anyone. We told him we have to leave now and he won't budge. He just sits there, staring at the sky."

"We can't just leave without him," Lacy said.

"I tried to get through to him," Charlie said. "But now he's shut me out."

247

"It's going to be light soon," Jim said. "We've got to get moving."

Charlie scratched the back of his head and sighed. "I guess I can just pick him up and haul him into the truck. He might put up a fight, but I'm out of ideas."

"No," Lacy said. "Let me talk to him."

Jim chewed on his lip, then nodded. "Okay."

Lacy walked along the white line of the highway, smelling the dew from the cool evening air. A stone bridge loomed ahead with a bubbling stream rushing beneath it.

Robby sat cross-legged on top of the wide stone railing of the bridge, facing outward and looking up at the stars. Lacy came up behind him, standing there silent for a moment. If Robby had heard her approach, he made no indication of it.

"Do you mind if I sit next to you?" Lacy said.

Robby continued to look up at the night sky, not saying anything. Lacy stepped forward and climbed up next to Robby, dangling her legs over the side of the bridge. She pushed her hair behind her shoulders so she could see him out of the corner of her eye. His cheeks were wet and shiny in the moonlight. The stream below sounded fast and strong, as it flowed underneath them for a ways before turning right, around a bend and into the woods.

"I know the pain is unbearable," Lacy said.

Robby sniffed and looked down at his hands.

"I'm not going to pretend I know what it feels like. I never had any family, and maybe that's easier because you don't have to lose anyone."

Robby glanced at Lacy, then looked down at the churning water.

"I never had friends either until I met those guys." Lacy pointed back down the road. "And now someone I love—" Lacy paused, thinking as she marveled at the clarity of the glimmering starlit sky. She gave a wry laugh and blinked her shiny eyes. "I guess I never really knew what love was until I met my friends a few years ago. Up until then, everyone who came into my life either wanted to use me or abuse me— usually both."

Robby's body stiffened, his breathing becoming more audible.

"Someone I love is being held prisoner, and he needs my help," Lacy said. "But I refuse to leave you here alone, in such horrible pain. So I don't know what to do."

They sat there in silence for a while.

Lacy looked up at the stars and then closed her eyes. She took a shuddering breath and let it out. Then Lacy reached her hand over and put it on top of Robby's hand, giving it a squeeze. Robby wiped his cheeks with his other hand and turned to look at Lacy.

"We'd better go," Robby said. "Your friend needs our help."

Lacy gave him a gentle smile and nodded. "His name's Tom," Lacy said. "He's an old man that loves hunting, camping, and fishing. I think you'd really like him."

Robby nodded, giving a hint of a smile. They climbed down off of the stone railing and onto the bridge. As they made their way along the road, heading back toward the truck and the others, Lacy turned and hugged Robby, holding him for a moment before letting go.

"Thank you," Lacy said.

Robby gave her a quick nod. "We'd better hurry," he said.

CHAPTER 37

J im sat on a boulder in the dark, staring out at the reflection of the moonlight on the dark ocean water. They were on a beach in the Florida Keys, and Jim felt an intense tightness growing inside his chest as he faced the reality of what they were about to do. The three hour drive from the Everglades all the way down to Cudjoe Key had been so nerve racking, he thought he would lose his mind. The single highway that spans over the ocean, along the Key islands, is heavily patrolled by police, especially at night. Every time they passed a cop car, Jim thought it was coming for them, and usually there was nowhere to go—nothing but ocean on both sides. But somehow, they had made it there unnoticed.

"You sure that's it?" Jim said.

Lacy stood at the edge of the water, hands on her hips, facing an island out in the ocean, about four miles offshore. There was a giant mansion on the island, looming in the dark. Many windows in the compound had lights shining out of them, looking like tiny white specks floating far off in the distance.

"Yeah, that's it," Lacy said. "That's where Kraig was when

I hacked him. This is our best chance of getting Tom back."

Jim turned around to look at Charlie and Robby. They had just come back from acquiring a couple of jet skis from a nearby resort, and were standing there, dripping wet.

"You up for this?" Jim said, giving Robby a nod.

Robby had been eager to help out ever since they left Alabama. He was still quiet and sullen most of the time, but whenever something needed to be done, he was the first to volunteer.

"I'm ready," Robby said..

"Good," Jim said. He sat down next to Emily and put an arm around her, pulling her close as he tried to gather his own wits. He listened to the waves crashing onto the shore and shivered, despite the heat. After everything they had been through, he could not remember being as afraid as he was in that moment.

"Can we really do this?" Emily said, seeming to read Jim's mind.

"I have to believe we can. We've come this far." Jim looked out at the island. "There's no army out there, just a big house." Trying to put an upbeat tone in his voice, Jim pointed to Charlie with his thumb and said, "Plus, we have a Navy SEAL with us."

"Ex-Navy SEAL," Charlie said. "And that was fifteen years ago."

"I think you're better and stronger now than you ever were," Jim said.

"Yeah," Charlie said, his voice going quiet and thoughtful. "I think you're right. So, are we clear on the plan?"

"I think so," Jim said. "You'll take one jet ski and I'll take the other."

Charlie folded his arms and nodded.

"Lacy and Robby will stand lookout on shore," Jim said. "Lacy, you'll have your signal jammer ready, just in case." Jim pointed up at a hill behind him, with a parking lot overlooking the beach. "Emily will be ready with the truck running in case something happens and you guys have to get out of here. Don't wait for Charlie and me if there's an emergency. If we get separated, we all meet back at the motel. Everyone got it?" They were all bobbing their heads, and Jim felt his legs go numb. All of them were looking to him for leadership in this deadly serious mission, and he was just a shipping dock manager. Well, not anymore, he supposed. He had become a bit more than that.

Jim got up and walked over to Robby, placing a hand on his shoulder and taking him aside.

"Robby, I'm going to depend on you to keep an eye out for anything that looks out of place."

Robby looked at Jim with wide open eyes and grim determination.

"All those years of hunting in the dark woods for survival," Jim said. "It's given you instincts that none of us have."

Robby's posture straightened up and Jim could have sworn he saw the hint of a smile. It was a start, he thought. It was something. Jim handed a flashlight to Robby. "If you spot anything that looks suspicious, you flick this light on and off three times. That way you can warn me and Charlie if there's danger. Got it?"

"Got it," Robby said.

Jim gave him a warm pat on the back. Then Jim turned around and motioned to Charlie. "Let's go."

Jim sped along next to Charlie on his jet ski, flinching as the cold water sprayed up in his face. The waves were challenging, but they were making progress. He became overwhelmed with the eerie feeling of being far out on the ocean water, in the dark, on a little jet ski. The island ahead became massive as they neared it. The lights along the roof of the mansion gave Jim an idea of where things where. As they came close, it was apparent that there was no way to get onto the island from the side facing the mainland. It was all sheer cliff and rock, with the waters raging and churning against the towering stone wall. Jim had to turn his jet ski around and give it full throttle to avoid being sucked into a current that threatened to grab him and slam him against the side of the cliff. They would have to go around to the other side.

Charlie came up close enough to Jim that he could shout over the thundering sound of the ocean.

"This side's no good," Charlie said.

Jim cringed from a huge roar as water crashed into the rocks near them. "Definitely not," Jim said.

"Follow me around it," Charlie said.

Jim gave a thumbs-up and they were off. They headed to the left and circled around until the rocky cliffs gave way to high trees with underbrush. It seemed the front of the mansion was facing out toward the ocean, away from the Keys. The whole side of the island was covered by dense forest. A long dock jutted out from the shore of the island, reaching toward the open sea. They took off toward the dock until they got to its furthest out point, then they slowed down and followed along it until they were close enough to examine the shoreline.

There was a path cut in the thick woods, where a road led up from the dock, through the trees, and ended at a red brick wall with an iron gate. Jim looked along the dock, all the way up the road to the gate, and saw that there were no visible guards. He assumed there would be people at the gate, and marching right up to it was not the way to get in. But if they could just get on the island, perhaps sneaking through the trees, they could probably find another way in. Charlie's face seemed to indicate he had seen all he needed in order to formulate a plan. With a jerk of his head, Charlie signaled that it was time to head back.

They were about halfway back from the island when Jim saw a flashlight flicker three times. He looked around, but saw only dark waves in every direction. Then a moving silhouette caught his eye and he let off the throttle of his jet ski. Charlie sped past him and a small boat came from the right side, plowing into the front of Charlie's jet ski and sending him flying high into the air. Jim cried out and turned his machine sideways, narrowly avoiding the boat himself. He saw a splash far away where Charlie's body landed in the water. Jim tried to circle around to the left, to get over to Charlie, but the boat got in his way. Turning his jet ski the other way, he tried to veer right, but another boat came skidding in front of him, its side clunking against the nose of his jet ski. Rifles clicked all around him.

"Hands behind your head," one of them commanded.

A spotlight flicked on, shining in Jim's face. He put his hands behind his head.

"You will come with us," the man in the boat said.

"And if I refuse?" Jim said.

"We shoot you right here."

~ ~ ~

Emily twisted around in the front seat of the truck, looking down at the beach where Lacy and Robby stood watch. The truck was parked, backed up to the edge of a small cliff, overlooking the ocean. When Jim and Charlie would get back to the beach, they could all run up the stairs and hop into the back of the truck. From there, Emily could floor it and drive the straight shot through the alley, onto the highway, and they would be gone in a flash. But Jim and Charlie were taking longer than she expected. Emily wondered why she always had to be the getaway driver, waiting and worrying. She was going to have a talk with Jim about that as soon as possible. Her nerves were worn out from not knowing what was going on;

she would rather be in the fray, no matter how dangerous.

Emily's stomach seized up into a painful ball when Robby flashed his light three times. Her eyes searched the ocean, but she only saw churning white waves in the moonlight; they were still too far out there. Someone pounded on the hood of the truck and Emily nearly jumped through the roof. She spun around and saw four men pointing machine guns at her through the windshield.

"Get out of the car!" one of them shouted.

A month ago, Emily probably would have obeyed such a command. She would have opened the door, stepped out, and assumed everything would be okay as long as she cooperated. At this point, she knew better. Emily ducked her head down, shifting the truck into drive, and hitting the gas pedal. Bullets pounded through the windshield, cracking the glass. Her truck slammed into bodies and it sounded like sacks of apples being thrown on top of the hood. She felt sick to her stomach as the truck bounced into the air while her tires rolled over someone. Emily looked in the rearview mirror as one of the men got back up, firing his machine gun into the back window. Keeping her head down as far as possible, Emily kept accelerating through the alley.

~ ~ ~

Lacy strained her eyes, trying to see far out into the ocean, her heart beating jack rabbit fast in her throat. "Are you sure you see something?" she said.

"Yeah, I seen it over there!" Robby pointed as he clicked his flashlight on and off. "A boat, moving fast. I could see the splash of the waves on its bow."

Lacy was about to suggest he was seeing things when she heard a horrible crash out on the water. She let out a shriek and ran into the churning froth, where a huge wave crashed into her, knocking her down and sweeping her back onto shore, her body tumbling and rolling onto the sand like seaweed. Lacy's head slammed into the rocks near the waterline and she saw a flash of colors in front of her eyes. Robby ran up to help her, when a chorus of guns cocking rang out around them. Taking a protective stance, Robby stood over Lacy, holding his flashlight over his head, ready to swing it at anyone who came near. Men in brown camouflage surrounded them, all of them holding automatic rifles.

A bright light shined in Lacy's face.

"It's her," said one. "Cuff her."

Lacy didn't intend to be taken alive, not by these guys. She rolled onto her belly, head still swimming, and slid one of her legs under her, preparing to pounce. Looking up, she saw a dark figure coming up behind one of the men. The figure lifted its arm, brandishing a gun. There was a pop, and the man who had spoken dropped to the ground. Three more quick pops sounded off before anyone knew what was happening, and more bodies collapsed in the beach sand. One man turned to see what had happened, and the figure grabbed his arm, twisted the machine gun out of his hand, and used him as a human shield as the other soldiers started firing rounds. The figure raised his own newly acquired machine gun and mowed down the remaining men.

Robby took a step forward. "I ain't letting you hurt her. You'll have to kill me first."

"I'm not going to hurt her," the figure said, tossing his hood back.

Lacy sucked in a breath, recognizing Ethan's face. "I . . . . what . . . . you?"

She pictured the night she met Ethan at the coffee shop in Night Harbor. He was just a laid-back, hip looking musician. The Ethan she saw now was deadly serious, with a look of pure urgency in his eyes. Ethan held out a hand to help Lacy up, but she hesitated. Robby squinted in confusion, looking down at Lacy, his eyes begging her to tell him what to do.

"I don't understand," Lacy said.

"You will," Ethan said. "But we have to get out of here first."

"I'm not leaving my friends," Lacy said. "They're in trouble out there."

Ethan looked out at the ocean. "I can help you save them, but there's nothing we can do tonight. We have to get out of here right now or we'll be captured too. Then everything will be lost."

Lacy looked up at the rock cliff, where Emily had been waiting with the truck, but Emily was gone. Lacy closed her burning eyes as despair consumed her.

"Also, Tom needs to talk to you," Ethan said.

Lacy's eyes popped open and she stumbled to her feet, her head spinning. "You know where Tom is?"

"Of course," Ethan said.

"Is he okay?"

"Yes, he's perfectly fine."

Lacy gave one more look out at the waves, then studied Ethan's face. "Okay, take me to him."

~ ~ ~

Jim's hands were still behind his head when he saw Charlie's face appear on the other side of the boat that contained men pointing rifles at him. Charlie's arm came up, grabbed one of the men and pulled him into the water. Then Charlie disappeared. The men leaned over, trying to look for him. Jim jumped backward off his jet ski, landing in the ocean with a splash. He tried to swim away but the rough waters kept him from making much progress. The second boat motored after him, getting up next to him. One of the guys in the boat slammed the butt of his gun into Jim's head. He felt a flash of pain and sucked in a mouthful of salt water, causing him to choke. The man reached over and grabbed Jim by the shirt, yanking him into the boat. Jim rolled onto the floor, coughing and gasping for air, as the boat sped off.

~ ~ ~

Emily thundered down the road in the truck, still staying low as shot after shot pegged the back of the pickup. The rear window was completely shattered now. She wanted to go back, to whip the truck around and drive back to the beach, but getting killed would not solve anything. No, she had to be smart, and Jim had said to meet at the old motel if they got separated. Emily bit down on her lower lip, cursing her indecisiveness. They had not been separated, she knew where they were. The people she loved were back there fighting for their lives.

Emily realized the shooting had stopped. Shifting her foot over to the brake, she cranked the steering wheel to the left, screeching into a U-turn as the tires squealed across the pavement. Then she flew back down the road toward the beach, leaning forward, gritting her teeth.

To her surprise, the streets were empty, without a person in sight. Ahead of her, she saw the lot with the overlook where she had been parked. She expected to see soldiers firing at her with machine guns. But there was no one. A cold tingle spread through her chest when she saw that there were no bodies lying on pavement where she had plowed through her attackers.

She came to a sudden halt and jumped out of the truck, running up to the cliff. By the light of a streetlamp, Emily could see a small pool of blood where she had run over a man, and shell casings all over the ground from the machine guns, but that was it. The only sound was the crashing waves down on the beach. Emily dashed over to the steps, shuffling down them so fast she was almost sliding like a skier. When she got to the sandy beach at the bottom, Emily ran out toward the ocean. She saw the footprints where Lacy and Robby had been, as well as dozens of impressions in the sand that seemed to surround her. Kneeling down, Emily searched around for clues on her hands and knees. She found a splotch of blood. Choking on tears, she crawled around and found another blood spot, then another. Then another.

The ocean roared in her ears, the waves having grown bigger and fiercer. Emily could see the lights from the mansion, far off on the island, but nothing in between. Her face wet with sweat and tears, she collapsed onto her stomach with her arms outstretched and sobbed into the powdery sand. She screamed with all of the force her lungs could muster, "I'm right here! Come and get me! I'm right here!" But her cracking voice was swallowed up by the massive sound of the crashing waves, making her feel tiny and helpless.

Emily lay there crying at the edge of the water until her shoulders and arms felt weak and numb. Finally, she forced herself to stand and stumbled through the sand back to the wooden steps leading up the hill. Her legs shook and almost refused to bear her weight. Reaching the top, she headed for the truck, still sitting there with the engine running. Glancing down at the pavement, Emily did a double take and she froze as adrenaline flooded her body. The blood spot and all the shell casings were now gone.

~ ~ ~

Charlie burst up out of the water again, right next to the

boat. He grabbed another man by the neck and pulled him overboard, twisting his head with a violent sloshing jerk. Then Charlie dove deep, hearing gunfire above the surface. He flinched as a bullet spiraled through the water next to his head. Charlie pictured what he had seen in the brief moment he had been above the surface. Jim was gone, and so was one of the boats. They had either taken Jim or killed him—most likely the second boat left because they had captured him and were bringing him to the mansion.

As he swam deeper, Charlie agonized over deciding if he should try to get to the island and go after Jim, or head back to shore and get the others first. Realizing that every second mattered if he hoped to get Jim back alive, Charlie swept his arms down to his sides, propelling himself toward the island. He needed to get far enough away from the boats to come up for air without them spotting him. His lungs felt like they were full of hot coals as he frantically shuttled himself to the surface and into the open air. He gasped, big and deep, twisting around to see how far he had gotten before plunging down again. He had gone twenty yards away from the boats, but they still seemed to be heading in his direction.

CHAPTER 38

The parking lot of the old motel was nearly empty. Emily eased the truck along, looking for the door number that matched her key. She found number sixteen and decided to park on the other side of the lot, so nobody could guess what room she was in.

Her eyes darting back and forth, Emily closed the truck door as the creaking of the hinges echoed throughout the lot. She hurried across the pavement, and large raindrops began to splatter onto the ground. A deep rumble rolled through the clouds above her, the sound continuing far away from her in the sky, like a crowd doing "the wave" at a baseball game. She quickened her steps, her hips fully rotating back and forth at that point where someone is on the verge of running but cannot bring themselves to cross that threshold. Rain was coming down hard by the time she reached the door. Emily used the key and slipped inside the room, flicking on the light. In that moment before the room became fully illuminated, Emily hoped she would see Jim sitting there, or maybe Lacy. Jim had the other key, and Lacy could have picked the lock if she needed to. But the room was empty. Emily turned the light back off, choosing to wait for the others in the dark. She felt a little safer that way, not advertising to the world that someone was in the room.

The wind had picked up outside and the pouring rain hammered against the window in gusts. As she sat in a chair, looking out the window at the storm, her mind churned over everything that had happened. Had the others been surrounded like she had? Were they all captured, or . . . . killed. Emily swallowed hard at this thought, a terrible dread overtaking her, making her want to crawl into a hole and never come out.

A car pulled into the parking lot, its headlights barely visible through the thick downpour. Emily's heart raced as the vehicle rolled up into a spot right in front of her door. She moved away from the window just before the light beamed into the room. A car door slammed shut, but the engine was still running. Emily held her breath and waited in the shadows, hoping to hear the key in the lock, which would mean Jim had made it back—that he had managed to find a car and get to the motel, hopefully with Charlie.

Instead, there was a heavy pounding on the door. It was not the code of knocks they had agreed upon ahead of time, to signal it was one of them. This was just heavy, wet slamming of a fist on wood. Emily froze, like a cornered mouse, her eyes searching for somewhere to hide. Under the bed. She dropped to the ground and lifted the comforter, but the frame was solid wood all the way around, with a drawer in the center. She cursed, then had an idea. Grabbing the drawer, she slid it out all the way, but it stopped at the very end, even as she pulled and wiggled it. Another flurry of loud pounding erupted against the door, and during that noise, Emily threw her weight backwards, yanking on the drawer. There was a crack of wood and the drawer came free, landing in Emily's lap. She set it aside and turned onto her stomach, shimmying her legs into the opening in the bed frame. Her butt scraped against the wood, not wanting to fit at first as she pushed against the floor with her arms to force herself through the opening. Once her body was inside, she had to turn her head to fit it through the drawer opening.

A thundering boom hit the door, shaking the entire wall of the motel. Someone had tried to kick the door in, but the deadbolt held. Emily reached her arms out and clamped her hands over the back of the drawer, pulling it into the opening as she squirmed backwards, sliding it into place. Another massive kick hit the door and it exploded open. Emily heard splinters from the frame hit the dresser and wall. Several sets of boots shuffled inside and heavy breathing echoed in the room as the door closed, shutting out the roar of the storm.

Emily lay still, the floor feeling sticky underneath her. She gagged on the smell of moldy carpet and struggled to keep herself from coughing. Footsteps clomped around the beds, a pair of them going back to the bathroom.

"You sure this is the right one?" said a voice.

"Yep, sixteen," said another. "You saw the truck out there."

"Maybe she ditched it," said the first voice.

"Yeah, maybe."

Someone kicked the bed frame a couple times with their boot. Emily's heart jackhammered against her rib cage.

"What now?" said the first voice.

"We drive around town. If she's on foot, she's not getting far in this storm."

The door opened and the loud sound of rain poured into the room. There were hurried footsteps, then the door closed again. Emily could not take the putrid odor anymore and went into a coughing fit, which ended with her vomiting all over the carpet. She shoved the drawer out of its slot and stuck her head through it, gasping for fresh air.

~ ~ ~

Charlie fought the massive waves as he sucked in a deep

breath before diving far underneath the surface to swim through the freezing water. He could not remember ever being so exhausted in his life. His arms and legs burned as though they had been set on fire. It was impossible to swim near the surface, since the crashing torrent up there just tossed him around like a piece of driftwood. Instead, he had to keep getting air for a brief moment before going down deep enough, where the water was calmer, and he could make progress. Charlie used all of the mental tricks he had ever learned to stay focused and avoid panic. After more than an hour, Charlie's arms became too numb to move, and all he could do was frog kick with his legs. He got to the point where he was barely gaining a few feet between trips to the surface, but he had calmed his breathing down enough so that he could continue the ritual until his legs would no longer move.

Taking a final breath, Charlie dipped his head down to dive, when his forehead bumped into a rock. He jerked his head up in pain and wriggled his feet, finding something solid to push off of. Finally, Charlie realized he was near the island. He shook his arms, trying to regain feeling, and managed to crawl onto the rocky shore at the bottom of the massive cliff. Charlie heard boat engines moving around in the water behind him. Turning his head, he saw dim spotlights sweeping back and forth across the water. The storm had picked up and the visibility had become almost nonexistent. Turning back to the cliff, Charlie looked around and saw a place where the rocks hung out from the wall, forming an alcove. Howling at the pain in his limbs, he crawled on his belly like a lizard until he reached the spot. Then Charlie rolled under the protection of the overhanging stones and lay on his back, wheezing for breath. Darkness overtook him and whether he lost consciousness or had simply fallen into a deep, involuntary sleep, he did not know. Nor did he care.

~ ~ ~

Lacy studied Ethan as he shifted his black sports car into fifth gear and sped around the curve in the road along the edge of the ocean. Robby sat in the back, staying quiet, fumbling with the flashlight in his hands as he watched out the window.

"I need to know who you are?" Lacy said. "And I need the truth."

"My name is Ethan and I am an agent from a group tasked with preventing The Supremalus from becoming more powerful than they already are."

"Where are you from?"

"The Netherlands."

"When I met you that night, you were—"

"Undercover."

"That was all an act?" Lacy's cheeks became hot.

Ethan gave her a quick smile. "Not all of it."

"Then it was you all along? Following us this whole way?"

"Well, I lost you after Colorado. I was worried you'd been captured, and I knew this is where they'd bring you."

"What about Tom? Why is he with you?"

"I snatched him."

Lacy turned in her seat, raising her eyebrows. "What do you mean you snatched him?"

Robby shifted in the back seat, his body going tense.

"I shot him with a dart, and hauled him to my car," Ethan said. "To save his life," he was quick to add.

Lacy felt a pounding in her chest. She swallowed hard. "You knocked him out?"

"There wasn't time to talk him into coming with me. I knew that army was coming up the mountain and you know damn well he would have died in that onslaught."

Lacy considered grabbing the wheel of the car and slamming her knuckles into the temple of Ethan's forehead. "Then you just left?" she said. "Didn't feel like helping us?"

Ethan sighed. "I helped you as much as I could. Do you happen to remember when I stopped those thugs from gang raping you?"

Lacy flinched, the recalled image filling her with terror all over again.

"Look," Ethan said. "My first priority is to make sure The Supremalus don't know I'm here. I cannot risk that for anything. The stakes are way too high. That's why I had to get out of there before you were attacked. Getting Tom to safety was the best I could do."

Lacy was shaking now. "But I thought it was them that had taken him! I came here to save him!"

Ethan was silent, watching the road as he increased his speed.

"You're trying to keep them from getting me," Lacy said. "You know what I created a few years ago."

Ethan nodded. "Yes, we do."

"Then why don't you just kill me?"

"That's not who we are." Ethan shook his head. "That's what The Supremalus would do. They are all about killing. We are about saving innocent lives." Ethan turned the car down a side street and came to a stop in front of a small beach house, mostly hidden in palm trees.

Tom stood up from the couch, his big rosy cheeked face smiling when Lacy walked in. She ran to him and gave him a squeezing hug.

"You're safe!" Lacy said.

Tom put his arm around Lacy, letting out a sigh. "I'm so glad you're here. I thought they had you."

Lacy stepped back, looking at Tom's face. "We got away." Her eyes started to water, her hands becoming frantic. "But Jim and Charlie! The soldiers surrounded them in the water—it's like they knew we were coming."

"We'll find a way to get them back," Ethan said. "If they're still alive—"

Lacy whirled around on Ethan, her mouth twitching. "They have to be alive," she said.

Ethan continued, nodding. "We've been studying their island from every angle, but we need your skill to crack their security. If you can do that, I may have a way."

Lacy walked over to a table where Ethan's laptop was sitting. She ran her finger along the top of the shiny computer, shaking her head. "No, it won't work, they can track anyone who tries that. They'd know what I was doing right away."

Ethan stepped up to the laptop, opening it and hitting a key combination. "Not if you go through our system. We developed a protocol that sends every packet through a different random node in the world."

Lacy's forehead crinkled. "What is the name of your organization?"

"I cannot tell you that," Ethan said.

Lacy frowned.

Ethan stepped closer to Lacy and placed his hand on her arm. "You're going to have to trust me on this. We've been connecting to their network for a year and they haven't been able to detect us. But we just can't get in. You are the only person we know of who could do that."

Lacy's pulse took off. "You mean me and Kraig Freestone," she said. "But they have Kraig."

Ethan nodded. "Yes," he said.

Lacy swayed on her feet and Tom came up next to her.

"I'm with you whatever you decide," Tom said.

Lacy remembered the sight of the boats surrounding Jim and Charlie in the ocean. Biting her lip, she sat down in the chair and placed her fingers on the keyboard.

~ ~ ~

Emily sprinted out of the motel room, not bothering to

close the door behind her. She took one sweeping look across the parking lot, seeing no one, and made a straight line for the truck. She ducked her head down as she ran, while hurricane like rain pelted her scalp, feeling like needles. Fear gave her speed and she was at the truck in an instant. She tried to stop in time but her feet slid on the slick pavement. She put her hands out to protect herself as her knees slammed into the front of the truck with a bang. Cursing the pain, she scrambled around to the door, yanked it open, and hopped inside.

They are watching me, she thought, but she did not care. She would rather have them chasing after her out in the rainstorm than be trapped like a rat in some dingy motel room. Emily recalled the feeling of hiding under that nasty bed while the boots pounded around it. She shivered. No, this was better. Emily fired up the truck and drove across the lot, her eyes casting glances in every direction. She went to the lot entrance and pulled up onto the highway, when something clanked behind her. Gasping, she spun her head around to see what had made the noise in the backseat, but there was nothing. Thoughts of Jim filled her mind, and her stomach lurched with the idea of never seeing him again. She could not stay away. Emily decided she would rather be captured herself, or even killed, than leave her husband with those horrible people. Once she got on the highway, Emily sped up, heading back toward the island. She glanced up into her rearview mirror and, far behind her on the road, saw headlights flick on.

Very aware that she was being followed, Emily drove through the town area next to the beach where she had last seen her friends. She was looking for a place to go, a public place with lots of normal looking people—folks who could not possibly be under the command of the group that inhabited the island. She wanted to be among people who would be alarmed if an army of soldiers came barging in and hauled her away. Even if police officers, under The Supremalus' command, came and tried to arrest her, she would put up one hell of a fight, maybe even get on the news. Anything, at this point, was better than doing nothing.

Then Emily spotted a place, a restaurant, quite fancy looking, with windows all around and a great view of the ocean. It was perfect. Emily cranked her wheel over, pulling the truck full of bullet holes up onto the curb with a violent bounce. She leapt out and walked up to the valet, who was standing there looking at her wide eyed, like she was some kind of grotesque creature that had crawled out of the sea.

With a forced smile, Emily handed her key to the valet and pointed to the pickup. "Take good care of my baby," she said.

The valet opened his mouth to say something, then hesitated. "Will do, Ma'am," he finally said.

Emily hurried inside the front door and turned to see the car that had been following her. It slowed to a crawl and rolled by the door, causing Emily to move her head out of view for a moment. At first, it seemed like the car would keep on going, but then it rolled over to the curb and stopped. Emily felt her body tremble, yet she could not look away. The car's driver side door opened, and a man wearing a trench coat stepped out. Emily squinted through the rain. There was something familiar about him. The man turned, and Emily's heart leapt into her throat. She blinked hard, trying to be sure she was not imagining it. But she was not mistaken, a grim faced Tyler Samsteen was striding toward her through the storm.

CHAPTER 39

T his is the most sophisticated security system I have ever seen," Lacy said. She examined the code on the screen, scrolling through thousands of lines.

Ethan nodded. "Of course, The Supremalus wouldn't remain the most powerful organization in the world if they didn't have the best of everything."

The window to the beach house was open, and Lacy breathed in the sea air, trying to relax as her mind worked. "Why hadn't I heard of them before?"

"Because they control everything, from elections to wars, while giving people the illusion that they are free," Ethan said.

"Our elections?" Lacy said. "I believe in a lot of conspiracy stuff, but that's pretty hard to swallow."

"Of course your elections, any elections that really matter. It's all a big show, and they make it more extravagant every time. It keeps people believing they have freedom and choice, which makes them much easier to control. It also keeps the public divided, fighting each other, which again, makes them easy to control."

Lacy's chest heaved as she absorbed this information. She stopped typing and looked at Ethan. Tom stroked his beard and looked out the window at the whitecaps rolling onto the beach.

"But what's the point? Just a lust for power?" Lacy said.

"That's part of it," Ethan said. "Ultimately, they think their cause is for the greater good. That they have the ultimate calling."

"Their cause?"

"To save the human race," Ethan said. "They believe that people, as a species, will destroy themselves if they are not culled. The Supremalus' primary goal is population control."

Lacy swallowed. "You mean, preventing reproduction?"

Ethan shook his head. "No, that's not enough. The Supermalus aim to kill as many humans as possible without the general public realizing they are doing it. This requires control of the world's most influential people, and the best technology. It's an art they have perfected."

Tom fidgeted in silence looking at Lacy with horror in his eyes.

Lacy stared at Ethan, feeling her body go numb.

"That is the most terrible thing I have ever heard," Lacy said.

Ethan tightened his lips and nodded once.

"And your team is trying to stop them?"

"Yes," Ethan said.

Lacy said nothing for a moment, then gripped the table in front of her with both hands. "I will do anything and everything to help you," she said.

Ethan gave her a grateful smile.

"We're not just going to that island to get my friends, are we?" Lacy said.

"No," Ethan said. "We're going there to destroy it."

"Someone is going to have to activate these security shutdowns at the right time," Lacy said. "From this computer."

"Tom will have to do it," Ethan said.

Tom stood up and walked over to the laptop. "Just show me what to do."

"We can't risk communication while we are out there," Ethan said. "It's too risky, they'll detect it. We'll just have to give you exact times to deactivate each system, and we'll make sure we're in the right place at the right time."

Lacy's fingers hammered on the keys, and a schematic of the island appeared on the screen. She studied it as Ethan looked over her shoulder. Lacy sucked in her breath and touched her finger to the screen.

"Did you know about that?" Lacy said.

Ethan shook his head, letting out an exasperated laugh. "No, I had no idea."

"What is it?" Tom said.

"It's a tunnel under the ocean floor," Lacy said. "From the mainland to the island."

Ethan looked out at the fading storm, shaking his head. The sun was starting to peek over the ocean horizon. "We'd better get some sleep, we can't go out there until tonight."

"I don't think I can sleep knowing my friends are out there somewhere, in need of my help," Lacy said.

"We have no choice," Ethan said. "We'll be sitting ducks if we try this in the daylight."

Lacy ran her hand through her hair and closed her eyes, trying to ignore how much they stung. She couldn't imagine what Jim was going through, that is, if he was even alive. Or Charlie—and did Emily get away in the truck?

Robby stood awkwardly by the window, silent, looking outside.

"Robby?" Lacy said. "Are you okay?"

Robby shifted his weight away from the wall and scratched his forehead. "I'm going with you, whenever you say it's time."

Lacy sat there rubbing her eyes for a moment, then stood up and walked over to Robby.

"I'm going to need you to stay here with Tom," Lacy said. Robby raised his eyebrows and he looked hurt. "I want to help," Robby said. "I'm a great shooter. I can protect you."

Lacy closed her eyes, biting her lip. She put her hands on his cheeks and tried to give him a warm smile. "Robby, I need you to stay here and protect Tom."

Robby's mouth opened to protest, but Lacy cut him off before he could speak.

"Nobody can interfere with Tom executing those commands; if they do, we're all dead. This is the best way you can help me."

Robby clamped his jaw shut and looked into Lacy's eyes in a way that made her heart ache. She could tell the poor kid was scared out of his mind, and he did not even fully understand what they were up against. Yet he insisted on sticking by her, facing certain death to find the others. We are all he has, she thought—the closest thing he has to family.

"Please," Lacy said. "I need you to do this for me."

Robby nodded. "Okay."

Lacy kissed Robby on the forehead, causing his stern mouth to turn up in a slight smile.

"Thank you," Lacy said. "I knew I could count on you."

Robby smiled broader and straightened up. Lacy held Robby's gaze for a moment, then dropped her hands from his face and turned around. "Okay, we'll try to get some rest, and we'll head out tonight."

But Lacy did not rest at all. She just lay there with her eyes open, going through her plan over and over in her head.

CHAPTER 40

Lacy sat in the passenger seat of Ethan's car, staring at her watch. It was 9:05 p.m.

"We've got ten minutes," Lacy said.

"This had to have been one of your trickiest hacks," Ethan said. "If Tom isn't able to do it right, this'll all be over real quick."

"It was one of the tougher ones," Lacy said. "But all Tom has to do is click a button. I laid it all out for him."

Ethan nodded, furrowing his brow at Lacy. "When did you dye your hair red?"

"After I got away at the airport," Lacy said. "I figured nobody had a photo of me with red hair. It couldn't hurt."

Ethan shrugged his shoulders. "I really like it," he said. He breathed in deep through his nose, then let it out slowly. "Okay, it's now or never."

The two of them got out of the car and closed the doors. Ethan led the way down a winding path on a grassy hill until they reached the beach. They hurried through the sand until they came to a restroom building with stone walls. There were three steel doors; the one on the left said "Men" and the one on the right said "Women," both of which had steel handles.

The door in the center was unmarked and had no handles, looking like some kind of maintenance room. Lacy looked up at a security camera above the center door, noting that its red light was blinking. She smirked, feeling relieved since the blinking light was a feature she had programmed into her hack to let her know that the camera was using a pre-recorded loop and not a live feed. Lacy had been careful to choose a recorded chunk of video from the same time of day, and with similar weather conditions, so anyone who happened to be watching the feed would not notice something strange.

"So far, so good," Lacy said.

Ethan nodded. Lacy looked at her watch, noting they had one minute to go.

The steel door in the middle clicked, and Ethan pushed it open. As they entered, lights flashed on, and they found themselves in a small room with brick walls. There was another steel door at the other end. Lacy flinched when the lights came on, spinning around in alarm.

"It's okay," Ethan said. "They're just motion lights, nothing more. All the alarms should be off right now."

Lacy nodded as the door they had come through closed behind them with an echoing clank. They walked to the other side of the room, standing before the next steel door, which was much bigger and solid looking than the first. Lacy looked around the room, spotting a camera up in the corner, its red light blinking. She looked down at her watch, then at the door, as a horrible feeling of being trapped came over her. She pictured Tom sitting in the beach house, waiting to press the next button. Ethan's forehead started to shimmer with beads of sweat as he walked up and pushed on the door. He grimaced when it would not budge, and stepped back, swallowing and looking nervous. There was a loud click and Lacy lunged forward, pushing the door open in fear that it would re-lock right away.

"What the heck happened there?" Ethan asked. "Did Tom

have to take a bathroom break?"

"I don't know," Lacy said, stepping through the doorway.

They entered a much bigger room, at least fifty feet by fifty feet, which must have been under the hill near the edge of the beach. The walls were lined with metal, and five air vents hung from a steel ceiling, as well as several lights. There were three small vehicles on the opposite end of the room; they looked like golf carts, but bigger and more heavy duty. A ten foot wide square hole was in the middle of the metallic floor, with a ramp leading down into the dark.

Lacy hurried over to the carts, studying them with interest. "I don't suppose we can take one of these?"

Ethan shook his head. "If there's anyone in the tunnel, they'll hear us coming from a mile away."

Lacy walked over to the edge of the ramp, looking down and dreading the fact that it was the start of a tunnel leading downward under the ocean floor.

Ethan walked up next to her. "We need stealth more than anything," Ethan said. "And for that, we'll have to be on foot."

"I know," Lacy said. "I was just hoping there would be another way."

"It's a long walk," Ethan agreed.

Lacy felt her insides start to churn. "And I'm claustrophobic," she said.

Ethan walked down the ramp, keeping his footsteps quiet. Lacy followed close behind him. The tunnel was square shaped, made of cement, ten feet high, and ten feet wide. Thick stone support columns lined the walls every twenty feet and each post had a light mounted on it. Lacy could see way up ahead, even though the tunnel felt dark and narrow. It was quiet down there, a terrible eerie quiet. The only sound Lacy could hear was a faint swishing sound, which she figured must be the ocean waters moving up above them. The air seemed thin and musty in her nose, which made her feel light headed. Lacy admired Ethan's ability to sneak along the tunnel, staying focused and seemingly unaffected by the suffocating feeling that was taking her over. He was, after all, an elite spy of sorts; something she was definitely not.

"I don't suppose we can run," Lacy said.

"It would make too much noise," Ethan said.

"You know this tunnel is four miles long, right," Lacy said.

"Yeah," Ethan sighed. "I know."

Lacy swallowed the ball of fear in her throat, trying to push it down, but it stayed put.

A new noise caused Lacy's skin to tingle. It was a faint whining sound, far away. Ethan put his hand up, signaling her to stop.

"What the hell is that?" Lacy said.

Ethan stood still, listening. His eyes widened. "It's a cart," he said. "Coming this way! Hurry, get against the wall!"

They dashed to the right, getting up against the wall, and then shimmied along until they were behind one of the support posts.

"This is no good," Lacy said. The post was too small to hide both of them. "They'll see us."

"You stay behind this one, I'll get my own," Ethan said. He darted across to the other side of the tunnel and pressed himself against the post opposite of Lacy. They waited for a few minutes, Lacy's nerves growing more raw as the sound grew louder with each passing second. Her body began to shiver as the cave-like cold seeped into her skin.

The tunnel got brighter, as the cart approached, lighting the way in front of it with headlight beams. Lacy pressed back against the wall as much as she could. Two men, riding an electric cart, flew past them in a blur. The driver wore casual clothes: jeans, sneakers, and a sweatshirt. However, the passenger was wearing a full suit and tie, and his posture indicated he was a man of high importance. He must have been leaving from some sort of meeting, and the driver was shuttling him out. There would probably be men waiting for him at the exit, personal bodyguards. Lacy hoped she had programmed the fake camera feed to turn off in time. If the activity of that man leaving did not show up on the cameras, it was game over.

Once the sound of the cart had faded to nothing behind them, Ethan moved out from the shadow of the post and started walking further down the tunnel. Lacy's body was now covered with a cold, clammy sweat. The swishing sound above them got louder. Lacy tried to feel the weight of her body in an effort to determine if the tunnel was angling upward yet. She could not tell and it was very disorienting.

Lacy's muscles seized up as the sound of another cart echoed through the tunnel, this time from behind them. Dashing off to the side, Lacy stood against another post. Ethan, seeming more relaxed this time, shuffled over to his own hiding place. The sound of this vehicle was different, more high pitched, like it was moving faster. Again, the tunnel became brighter and an electric cart zipped past them. The same man appeared to be driving the vehicle, but the passenger looked much different. The man riding in this cart was old, at least eighty years, maybe more. He wore a shiny black suit with a trench coat pulled over his shoulders. Lacy shivered and found it hard to take a breath. As the cart drove past, Lacy was certain that the old man had turned and looked directly at her, peering right into her eyes. His expression, which she now saw clearly in a snapshot within her mind, was ice cold, like a tiger hunting its prey. She sat there still, waiting, though Ethan had popped out of hiding right away.

"I think he saw me," Lacy whispered.

Ethan stiffened, turning to look down the tunnel. They both stood still, listening to the sound of the cart, which kept fading softer and softer until it was gone.

"I don't think he did," Ethan said. "I couldn't even see you, and I knew exactly where you were."

"I swear, he looked right at me," Lacy said.

Ethan rubbed his hand on the stubble of his cheek, continuing to listen with an ear facing into the dark ahead of them. "We've got to keep going."

"Okay," Lacy said. "But I think that guy was the devil."

"He did look like he had one foot in the grave," Ethan said.

"Exactly," Lacy said.

Ethan started slinking down the tunnel at first, then he straightened upright and walked with long, determined strides.

There were no other carts for the rest of the way through the tunnel. Lacy had counted one-hundred and sixteen cameras along the way, all with blinking lights. Ethan came to a stop, staring up ahead. At the end of the tunnel, a large set of elevator doors loomed.

"They drive the carts right into the elevator?" Lacy said.

"It looks that way," Ethan said, his pace quickening. As he drew closer, he crept up to the doors. "You disabled the security on this?" he said.

Lacy checked her watch, shaking her head. "We've got twenty minutes before Tom deactivates it. I gave us some cushion, just in case."

Ethan smirked. "I guess we went too fast."

They moved off to the side to wait, leaning against the wall next to each other. Lacy kept an eye on the lights, her stomach doing flip flops over the idea of someone coming down while they stood there.

"Do you know if there are guards at the top? Did you see them when you hacked the cameras?" Ethan said.

"There were usually two," Lacy said. "Guarding double doors in the room up there."

Ethan nodded, pulling his silenced pistol out of his belt and holding it down by his leg. "That I can handle."

"We have three more minutes," Lacy said.

Ethan looked up at the light above the elevator doors, which still indicated that it was at the top. When he turned back to Lacy, she was aiming a gun at his face.

~ ~ ~

Her hand trembling, Emily took a sip of her coffee and looked out the window where she knew the island was, even though the only sign of it was an array of tiny lights, far out in the ocean. The waitress approached them, offering to fill her cup. Emily lifted her hand to signal she did not want more.

"I can't sit here anymore," Emily said. "I've fallen asleep twice in this booth, and the restaurant owner keeps looking at us like we're vagrants. You told me you had a plan, but we're doing nothing and I'm going crazy."

"I know," Tyler said. "I guess I can't put this off any longer, so I'm just going to show this to you and see if you think it's legitimate. You know her much better than I do."

Tyler pushed up his sleeve, revealing a smartwatch with a blank screen. He touched it and it lit up. After tapping the watch a couple more times, he turned his wrist so that Emily could read it. Emily stared at the watch for a few seconds, reading the text several times. Her pulse raced and she felt dizzy.

Tyler leaned in toward Emily. "Right before you passed me on the road, I got a message telling me to follow your truck. And a little later, I got this. Do you think it's really from Lacy?"

"I don't think so," Emily said. "She never risked sending messages—said they were always traceable. She didn't even want to go online. Those people were capable of tracking her if she did."

Tyler covered the watch back up with his sleeve and rubbed his eyes with his hand. "Maybe she found a way. What if she figured out how to locate us and send texts to me without being detected?"

"She couldn't do that the entire time we were on the road," Emily said.

Tyler nodded, looking out the window for a moment. "But circumstances have changed."

Emily tried to sort it out in her mind. She wanted to believe the message was truly from Lacy, but it seemed insane.

Tyler cleared his throat, seeming to have come to a conclusion. "Jim once told me there was something about Lacy that really worried him. He said the more frightened she gets, the more ingenious her mind becomes. It's as though her brain is designed to run on adrenaline. He said on a normal day she's just a world class genius, but get her riled up enough, and you can't fathom what she's capable of."

Emily's mouth went dry and her temples pounded. She pushed her fingers into her hair, scratching her head. "If we follow that message, and it's fake, we'll be killed for sure."

Tyler nodded. "But if it's real . . . . "

~ ~ ~

"Drop your weapon," Lacy said, keeping her pistol aimed at Ethan's head.

"Lacy, what the—"

"Drop it now or I'll blow you away, and trust me, I won't hesitate. Not after everything you've put me through."

Ethan let his gun slide out of his hand and clatter to the ground. "I don't understand, we're saving your friends." Ethan blinked hard, his face turning white. "Why are you doing this?"

"You're one of them," Lacy said.

"What? No, I'm—"

"You're in The Supremalus."

"I'm trying to fight The Supremalus!" Ethan shouted.

The light above the elevator flickered, then went out. After a pause, the doors slid open.

Lacy swept her foot in a semi-circle, kicking Ethan's gun across the floor. "I don't have time for your shit, keep your hands up and move." She slammed her hand into Ethan's shoulder, shoving him toward the elevator. He hesitated, then walked ahead into the elevator with Lacy following behind, keeping her gun aimed at his head. They both stood there in silence until the doors closed and the elevator started moving upward.

"How long have you known?" Ethan said.

Lacy tilted her head to the side, raising an eyebrow and saying nothing.

"When did you figure out I was part of The Supremalus?"

"On the drive to the beach house," Lacy said.

Ethan shook his head and smirked. "You have no idea what you're up against here."

Lacy brought her other hand up to the gun, steadying it with her palm underneath the handle. "You know, everyone keeps saying that."

The doors slid open and Lacy moved behind Ethan.

"Drop your weapons or I shoot him," Lacy shouted to the two guards across the room.

"Do as she says!" Ethan said.

The guards looked at Ethan with confused expressions.

"Do it now!" Ethan said.

They threw their rifles onto the floor and lifted their hands.

"Now back away from those doors," Lacy said.

Looking at each other first, the men stepped back a few paces.

"Move," Lacy said.

Ethan walked to the doors, and Lacy kept the gun firmly aimed at his back. He opened the doors and entered a hallway.

"Where's Jim?" Lacy said.

"At the end of this hall," Ethan said.

CHAPTER 41

Ethan pushed through a final set of doors and Lacy almost dropped her gun from shock at what she saw. It was an enormous round room, much like a rotunda in a government building. The walls were marble, polished and white. Across the room, there was a balcony about ten feet from the floor, all decked out in red velvet with a golden railing around it, as though it were prime seating at an opera house. The thin old man that Lacy had seen riding in the tunnel was sitting in a single chair on that balcony.

The old man rose as the doors closed behind Lacy with a loud metallic boom.

"Welcome, Ms. Chase," the old man said, his voice echoing against the marble walls. "My name is Francis—"

"I don't give a fuck what your name is," Lacy said. "I just want my friends back."

Lacy caught movement above and looked up to see that there were windows all around the room, in a complete circle just above the balcony level. The windows were tinted, but she could make out people, lots of people, and they were very well dressed. She could tell by their outlines that most wore suits and were holding something in their hands; it looked like champagne glasses, though some glasses were of the wider, wine variety. The people were moving closer to the windows, hundreds of them, their heads tilting down to watch her. These were the most powerful people in the world, some of them famous, and some, nobody had ever heard of. They gathered here in secret. Lacy had just walked into the most dangerous lion's den on the planet, and they were watching her, as though a show were about to begin.

Francis' mouth turned into a creepy, lustful smile. "Ms. Chase, you will not need that weapon. Though Ethan is my nephew, and a very talented man, his death would be of little consequence compared to the marvelous event that is about to occur." Francis took a step forward, placing his hand on the golden railing, his beady eyes penetrating Lacy. "You can shoot him now, if you like, just to move things along quicker."

A trickle of sweat rolled down Ethan's neck. He looked at Lacy out of the corner of his eye. "He's not bluffing. Killing me changes nothing."

"Or, you could take a look at your friend," Francis said, gesturing to a round opening in the middle of the floor.

Lacy's chest seized as her heart began to pound against her ribs. She looked at Ethan, then up at Francis. Keeping her gun pointed at Ethan, Lacy sidestepped over to the round opening, twenty feet in diameter, in the stone floor. As she did so, more people behind the windows crowded in closer to watch. There was a single table sitting on the floor near the hole, with a keyboard and monitor on top of it. Lacy gave the table a quick glance as she passed by and then turned her attention to the hole in the floor. She reached the edge, leaning her head over to peer down, and her gun fell from her hands, hitting the floor with a clang that reverberated throughout the marble room.

A few feet below the floor, there was a giant round screen. The video image on the screen was so crisp that Lacy thought it was real for a moment. Lacy saw Jim, lying strapped to a steel table that was angled upward at forty-five degrees. His head, arms, and legs were secured and could not move. A giant metal arm stood in front of Jim, holding a glistening needle a few inches from his chest. Lacy choked and her eyes went blurry. She almost fell onto the screen and managed to stumble backward, away from it. She looked at Francis in horror. Then she looked at Ethan.

"You," she spat at Ethan. "You wanted me to come here like this." She looked up at Francis. "You let me in!"

Francis chuckled. "No, you legitimately hacked our security system." He waved his hand around the room at the tinted windows. "Much to all of our entertainment. You wouldn't have come willingly if you didn't have to earn your way in."

A new lump formed in Lacy's throat. "Tom," she said. "Robby."

Francis brushed their names aside with his wrinkled hand. "They know way too much. We have soldiers on their way to visit them right now. They have finished their purpose of helping you get in."

Lacy winced, her knees going weak. She felt her body attacking itself, a war raging within her. She looked at the floor, trying to focus, trying not to faint. Then she raised her head back up to Francis.

"Charlie," she said. "You captured Charlie too."

"Oh, your hero died at sea trying to fight off our men," Francis said. "Quite fitting for a SEAL, I should say." Francis gave a gravelly chuckle.

The room spun around Lacy as her mind tried to find footing. She fell to her knees, gasping for breath. Then, her brain began to move faster as adrenaline surged into it. Her fight or flight reflexes flipped into overdrive and she started seeing images in her mind.

Images she had not seen since . . . .

Her head jerked up. "All of this," Lacy shrieked. "All of this has been part of your plan, since the moment I met him in Night Harbor." Lacy pointed at Ethan.

Francis raised his eyebrows, his face brightening. "Very impressive, Ms. Chase. Very impressive indeed." Scratching his chin, Francis regarded Lacy while pausing for a moment. "We did our research. Studied all the footage," Francis said. "You see, we have eyes and ears in far more places than even you can imagine—mostly electronic of course. And almost entirely unknown to the people who actually own those electronics."

Lacy was beginning to feel her head clear, as though she were comprehending everything in absolute clarity. Seeing things in a new light, as they say, yet this light was filled with terrible horrors.

Francis cleared his throat. "The first time you developed your wildfire program, it took days of paranoia, running and hiding, in order to set the tumblers in your mind into the unique state which allowed you to create the impossible algorithm. That's not something that can be turned on easily. We had to simulate the same instincts. We had to get you fighting for your life, long enough to make it happen."

Though her mind was churning in high gear, Lacy's muscles were still refusing to obey as the memories of everything they had been through paralyzed her with hot rage. She lifted her left knee, trying to stand.

Francis raised an eyebrow at Lacy and said, "Granted, I must admit, you and your friends eluded us much longer than we had anticipated. You were not supposed to make it out of Colorado." Francis shot a glance at Ethan and shook his head. "We even had to use Kraig to stop you from hacking our satellites. Yet, it turned out you beat your old nemesis, and it was you who found us. Either way, you are here, and that's precisely what we wanted."

"But so many people died," Lacy said. "So many of your own people."

Francis blew air through pursed lips. "My people? I have more people than I could ever need. Too many people, actually. But you have a gift that can change the world, and it is only right that I obtain that gift."

"But I almost died, many times," Lacy said. "What would you have done then?"

Francis shrugged. "It was a risk that needed to be taken in order to pull your gift out of you. If you had died, at least no one else could get your wildfire program, and that's almost as good as me having it."

Lacy spat on the floor and rose to her feet. "Well you're not getting it from me, you sick old bastard."

"Oh?" Francis said. "I think I will. Go look at your beloved Jim again."

CHAPTER 42

The beach house stood silent in the cool salty breeze. Ronald Cornwell, a former U.S. Marine, was growing impatient. Looking across the ocean, he noted that the sun would be coming up soon. Kicking at some gravel in the driveway, he sighed. Ronald had been hard on his luck after leaving the Corps, but then this private contract came along. It was good money, but he was tired of getting jerked around all the time. Go wait here for more orders, only to sit somewhere for days not hearing anything. Now go kill this guy and make it look like a random shooting. It was getting old.

Ronald checked his phone. Nothing. The twelve men under his command were holding their positions, surrounding the beach house. Ronald turned to the soldier next to him, who was leaning with his back against his truck, his assault rifle cradled in his folded arms.

"You hear anything yet?" Ronald said.

"Nope," said the other soldier.

Shaking his head, Ronald took a step forward, peering at the window of the beach house. The light was on, but he had not seen any movement.

"It's gonna be light soon," Ronald said, "and we'll all look pretty damn stupid standing out here with machine guns."

The other soldier shrugged. "Oh well, no one seems to give us any trouble when we're following orders from those guys."

Ronald frowned, spitting onto the ground. It was true, those damn TS orders. Tell any person with some sort of authority that you were following TS orders, and they just back away, no questions asked.

Ronald's phone vibrated in his pocket. He fished it out and read the message:

"Two males in the beach house. Eliminate them, leave no trace."

Grunting, Ronald stuffed his phone back into his pocket and signaled the others to move in.

The door slammed open and Ronald came storming in, stopping and looking around. There was another smash and two of his men busted through the back door. A laptop sat on an empty table in the middle of the room.

"Check the other rooms," Ronald said.

His men hustled down the hallway, but Ronald already knew. He had known it the second he stepped inside and did not hear that slight reverberation in the air that a human presence makes. No one was there.

~ ~ ~

Trembling, Lacy edged up to the hole again, looking down at the screen. The image of Jim zoomed out and Lacy saw that he was inside a dome, made of shiny one-way-mirror glass. People were walking past it—men, women, and children. Hundreds of people went about their day, looking at their reflection as they passed by the dome without a clue as to what was inside.

"He's in the middle of downtown Miami," Francis said. "He will die soon, and none of us could stop that, even if we wanted to. You are the only one who can do that." Francis looked over at the table with the computer sitting on it.

Lacy stared at the table as well, barely noticing Ethan coming up next to her.

"You love him, don't you?" Ethan said.

Lacy stiffened, blood pounding in her head. "No, not in that way," she said.

"Don't lie to yourself," Ethan said. "Even we know how you feel about him. Why do you think we posted your coordinates on that website so he could find you? We needed him too—for leverage."

Lacy was silent.

"You know the entire world will change if you are able to write this program. Countless people will die because of it. But you can't lose him." He pointed down at Jim on the screen.

Lacy's mouth tasted like salt and she realized she had bit her lower lip so hard it was bleeding.

"Jim has one hour to live," Ethan said. "The passcode that can save him is in a binary file containing your full name. It's stored on a computer somewhere in the world. I'm assuming it took you a lot longer than an hour the first time you made wildfire. I wouldn't waste any more time."

Tears streamed down Lacy's cheeks. Her hands twitched at her sides, as she kept looking to the screen with Jim on it. She looked away, keeping her gaze fixed on the floor. The first time she wrote the wildfire program, it was for herself. She knew she would never do it again to save her own life; she'd rather die than let these monsters get their hands on it. Yet, there was another thing she knew: She would burn the whole world and everything in it to the ground in order to save one person—Jim.

Lacy blinked once and walked to the keyboard in a trance

like state. She began typing, her fingers flitting over the keys so fast they became an invisible blur. Ethan watched as line after line of code materialized on the screen. After five minutes, she stopped typing.

Lacy stepped back and the computer started making a dinging sound. Ding. Ding. Ding.

"What does the bell sound mean?" Ethan said.

"Each ring means it took over another computer."

The dinging sound chimed faster and faster until it turned into one long tone. Then it stopped. Lacy looked up at the windows all around her, the deep tint suddenly disappearing to clear glass. She looked at the people, seeing the details in their suits and their arrogant faces, so many of them. Lacy was sure she would even recognize a few of them, the world's most powerful people, if she took the time. She glanced at her watch; no, she did not have time for that.

The lights went off inside the windowed room where all the people stood. A few panicked and headed for the doors in the back of the room, trying to pull them open, but they would not budge.

Ethan's eyes swept around the room. "What was that?"

But Lacy was not paying attention to Ethan. She was looking up at Francis, standing at the railing on the balcony. Francis' eye was twitching as he stared at Lacy with an icy, penetrating gaze.

"The untraceable server you had me use last night," Lacy said. "It was flawed. It was in a fixed location that you controlled. So I created a new one of my own."

Ethan stared at Lacy a moment, then ran up to the computer; it turned off right before he got to it. Ethan slapped his fingers on the keyboard, but it did nothing, the computer was dead.

"I wrote a lot of code yesterday, Ethan. While you were asleep."

Ethan grabbed the computer and shook it. Lacy shot

another glance at Francis above. His face was contorted, his one eye twitching so hard it looked like he was winking.

"That code I wrote was just waiting to be downloaded and executed—downloaded from my brand new untraceable server."

Ethan picked up the computer and threw it across the room with a roar. It smashed against the wall with a crash.

"But I just couldn't complete the last bit," Lacy said. "That last algorithm wouldn't come to me. Not until you brought me here and put me through this."

"Wildfire?" Ethan said, looking over at the smashed computer and breathing heavily. "It had to get stored somewhere, we'll find it."

Lacy shook her head and smiled. "It's on my new untraceable computer."

Francis growled from above, his hands clawing into the railing. "Wheeeere is it?" he shouted.

Lacy looked up at Francis, then down at her watch, then back to Francis again.

"Up until five minutes ago, it was somewhere," Lacy said. "Now, it's everywhere."

A screeching sound came from outside, and the wall behind Francis exploded, sending him flying through the air. Francis landed on the ground with a thud and a crack, his arm twisting at a grotesque angle under him. He stirred but did not make an effort to get up. Ethan crouched down to one knee, looking up at the hole in the wall. Lacy bolted at Ethan, and he turned toward her just in time to see her knee smash into the front of his face.

Then Lacy walked over to the hole with the video screen and saw Jim staggering out of the dome into the streets of the city, with people looking at him like he was a drunk stumbling out of a bar.

Bending down, Lacy picked up her pistol. She could hear the muffled sounds of the people up in the glass windows.

Some were still trying to get out, others were shrieking in fear. And some just stood and watched her with a cold stillness.

Ethan had gotten to his feet and stood there, staggering with his nose smashed in, blood blinding his eyes. He wiped his arm across his face and blinked so that he could see. Francis was trying to push himself up with his one good arm.

"You are going to die." Ethan was spitting out blood as he spoke. "All of your friends are going to die because of your stupidity."

Lacy smiled. "You have no idea whom you're dealing with." She pointed her gun down at Francis in a nonchalant, one handed gesture and fired five shots into him. Francis collapsed to the ground on the first shot, his bony old body twitched with each of the next three, and then the back of his head burst open with the last one. Ethan's face twisted into a growl of rage. He ran at her as she raised her gun to head level. Just before Ethan was about to crash into her, Lacy pulled the trigger and shot him in the face, sending him flying backwards onto the floor. Lacy stood there for a moment, still holding the gun extended out in front of her. She opened her hand, dropping the gun to the floor. Then she turned and walked out of the room.

The doorway to the outside was in sight and Lacy hurried her footsteps, knowing she had limited time to get out of there. The hallway was long, endlessly long, it seemed, with doors on either side along the way. All of the doors were locked, mechanically, she had made sure of that. But a door on the left, at the far end—the light above its handle changed from red to green, and it opened. Kraig Freestone stepped out, holding a machine gun. His expression was crazed, his mouth gaping open in a giant smile. What used to be hair slicked back in a perfect ponytail was now a wild mess. He looked like he had aged twenty years.

"You may have outsmarted them," Kraig said, snarling.

"But you didn't outsmart me."

He was right. She thought no one would be able to open any of the doors once her code had locked them, not even Kraig. But he had. Lacy swallowed hard and looked into Kraig's insane eyes as he walked toward her, smiling, machine gun aimed at her stomach. She saw a change in the lighting behind him, like a shadow that appeared and was gone. She heard a grunt, then a whirring sound, like a jump rope when someone spins it fast for a double under. Kraig's mouth opened wide in shock, his eyes bulging out of his head. The machine gun dropped to the floor and Kraig stood there like a statue for a moment, before collapsing with a dull thud. There was a knife sticking out of Kraig's back, its blade buried in all the way to its black handle. Lacy read the name "Trevor," engraved on the handle in a flowing script. She looked up and saw Charlie standing at the end of the hallway, his hands on his knees, his torso billowing in and out with deep shuddering breaths.

Relief flooded Lacy like a title wave, not because she was going to live, but because she had thought Charlie was dead. She ran to him, crashing into his chest and grabbing ahold of him.

Charlie looked at her with tired eyes. "Lacy, someone's firing missiles at the island. I think this is the end for us."

Lacy patted Charlie on the chest and took a step back, giving him a reassuring smile. "I'm shooting missiles at the island, and this is only the beginning."

The hinge of Charlie's jaw fell open as he stared at her. A deep crease appeared on his forehead as he tried to make sense of what Lacy was saying. Then his eyes grew wide and he looked at Lacy with a mixture of awe and fear. "You hacked the Naval base?"

"I hacked many bases," Lacy said.

"When?" Charlie's voice was low and barely audible.

"I wrote all the code for it yesterday," Lacy said. "But I

didn't have enough horsepower for it to work until I created the wildfire program."

Charlie's large Adam's apple bobbed in his neck as he swallowed. "You created wildfire?"

Lacy smirked. "More like wildfire 2.0."

Charlie's face went pale and he stood there speechless until a nearby explosion made him flinch.

"Follow me," Lacy said.

Lacy walked out of the building with Charlie following behind her. Charlie kept looking all around with frantic movements of his head. Another burst of screeching noise filled the air, then booming thunder shook the ground and parts of the mansion burst into flames behind them. Walking fast, but calm, Lacy strode across a grass courtyard until she came to a long set of stairs that led upward. She marched up the steps, heading toward the rock cliff that spanned the side of the island facing the Florida Keys. A different sound filled the sky—not a screeching sound, but a roaring grumble, like jet planes. Charlie crouched down, covering his head as three missiles rocketed straight into the center of the island, sending an eruption of rock and dirt into the air. A wave of dust flew past Lacy, but she did not flinch. Reaching the top of the stairs, Lacy walked onto a flat area at the top of the cliff, which was about a hundred yards across. The wind whipped Lacy's auburn hair around like wild red flames. She kept walking toward the edge, looking out at the pure blue sky. Now she was ten feet from the edge and she could hear the ocean waves crashing far below.

"Lacy!" Charlie said. "Wait!"

Lacy stopped, turned, and smiled at Charlie. Closing her eyes, she arched her back and breathed in deeply, stretching her arms outward in triumph. The wind picked up, howling so loud, nothing else could be heard. Lacy's clothes fluttered wildly against her skin as the air swirled around her.

Then a helicopter appeared from below the cliff, rising behind Lacy until it was level with the edge. Tyler Samsteen was flying the chopper. He guided the helicopter over onto the flat rock surface and Lacy stepped inside. She turned and looked at Charlie. His mouth was agape and he stared at her in wonder.

Far in the distance, there was another roar. Lacy stuck her head out of the helicopter door and gave Charlie a firm wave of her hand to hurry. Charlie sprinted to the chopper, jumping inside. Tyler pulled the control lever, banking away.

Lacy and Charlie turned to watch, as they sped off over the ocean. There was a sound, like hundreds of thunderclaps at once, and the entire island disintegrated in one massive explosion.

CHAPTER 43

Tears rolled down Tom's cheeks as he drove a shiny new forest green pickup down the road. Robby sat next to him, watching out the window, bewildered. Then Robby glanced at Tom, but looked away when he realized that Tom was crying.

They rode in silence for a while before Robby cleared his throat and spoke. "Will we ever see them again?"

Tom looked at Robby and tried to give him a reassuring smile. "I'm sure we will." Tom reached over and patted Robby on the shoulder. "We'll see them again."

"Even Lacy?" Robby said.

Tom swallowed hard, causing the pain in his chest to intensify for a moment. "Yeah—" his voice cracked. "Even Lacy." Though Tom was not sure if that were true.

"I wish I could have said goodbye," Robby said.

"Me too," Tom said. "But she wanted to keep us safe."

Robby sighed and went back to looking out the window. Meanwhile, Tom kept reading the message over and over in his mind; the message that had popped up on the laptop screen as soon as he had opened the door to the tunnel for Lacy:

My Dearest Tom,

I love you so much, and that is why I can no longer put you in danger. You must leave, right now, because they will be coming for you, and they will kill you on the spot.

The rest of the security shutdowns to get me inside will be automatic. I found a way to pull it off without detection. I have arranged for a new truck to be waiting for you a block behind the beach house. Take Robby with you. He's a good kid and he desperately needs someone like you to help him find meaning in life again. You two can go back to your shop in the Minnesota woods, he would love it there.

They will not come after you anymore, I am making sure of that. But there will always be someone after me, so I have to go somewhere far away, and no one can know where I am. That is the only way all of you will be truly safe.

Thank you for everything. I would have been lost without you.

Love,

Lacy

CHAPTER 44

Emily cried out when the island vaporized into rubble. "Where's Jim?" She was frantically pressing her face against the helicopter window. "Was he still on the island?"

Lacy snapped out of her triumphant daze and dove forward to grab Emily's hand. "No, he wasn't. I know where he is."

Emily breathed a deep sigh, trying to wipe the tears from her eyes.

"Fly to downtown Miami," Lacy said to Tyler. "But hurry, we don't have much time."

"You got it," Tyler said.

They sped over the city, swooping close to the buildings as people looked up in shock at the chopper banking and turning while it flew just above the streets.

"There!" Lacy pointed. "I knew he'd be heading back for the beach!"

Jim was running along the sidewalk, a worried look on his face. When he saw the helicopter, Jim stopped in his tracks and looked up. His eyes opened in alarm and he started running, faster this time.

"He must think we're The Supremalus," Charlie said.

"Try to get in front of him," Lacy said.

"I'm not really that good of a pilot," Tyler said.

"I think you're doing quite well," Lacy said.

Tyler sped the chopper past Jim and turned it around, bringing it down to face him. Emily waved both hands, and Jim caught sight of her. He stopped and scrunched his eyes in confusion. Then the helicopter touched down as Emily flung the door open. She jumped out and ran to Jim. He gave an exhausted smile and caught her in his arms.

Charlie leaned out of the side door and shouted, "Come on, let's go!"

Jim and Emily sprinted to the chopper and dove in. Tyler pulled up and they were storming off.

"Where do we go now?" Tyler asked.

"An airport," Lacy said.

"Which one?" Tyler said.

"A small one, farther south. I'll give you the coordinates."

"We're taking a flight?" Charlie said.

"Not we," Lacy said. "Just me."

CHAPTER 45

They all stood there without saying a word: Lacy, Jim, Emily, and Charlie. Tyler had flown off, taking the helicopter back to Key West, having said something about needing to return it before he lost his deposit, which was around one million dollars. He was going to come back for them later with his car. The bright sun beat down on them as they huddled near a small private plane on the tarmac.

Emily broke the silence with her soft voice. "So you're going somewhere by yourself?"

"It's the only way," Lacy said. "All of you almost died because of me. I can't let that happen again."

"But where are you going?" Jim said.

"It's better if you don't know," Lacy said. "I don't want anyone going after you in order to find me."

"You killed all of The Supremalus," Charlie said. "I don't think there's a threat anymore."

"I'm not sure if that was all of them, but it would at least take them awhile to regroup." Lacy looked off in the distance, tears brimming in her eyes. "There'll always be someone who wants to use me. I need to be hidden somewhere, alone."

"Did the wildfire program erase itself again?" Charlie said.

"No, it's dormant. Encrypted and sitting on millions of unknowing people's computers, in case I ever need it again. I know the passcode to activate it, and I'm sure there isn't anyone alive who could crack it."

Emily stepped up to Lacy, hugging her. "We love you, Lacy. You sure we can't come with you?"

Lacy shook her head. "I'm sure." Then Lacy's eyes went to Jim, but she could not look him in the face. Her heart shuddered, her arms trembling. Jim came up to her, putting his arms around her and squeezing her. Lacy could not breathe. She fought with all her might to keep the tears from spilling out of her eyes, because it would be the most horrible thing she could imagine; to show him how much pain she was really in. Lacy gave him a gentle push and stepped back, unable to see through her burning eyes.

"Will we see you again?" Jim said, his voice cracking.

He was trying not to cry, Lacy could both hear it and feel it. That made her feel both better and worse at the same time.

Lacy shook her head. "I don't know." Her lips were barely able to move as she spoke. She had to get away, before she could not.

Charlie cleared his throat. "If you need anything, you'll find a way to contact us."

Lacy forced a sad smile. "You know I will." Then she turned, deciding she could not handle one more second of this goodbye.

She walked toward the plane.

Jim called out, "You know how to fly that thing?"

"I took an online course," Lacy shot over her shoulder. But she did not look back. Looking back would have killed her. She marched ahead and climbed up the steps into the airplane.

CHAPTER 46

A vicious looking dog came running at Jim as he walked by a shambled house in St. Louis. It looked like a Rottweiler and it had a deep growl brewing in its throat that made the hairs on the back of Jim's neck tingle. When a dog like that is barking loud, it can be intimidating; but when they have that angry rumble deep in their chest, it's worse. Much worse. They have one thing on their mind: hunt and kill.

A glint of silver being dragged across the long grass gave Jim a feeling of relief in knowing that the beast had a chain around its neck. He only hoped the leash was short. Sure enough, the dog barreled at Jim, only to be stopped by a jerk when the chain went tight. It gnashed and growled in a flurry of twisting movements, as though it could break free.

The owner opened the door of the house and yelled out at the Rottweiler. "Bruno! Get back here!"

If the dog heard its owner, it did not care. It continued to snap at Jim with long yellow teeth clamping together like a bear trap. Quickening his pace, Jim hurried along the street. He looked at the house numbers as he went, sidestepping a broken bottle and a beat up baby stroller just sitting there next to the curb.

Finally, Jim found the house he was looking for. There was no number on the house, but the dented mailbox at the end of the driveway had the address written on it with black marker. The house was a small rambler, not much bigger than a double-wide trailer. Knee high grass surrounded the house, hiding most of the junk laying around in the yard, though a few tires could be seen on the ground. A plastic kiddy pool sat out front, filled with brown water. The garage door was open, though the garage itself was filled to the brim with junk; including an old dish washer, a smashed in tube television set, and a couch with flower print upholstery.

Jim walked around the side of the house to see if anyone was in back. The backyard was surrounded by a chain link fence. A swing set, which was brown and rusted, sat in the middle of an area where the tall grass was matted down. With a sigh, Jim made his way back around to the front and stepped up to the door. He knocked and took a step back.

A bony young woman with sunken eyes answered the door. While Jim could tell she was in her twenties, the woman looked like she had aged to about sixty. Jim swallowed and tried not to stare at the track marks on her arms.

"Hi, my name is Jim."

The woman put her hand on the doorframe to support herself and chewed a wad of gum with long, circular chomps. "Yeah? You need something?"

"Well, I was wondering if I could speak to Darrian for a moment."

Her eyes narrowed and she closed the door halfway. "What do you want with my boy?"

"Well, I have a message from his father."

The woman snarled. "Jake sent you?" She spit her wad of gum at his feet. "You'd better get your ass out of here before I call the cops."

She tried to slam the door shut, but Jim stuck out his foot, stopping it from closing all the way.

"Something happened to Jake," Jim said. "He . . . . was shot down."

"He dead?" she said, flashing a smile.

"Yeah," Jim said. "He is."

"Who got 'em?"

"It was some hired soldiers in Minnesota. But he gave me a message for his son before it happened."

The woman gazed at Jim for a second, then shook her head. "I don't give a shit if Santa Claus gave you a message, you ain't going near Darrian. Now get the hell off my property and don't you ever come back."

Jim heard footsteps elsewhere in the house. "Please," he said. "I made a promise."

She gritted her teeth. "No! Now go, before I get my gun."

Jim blinked, then took a step backward. She slammed the door shut and bolted the lock.

Walking with his head down, Jim moved to the other side of the road to avoid the yard with the rabid dog. As he plodded along, he heard the sound of thumping bass from a car, and it was getting closer. He looked up and saw a tan 1985 Plymouth Gran Fury coming down the road. Jim glanced inside as the car passed by. The driver was a scrawny man with a bald head, and he had what looked like a gold chain with one end pierced through his ear and the other end pierced through his nose.

The old car continued down the street and turned into the driveway of the house Jim had just visited. Jim watched as the man got out and went up to the door. After a few minutes, the man and Darrian's mom came out, got into his Plymouth, and started backing out of the driveway. Jim looked around and darted into a row of shrubs in the yard next to him, crouching low. The car rolled past him and continued down the road until the low bass sound had faded to nothing in the distance.

Jim jumped out of his hiding place and jogged onto the

road. He ran along the curb until he reached Darrian's house, then he turned up the driveway. Peeking in the window next to the front door, Jim saw no movement. He went around to the side of the house and stood up on his toes to peer inside. There was nothing but a kitchen with dishes piled up in the sink. He went back to the front door and knocked, then listened. Nothing, not a sound. He rang the doorbell, its loud chimes making him flinch. Nothing. Sighing, Jim started walking back down the driveway, when he heard a sound coming from the back yard. It was a rhythmic squeaking sound, like rusty metal.

Creeping around to the back of the house, Jim froze and stared at a little boy, swinging on the swing set in the middle of the fenced in backyard. The boy kept swinging, pumping his legs and leaning way back when he swung forward. Jim moved closer and put his hands on top of the fence.

"Darrian?" Jim said.

The boy's head whipped around and he jumped off the swing when he saw Jim. Stumbling and landing on his knees as he hit the ground, the little boy got to his feet and turned to face Jim. A tightness formed in Jim's throat when he saw the boy's face—he looked like a tiny Jake.

"Hi, what's your name?" the boy said.

"My name is Jim. I was your dad's friend."

Darrian frowned. "Mommy says my dad is a bad man."

Jim took a deep breath and exhaled. "He was, but he didn't want to be bad anymore. So he became a very good man."

Darrian's eyes lit up, his mouth forming a little smile. "Will I get to see him then?"

Jim's eye started to sting and he tried to blink away the pain. He shook his head. "Your dad saved my life, but in order to do that, he had to go away."

His shoulders slumping, Darrian pushed his lower lip over his upper lip and drooped his head.

"But he made me promise to come here and see you,

because he loved you, Darrian. He loved you so much."

Smiling at this, Darrian's chest puffed up a little. He walked closer to the fence and looked up at Jim. "Do you want to stay and play with me?"

Jim felt a pang in the pit of his stomach. He scratched his head, looking around. "I don't think I can, buddy. Your mom will probably come home soon and she'll get really mad if I'm here."

"Oh, she left with Jaxon," Darrian said. "When she leaves with him, she doesn't come home until it's been dark for a long time." Darrian looked up at the sky. "Sometimes, she doesn't come home until morning."

Jim closed his eyes, willing his tears to stay at bay. "Okay, we'll play for a few hours and then I'm going to have to leave. I can't risk getting us in trouble."

After three hours of playing cops and robbers, building forts, and digging in the dirt, it started to get dark.

"I'd better get going," Jim said. "What do you usually do when it gets dark?"

"I go inside and watch TV," Darrian said, "until I fall asleep."

"Okay," Jim said, crouching down in front of Darrian. "Well, I really enjoyed playing with you."

Darrian took a step forward and put his arms around Jim, squeezing him tight. Jim hugged Darrian back, as a dull ache throbbed in his heart.

"Will I see you again?" Darrian said.

"Yes, someday," Jim said. "And when you are old enough, I'll tell you more about your dad, okay?"

Darrian nodded. "Okay, bye Jim." Then Darrian turned and ran into the house through the patio door.

Jim watched as the TV set turned on, illuminating the living room with flickering light. He started to cry as he climbed over the fence and ran down the road to his car.

He sat there for a while, gripping the steering wheel and weeping. Then he straightened up and started the car. He had a long drive back to Minnesota. Maybe he could get there in time to have breakfast with Emily.

CHAPTER 47

The gravel crunched under Tom's slippers as he walked down his driveway in his bathrobe. Squinting his eyes at the horizon, he admired the sunrise coming up over the trees. The smell of morning dew on spring flowers surrounded him and he took it in with a deep breath. He came to a stop where the Friday newspaper lay on the ground, wrapped in a green plastic bag. As he picked it up and turned to head back to the house, he saw movement coming up the ridge.

Robby appeared among the trees, carrying a fishing pole and a stringer full of fish. He smiled when he saw Tom and started running toward him.

"How're they biting?" Tom called out.

"Like crazy!" Robby said. He came to a stop in front of Tom and held up his stringer, his eyes beaming.

Tom chuckled. "Looks like we're having bass for supper tonight."

"We might have to freeze some," Robby said. "Look at how many I caught."

"Actually, we should cook it all up. We have guests coming."

Robby raised his eyebrows. "Guests? Really? Who?"

Tom's smile grew bigger as he stared at Robby and waited.

Robby's face lit up. "Jim? And Emily?"

"Yep," Tom said. "And . . . . "

"Charlie?" Robby said.

Tom nodded.

"Yeah!" Robby said. "Awesome! Wait until I show him my target range."

"I'm sure he'll love it," Tom said. "You'd better go get those fish cleaned so we can get ready."

Robby nodded and started heading for the house. Then he stopped and his shoulders slumped, his head dropping low. Tom sighed and a small pain nagged in his chest. Robby turned his head, looking at Tom over his shoulder.

"I wish I could see her again," Robby said.

Tom nodded. "I have to believe we will."

"I hope you're right," Robby said.

Tom ambled inside and poured himself a cup of coffee before sitting down at the table. He opened his newspaper and flipped through the pages, scanning each article briefly before moving on to the next. He turned to the back page and felt a shiver run through him. The headline at the top of the page said:

Cause of Explosion in the Florida Keys Found

Tom tried to swallow, but his mouth had gone dry. He lifted his mug to his mouth with a shaky hand, took a sip, and set it down. Then he leaned over the table and continued reading the article.

United States officials are reporting that they have found the cause of the massive explosions which rocked the Florida Keys a month ago. A private island, known as Saints Villa, went up in flames due to a faulty gas pipe. Saints Villa was a highly exclusive vacation resort for the ultra-wealthy. Sources indicate that there were several hundred people on the island, attending some sort of celebration, at the time of the accident. No survivors were found.

The owner of the island was among those killed in the catastrophe and no living beneficiaries can be found. The island will be held under state ownership until further cleanup has been completed, at which time an estate auction will be held.

Tom sat back and took his glasses off, rubbing his eyes. He stared at the table, deep in thought. No survivors. No one claiming ownership of the island. He had assumed there would be a cover up, but seeing it in print was so surreal, it made him feel light headed. The truth, he mused, was definitely not something fit for public consumption. As he rested his face in his hands, Robby came walking in through the back door holding two Ziploc bags of fish fillets.

"What's wrong?" Robby said.

Startled out of his thoughts, Tom snatched the newspaper from the table, folding it in half and tucking it under his arm. "Nothing," Tom said. "Just daydreaming." Getting to his feet, Tom went to Robby and took the bags of fish, holding them up and examining them.

"What d'ya think?" Robby said.

"Perfect," Tom said. "How'd you like that new fillet knife?"

"I love it," Robby said. "It's the best one I've ever used."

"Good, cause that's the brand I sell in my store." Tom opened the refrigerator and placed the Ziploc bags on the top shelf. Then he walked over to the sink and opened the pantry door underneath, tossing his newspaper in the trash can. He decided not to worry about conspiracies anymore. Instead, he would enjoy being in his home among the peaceful woods and try to give Robby the best life he could. He had to trust that the people he cared about were safe. And most of all, he needed to have faith that Lacy had found peace, wherever she was.

CHAPTER 48

L acy walked along the edge of the ocean, letting the cool water wash up and tickle her toes. She looked out at the vast sea and marveled at its color, the deepest blue she had ever imagined. Having walked around most of the island that day, Lacy decided to go to her favorite clam digging spot. She stopped at a place where a massive rock, the size of an elephant, jutted out of the ocean about fifteen feet from shore. There were a lot of oysters nearby, but clams were Lacy's favorite.

Lacy had a staff which she had carved from the branch of a rubber tree. The top of her staff was shaped like a two pronged fork, which was handy for many things, one of which was digging for clams. She flipped her staff upside down, grasping it like a shovel, and worked at the sand for several hours. By the time she was done, Lacy had filled her entire backpack with clams and was ready to head back. She lifted her wide brimmed straw hat to mop her sweating brow and turned toward the jungle. Lacy always wore her hat when she was outside, just in case—the satellites. She was confident that she had wiped out The Supremalus, but she also knew that whenever there is a void of power, it will always be filled. It was better to be careful. Lacy was so diligent about this precaution that the natives of the Marquesas islands referred to her as "hat girl."

As she walked through the sand toward the jungle, Lacy shot a glance over her shoulder at the horizon. Whenever she looked out in the distance, she always felt like she would spot a ship out at sea, heading her way. But she never did.

Lacy made her way up a rocky path, climbing higher along the trail to the top, which she had created herself through her daily ritual. She finally reached the top of the small mountain, which was the highest point on her island. Walking to the edge, Lacy plopped down in her usual place, where the grassy vegetation was all matted down.

As Lacy sat there, high in the sky, she took a deep breath and soaked in the ocean air. The cool, salty breeze filled her nostrils with a sense of peace that she desperately needed. The jungle all around her, far below, was thick and green. From her vantage point it looked like miles of shredded spinach, covering a heart stopping landscape of valleys and hills.

Lacy's home was now a small island near the Marquesas, which she had chosen quite randomly through a process of shaking dice and ruling out places that would not be sufficient. She was thrilled with where she had ended up. It was as close to paradise as she could get. If a person had to disappear from civilization, there was no better place to do it.

With a sigh, Lacy stood up and walked down the mountain trail to her hut. She had two laptop computers, which she powered with solar cells, though she had no connectivity to the outside world. Lacy just liked to write computer code for her own enjoyment—she typed hundreds of lines each day. She would set up virtual networks on her computers, trying to make them as hack proof as possible, then find a way to hack into them.

Lacy's existence was simple, yet ingenious. She invented new contraptions all the time. When the loneliness would start

to get to her, Lacy used her boat to row over to the more pop-
ulated Marquesas islands, where she visited the villages,
bartering and making casual friends. She would often trade her
inventions to people for supplies and food, even though she
was self-sufficient on her own. She didn't have a need for
money or goods, given her ability to thrive in the wild, but it
felt good to make a trade and interact. Perhaps she would go
and live somewhere more civilized, someday. But for now,
complete isolation was best.

~ The End ~

ABOUT THE AUTHOR

Criminal Utopia II: Wildfire is the third book published by J. Arthur Squiers. He lives in Minnesota and draws inspiration for his writing from the vast forests and lakes, where he likes to spend his free time. J. Arthur is also an avid runner and fitness enthusiast.

Follow J. Arthur on Instagram at **j.arthur.squiers_author**, or send him an email at j@jarthurbooks.com. Be sure to visit jarthurbooks.com for more information about the Criminal Utopia series.

Made in the USA
Lexington, KY
13 August 2017